SEDUCING THE DOCTOR

BOOK 3 - THE HARTFORD BROTHERS SERIES

JA LOW

Cover Design by Outlined with Love
Editor by Briggs Consulting
Proofing by More than words

❀ Created with Vellum

1

PORTIA

"I'm free, babe," my boyfriend Axton Walsh yells as he wraps his arms around me and kisses me. He didn't want me to come to his graduation ceremony; he only wanted to meet up with me at the after-party, which I get because he wanted to spend time with his family. I met Axton at a friend's frat party he invited us to at Columbia. The six-foot-three, blond hair, blue-eyed Viking had me at hello. He was cute, intelligent, funny, and *that body*. We've been seeing each other for two years and his star on the football team has risen considerably since we first began dating. He started out as this sweet southern gentleman, but I could see over the years the accolades and adoration were going to his head. I never held him back, even if I thought he was partying too much and making friends with the wrong people. He's an adult; he can make his own decisions. Did I voice concern? Of course, but it never went over well and would end in terrible fights. So, I stopped and now I keep my mouth shut.

He's been offered a contract to play for a New York NFL team and is moving to Jersey. We've been looking for places to rent together as I'm still in school, so I'll commute to the city as he needs to stay close to the team. Axton was a year ahead of me at school. I have another year to go before I finish my interior design degree at FIT. Mom was able to get me an internship with her best friend Carrie Hartford, one of New York's best interior designers. I've known Carrie my entire life as the Hartford and the Garcia families are close. She's also my godmother, and I can't wait to work with her. I've admired Carrie most of my life. She's insanely glamorous, funny, kind, and a smart businesswoman.

"I'm so proud of you, Axton," I say as I wrap my arms around his neck. I can smell the beer already lacing his breath as he kisses me again. *Ew, I hate the taste of beer.* Someone calls his name from behind us, and I can already see on his face he's ready to go. *He's graduated college, Portia, give him a break. He wants to hang out with his friends before they start their adult lives. They will be dotted around the country and he's never going to see some of them again. Let him have this time with his friends because you are about to spend two weeks in Mexico together. You can grab some alone time then.* I mentally tell myself all of this as I uncurl my body from his enormous frame.

"Sorry, babe, got to go," Axton says, kissing me again before disappearing into the drunk crowd. I let out a heavy sigh and head to the bar; might as well drown my sorrows.

"Hey, what are you doing here alone?" Cora Jeffries, one of my best friends, asks as she takes a seat on the couch beside me.

"Just taking a break," I tell her as I turn and give her a smile.

"Is Axton drunk again?"

"Yeah. You know what he's like when he gets that way."

She nods in understanding. "I'm so looking forward to going to Mexico tomorrow."

"Wonder how everyone is going to feel in the morning? Or if they are just going to keep going?" I like to party as much as the next person but getting on a plane with a hangover is not my idea of fun.

"Guess we better have the buckets ready," she says with a chuckle.

"What are you two doing sitting here looking lame?" Hannah Randoff, my other best friend, asks, taking a seat on the other side of me on the couch.

"Axton's drunk and Portia needs a time out from all that," Cora explains to her.

Our eyes travel over to where Axton is with his gaggle of groupies surrounding him. He has his arm slung around some girl's shoulder as he talks, everyone giving him the attention he is always chasing. I'm not a jealous person; I can't be, especially with Axton being the charming flirt that he is, but sometimes dealing with his groupies who seem to forget he has a girlfriend is exhausting when he does nothing but court their attention.

"Ugh, is that Raylene who has her hands all over your man?" Hannah sneers, looking at the blonde who has heart eyes for my boyfriend.

"Yeah. But she's harmless. She's been after Axton for years, but he's not interested."

"He seems a little more flirtatious than normal with her though," Cora adds.

I can hear the concern in her voice. "It's graduation, guys. He's letting loose."

"He does that a lot," Hannah mumbles under her breath.

I understand what she is saying because I have noticed it too these last couple of months. For someone who is a professional athlete, he's partying a little more than usual. He's begun hanging around with a different crowd, his social media profile has exploded, his DMs have become full of thirsty women's requests. I'm secure in myself, and I trust him. I mean, the boy shows me his DMs, so I know he's not hiding anything. I know my friends are trying to look out for me. They have and always will. I also know they are not Axton's biggest fans. But I love him.

As the night continues, Axton is becoming drunker and more obnoxious. I hate when he gets like this. His evil twin kicks in and there's no reasoning with him. I walk over to where he is sitting with his boys; he looks up at me and gives me a lazy smile.

"Hey, babe. Come sit here," Axton says with a slurred voice as he pats his lap.

I take my seat and wrap my arms around his neck. His blue eyes are red from, I'm guessing, smoking some weed. I shake my head at him.

"What?" he asks angrily. "Why are you giving me that look?"

I'm surprised by the viciousness in his tone. "Nothing, babes. I'm tired, is all," I whisper, not wanting him to blow up. He looks like he's ready to argue, and I don't want to be in the firing line.

"I've graduated, Portia. We should be partying all night long. Don't tell me you've turned into a bitch."

I frown at his words, hate how they cut me, but I ignore him as he's trying to bait me into a fight. "I wanted to take you home and have a celebration of our own, babe," I whisper into his ear seductively.

He looks up at me and his face turns into a wide smile. "Do you now?" He raises a brow in my direction.

I nod, which seems to have dispersed the tension in his shoulders. The next thing I know, he's picking me up from his lap and placing me in a straddle position against him. My dress is riding up, exposing my ass to all his friends, which he doesn't seem to care about. I try to tug it down, but his hands grip my ass tightly while his hardening dick presses against my core.

"You're so fucking hot, Portia," he purrs into my ear as he grinds his dick against me.

I give him an awkward smile so as not to anger him, but the way he is looking at me it's as if he's moments away from fucking me in front of everyone at this afterparty. I'm not into exhibitionism.

"Come on, baby, let's go home," I ask, trying to get him to leave.

"No, I'm not going anywhere, yet."

Then the next thing I know, his hand is up my skirt as his fingers insert inside of me. "Axton," I hiss into his ear as panic rolls over my body. I'm sitting in front of all his football buddies, and he thinks now is the best time to finger bang me. Oh, hell no. I let go of his neck and place my hand gently on his wrist, halting the movement of his hand beneath my dress. "Please, stop." I stare down at his face, hoping he understands how uncomfortable he is making me.

"But you like my fingers in your cunt," he states loudly, which draws sniggers from his friends.

"Not here I don't."

He looks over my shoulders at his buddies and then back at me. "They don't care. Do you have any idea how many times I've seen them fuck someone?" He chuckles as if it's no big deal. To me, it is.

"I don't feel comfortable," I plead with him.

"You fucking love it." He wiggles his fingers inside of me as if trying to prove his point.

"Stop." I raise my voice. People must hear as the talking stops and silence follows. Axton's blue eyes turn from lust to anger in a matter of seconds, and I feel his entire body stiffen.

"My dick needs you, Portia. Wants you. Are you turning me down?"

"Babe, of course not. I don't want to do anything in public, is all," I whisper, trying not to upset him in front of friends.

"I need you now though."

"I understand, baby. The bathroom is over there. You can

have me whichever way you want in there," I tell him, looking over his shoulders at the club's toilets.

"No. These fuckers need to know you're mine. I hate hearing them speak about how much they want you. I wouldn't put it past any of them to come and take you from me."

"I don't want them, I want you. I love you," I say, cupping his face.

"If you loved me, then you would let me make you come right here, right now. They can't see anything," Axton tells me as he leans in and nips the skin on my throat.

"I told you I don't feel comfortable."

"Other chicks would. Do you have any idea how many chicks would get down on their knees right now and blow me in front of my friends? I could snap my fingers and have one right here now."

My body tenses at his words. What the hell? He's drunk, and now he's being a dick.

"Get your hands off me, Ax," I ask him through gritted teeth.

"If I take my hands off of you, know someone else is happy to take your place." He hisses his words and they feel like a slap in the face.

"If you want someone who's willing to fuck you in front of your friends, then so be it. But it's not me." I push off him and stand up on shaky legs. The look Axton is shooting at me is pure venom.

He then tilts his head and smiles. "Raylene, there you are. Portia was just leaving, so why don't you come and party with us." Axton grins at her before looking over at me. "Like I said, there are plenty of women willing to please me."

My heart breaks. I watch in slow motion as Raylene takes a seat beside Axton with a smile on her face, looking like the cat that got the cream. I won't let him or her see me break.

"Have fun, Axton, just know what you can do, I can do as well," I say with a wide smile on my face. I give him a wink, which makes his entire face turn bright red with anger, and I waltz out of the area.

"Are you okay?" Cora asks.

"No. I want to go home," I tell her, trying to keep my tears at bay.

"Your wish is my command, babe. Let's go."

2

PORTIA

I'm a bundle of nerves as Axton never messaged me last night after our fight. Raylene's smug face as I left the club is burnt into my retinas. If Axton and Raylene hooked up, then I'm done. What Axton did to me last night was fucked up. I made excuses last night about his actions to my girls when we got home, only because I was embarrassed and stupidly still in love with Axton. Also, it's become a pattern excusing away his behavior. And I know my girls are trying to look out for me because if the roles were reversed, I would tell my friends to dump their man's ass too.

But here we are, stepping out of our car at the private airport to get ready to go to Mexico with my boyfriend and all his friends, so it was hardly the time or place to break up with him. Hopefully, he's sobered up and we can talk about what happened last night like adults. My steps falter as I see an angry-looking Axton running down the stairs of the private plane toward us.

Axton asks as he stops in front of us, glaring at me, "What the hell are you doing here?"

"Going to Mexico," I tell him. I get he's angry with me, but we can worry about that once we are on the beach sipping cocktails.

"No, you're not," he yells at me.

Wow, hang on.

"I told you last night we're done."

I stare at him in confusion as I try to think back to our conversation last night. We had a fight, but I didn't think we had broken up. I wanted to, but I didn't.

"You made your choice last night, you left," Axton tells me angrily.

"After you tried to force her to fuck you in front of your friends," Hannah tells him angrily.

Axton glares at my best friend. "Portia needs to learn how to have fun. She's always had a fucking pole stuck up her ass, thinking she's better than everyone else. You all do because you have rich daddies," Axton sneers.

"Actually, it's my mom who's rich, thank you very much," Cora adds, crossing her arms and glaring at Axton.

A small bubble of laughter falls from my lips at her comment, which earns me death daggers from my boyfriend. Oops, sorry—my now ex, according to him.

"Come on, baby, we're ready to go." Raylene's voice echoes down the tarmac.

I turn and look at her dressed in a skimpy outfit with a glass of champagne in her hand and a smile on her face. "I see," I say, taking a step toward Axton, anger boiling through my veins. "That's fine. Have your fun with little miss gold digger. It's not like she hasn't fucked all your friends. Guess she needed your name on her list to call out Bingo."

Axton flinches at my words, but he knows it's the truth.

"Well, it's been a blast dating you, Axton. All the best. Make sure you wrap it up; don't want someone trying to trap you now you're actually worth something." And with that parting barb, I turn on my heels and walk back to our waiting car. The driver grabs my bags as I haul my ass into the back of the car and burst out crying.

"That motherfucking piece of shit," Hannah curses as she hops into the car.

"I can't believe he's taking Raylene to Mexico. What a fuck face," Cora adds, taking the seat beside me.

"What the hell happened?" I ask my best friends as tears stream down my cheeks.

"You had a lucky escape, that's what happened," Hannah says to me.

"You deserve better than him, Portia," Cora explains, wrapping her arms around my shoulders as she pulls me into her.

"Damn right I deserve better. I also deserve a fucking holiday in Mexico." I pout, thinking about the gorgeous villa we rented and now he's sharing it with her.

"Fuck him, we still have my family's villa in Cabo San Lucas where Cora and I were staying while you were at the other villa."

Axton refused to stay at Hannah's family's villa. He wanted to stay with his boys at another place and I, of course, sided with him. I'm an idiot. I should have listened to my girls these past couple of months telling me I could do better, that he didn't deserve me. But I couldn't see it. I was too damn close to it all, but I see it now. Last night Axton showed me his true colors, and it's the first time I actually paid attention to them.

"Mom said we could take her jet to Mexico," Cora interrupts us, waving her phone in the air. "I texted her what happened, and she said take it. It's in a hangar here somewhere. She's organizing the pilot; it should be ready within the hour." She grins.

I stare at my girls and squeal with delight. Fuck you, Ax, and fuck you, Raylene. I am going to enjoy my vacation and no wannabe player and groupie is going to put a dampener on it.

There's a limousine waiting for us when we arrive at the airport in Mexico to whisk us away to Hannah's family's holiday home in Cabo. It's not a long journey from the airport to her cliffside villa by the ocean.

"Welcome, Miss Randoff, Miss Jeffries, and Miss Garcia." Hannah's butler greets us with a tray full of margaritas. *Hell yes.* I take mine and throw it back quickly after the shit morning I've had. Being dumped publicly then my ex flying off with another woman? A cocktail in the morning is warranted.

"Julio, I'll show the girls to their rooms if you could make us some of your amazing tamales?" Hannah asks the older man.

"Silvia is already making them. As well as more drinks." He gives her a warm smile.

"You're the best, Julio," Hannah tells him before dragging us up the large spiral staircase which leads to the second floor, which has a mezzanine. All you can see out the windows is the blue of the ocean.

"Here you go, girls!" Hannah opens the door to my room, and I'm blown away. It's all white with a gorgeous four-poster bed with white linen cascading down like silk around the bed. The glass doors open out to a terrace that overlooks the ocean. There's a day bed set up I can see myself laying against, reading a book relaxing, and putting my breakup behind me.

"Thank you," I say as I turn and give Hannah a big hug. Cora joins in and hugs me, too. "Thank you both for saving me this morning. I honestly don't know what I would have done without the both of you there. I would have frozen in my humiliation and probably gone home and sulked in bed."

"He's not worth your tears, Portia. The man is a self-entitled dick. I should know; my brother Walker was one of them. He's reformed now, but the stuff he did to his poor ex-fiancée because of a gold-digging groupie is disgusting," Hannah says seriously.

Hannah's oldest brother is Walker Randoff. He's twelve years older than her. He was one of the best football players in the league until he got tied up in an enormous scandal where his fiancée left him at the altar as he had impregnated his fiancée's best friend. Then things turned a little dark Walker ended up getting shot in the leg as he saved his ex-fiancée from his baby momma who had kidnapped her. Unfortunately, it put an end to his football career.

"On the bright side, you found out what he's like before moving in with him," Cora adds.

This is very true.

"Least you're still smiling," Hannah tells me.

"I'm all out of tears. Plus, how could you not be smiling looking at this view?" I say, turning in my girlfriend's arms and staring out into the blue nothingness. We stay there in silence for a long while, letting the sun warm our bones and the sound of the ocean crashing against the wall below lulling us like a lullaby.

"I'm starved and Julio has food," Hannah tells us, breaking the silence.

We spent the afternoon eating and drinking by the pool. The perfect antidote for a broken heart, but my Zen doesn't last long.

"Can you believe he's already updated his status to single?" I moan to the girls. Not like I was intentionally stalking Axton, I wanted to make sure I had updated my status before him.

"Of course, he did," Hannah answers as she rolls her eyes. "I bet if you look at Raylene's photos they are of her all over him."

My stomach sinks as I search for Raylene's account and sure enough, there it all is in color, her all over Axton last night. Photos of her doing shots on the plane with the boys. *She's such a bitch.* Stupidly, I scroll through Axton's friend's profiles and unwittingly I stumble upon images of Axton in the background making out with other chicks.

"Shit," I curse out aloud. Hannah and Cora look over at me as I stare blankly at the photos I've uncovered. The date of the images was while we were dating, while we were supposedly happy. Shit. I try to hold back my tears, but I can't seem to, and they slide down my cheeks.

"What did he do?" Hannah asks angrily.

"He's been cheating on me for a long time," I tell them through a sniffle, turning the phone in my hand around to them. Cora grabs it out of my hand and starts scrolling.

"I can't believe these girls. They're supposed to be your friends. What bitches," Cora states, glaring at the phone.

"Always knew Shay was a snake in the grass, and Kendra too. The balls of these girls to hang out with us and all the while they're hooking up with her man. Fuck them. I hate cheaters. I hate women who know the guy they are with has a woman. Fuck them all," Hannah says loudly and angrily. "I know it's day one, Portia, and you're still, like dealing with shit. But I'm in a petty mood, so tonight we are going to go out, we are going to find where they are hanging out and we are going to find you the hottest available man in the club, and you are going to make out with him all night long. Give the fucker a bit of his own medicine. He doesn't give one shit about you, Portia." I wince at Hannah's truthful words, which she catches. "Sorry, babe, no offense, but the internet doesn't lie. He's been unfaithful, by the looks of it, your entire relationship. I bet he thinks you're sitting here in tears, pining over him as if he is the best thing that ever happened to you. Little does he know he wasn't the main character in your life. He was an insignificant side character that no one will ever think about." Hannah's passionate rant has me smiling and chuckling.

Gosh, I love my girls.

"I'm in," I say as I turn and look over at my best friends. "Get me on the petty train. Toot, toot, motherfuckers," I tell her, which has us all falling in a heap laughing, maybe one too many margaritas in the sun have gone to my head.

3

PORTIA

We found the sexiest dresses we could find in our luggage and wore them out to the bar. We knew where they would be at, thanks to them checking in online. I wore a white halter mini dress with a cut-out front, exposing my entire stomach and back. I usually dress sexy and simple, not flashing my junk to everyone, and this outfit is way sluttier than I normally wear, but I knew it would have the desired effect I was after. Yes, it's petty, but damn, it makes me feel good. We walk into the club looking like we've stepped off the runway. We own the looks, the stares, and the catcalls as we look for our table, which is right past Axton and his friend's table. The petty gods are on my side tonight I think as I walk past his table, making sure my hips do the talking. Two boys from his table spotted us and call us over until they realized who we were the closer we got. Yes, the entire table went quiet as we walked past them and toward our table. Little did we know the table across from us would be filled with hot guys who call out to us as we take our seats.

Thank you, karma.

As soon as we had ordered our food and drinks, the other

table of guys was up and over to us. Oh yes, we had hit the jackpot with a group of male models who were here for a photo-shoot, and they finished it today. They were out to celebrate before heading home. *Perfect timing.*

My phone buzzed continuously throughout the night, but I ignored it when I saw it was Axton messaging me. I read some messages as they flashed on the screen, but as soon as I saw the word slut, I ignored them, which only infuriated him more I'm sure. Honestly, I don't care because what this night has proven to me was my rose-colored glass have firmly been pulled off and smashed into smithereens. Axton is an entitled jerk who never loved me. He liked the idea of me. He only cared about his ego and big man on campus persona. Guess he's going to have his ego cut down when he hits the NFL as a small fish in a big pond. His arrogance will surely be cut down to size.

I'm on my way back from the bathrooms when someone grabs me and pulls me to the side.

"What the hell do you think you're doing?" Axton yells at me. His fingers dig into the flesh of my arm which will definitely be bruised.

"Having fun."

Axton lets out an angry chuckle at my answer. "Please, you're trying to make me jealous. But it will not work."

"And yet here you are accosting me in the hallway," I tell him, as I glare at where his fingers grip my arm forcibly.

"I'm looking out for you. Those men only want to get into your pants, Portia," he states coolly as his blue eyes flare with anger.

"Let's hope so."

Axton's face twists angrily at my answer. "If I'd known you were such a slut, I would have asked to share you around with my friends earlier. They seem to like what's mine."

A loud crack echoes down the hallway as my hand connects with Axton's cheek. My blood is boiling, my back stiffens, and

I'm moments away from punching him in his nuts for his disrespectful comments. "Fuck you, Ax," I hiss at him. Next thing I know, he is grabbing me and pushing me up against the wall and his chest is moving heavily, trying to rain in his anger. Panic runs through my veins as I scold myself for stupidly provoking him.

"I miss you, Portia," Axton whispers into my ear as he presses his hard body against me. "I fucked up, okay. Raylene found me in a vulnerable situation and made her move. I was drunk and fucked up on weed. You know how I get. I'm not in control of myself. I don't know where I am half the time or who I'm with."

I listen to his pathetic ramblings. All the while, my stomach turns nauseated by him. "Did you fuck Raylene?" I ask him point blank.

"Baby, I told you I messed up. She took advantage of me. I thought she was you."

"Have you slept with her since arriving in Cabo?" It's been a day. Let's see how he thinks he can weasel his way out of this.

"Babe, I'm single. We broke up," he answers.

"You dumped me on the tarmac before flying out on our vacation with another woman," I explain to him.

"What was I to do? You rejected me. You humiliated me in front of my friends. I had to save face, babe; you know that. I miss you. I need you," he purrs in my ear as he rubs himself against me. I want to be sick.

Placing my hands on his hard chest, I give him a shove. "I don't fucking need nor want you."

Axton stumbles back surprised by the action, his face turns from heated lust to anger lightning fast. "You'll come back to me because no one knows you like I do, Portia. No one is going to love you like I will, and no one is going to fuck you like I do," Axton sneers at me.

"You're no one special, Axton. The sooner you realize the better it will be for everyone else." And with my last barb I turn on my heels and stalk back into the club on shaky legs and take a seat back at the table, where one of the male models wraps his arm around my shoulders and pulls me into him. I let him, needing the connection of someone else to rub out the lingering touch of Axton from my skin. I watch as Axton walks back to his table and pulls Raylene into his lap and starts making out with her right in front of me. I still for a moment, my heart stopping for a beat as seeing them together hurts. I try to shake the feeling. I'm not a robot, no matter how strong I think I'm being. My feelings can't flick off as easily deep down inside.

"Are you okay?" Toby, I think he said his name was, asks. As he looks over at Axton's table and sees the performance, he is putting on for me.

"Do you know that guy?" he asks.

"Unfortunately, he's my ex who literally dumped me this morning at the airport before we stepped on the plane to come down here," I tell him quietly, embarrassed by the entire situation. Toby stills beside me, and I can feel his questioning eyes on me and then back on Axton.

"Let me guess, he's been cheating with that girl during your relationship and now the side piece thinks she's the main piece when clearly he only has eyes for you," Toby muses as his fingers run up and down my arm.

I turn and look up at his handsome face. "Her and many others."

He raises his brows in surprise at my remark. "His loss. I don't understand how he could look at anyone else when you're standing in front of him." Aw, that's sweet of him to say. My mind is all over the place. The more I play over Axton's words, the more I realize how toxic our relationship was without ever knowing it. "If you want some revenge. I'm happy to help," Toby states honestly, giving me a flirty grin.

"Is that so?"

"Yep. My superpower is being a great rebound guy." He gives me a wink, which makes me smile.

"That's an interesting superpower; don't think I've heard of it before."

"It's because it's a secret." He grins while those chocolate eyes look over me hungrily.

"And how does one sign up for this kind of help?" I ask flirtatiously.

Toby leans in and whispers in my ear. "You already have," he says as a hand cups my face and his lips crash down against mine in a blistering kiss which takes my breath away. Moments later, the sound of crashing glass pulls my attention and I look over at Axton's table where his boys are holding him back from coming over to us. They are screaming and shouting at him as they drag him out of the club.

"Told you I had superpowers." Toby chuckles.

And oh boy does he ever. I spent the entire week in bed with Toby, letting his superpowers put me back together again and again.

4

MILES

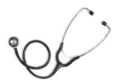

"**W**hat the hell are you doing here?" I ask my brother Remington as he lazily leans against the nurses' desk, flirting with them. I get it, the guy is good-looking, he's athletic since he's a professional polo player, he has a good style, and I guess he's charming in an egotistical way. The complete opposite to our other brother Stirling, who's all serious and conservative.

"Mom made me come and get you. She didn't want you to be late for dinner again. Her exact words were *'give me one dinner with my sons for the year'*," Remi repeats.

Sounds like something Mom would say. She should be happy she has birthed three successful sons, but I get we don't make as much time as we should for them both. It's not like they have time for us either with their busy lives. Dad's an ex-polo player from England, he's best friends with Nacho Garcia, who Remi plays for. Dad never continued with polo after he had his car accident, which ended his promising career. Mom was pregnant with Remi; they had gone out into the city for one last dinner before he was born. We were staying with our grandparents in The Hamptons, and a drunk driver ran into them on their way home and Mom went into early labor with Remi, while Dad's legs were crushed from the impact. We call him the bionic man because he's made of steel from being put back together again. He's lucky he didn't lose any limbs; it was close. I remember visiting the hospital in the city and it's where I fell in love with medicine. I wanted to help my father get better, help him learn to walk again after his legs came out of casts.

Dad lost his career, but luckily, our mother is a celebrated interior designer with her own company and kept us going until he could get back onto his feet again. Dad had to give up on his polo career, which affected him. He sank into a bit of depression during Remi's first two years. Mom and Dad went through a real tough time in their marriage. Mom told Dad he needed to come to work with her as she was worried he might harm himself. Him seeing my mother work and love what she did slowly pulled him from the grips of darkness. Dad fell in love with it and wanted to take her business further, so he went back to school, got all his licenses to become a builder, and now here they are all those years later with Hartford Construction & Design Company, one of the largest companies on the East Coast which build and design luxury homes. To this day, they still work together. They haven't killed each other after all these years of living and working with each other. Their love is strong. I've looked up to them, hoping one day I could be as happy as the two of them.

I'm not looking to settle down yet. Oh hell no, I'm not Stirling, who's been in love with his best friend's sister for years. I know something is happening between him and Audrey as much as he denies it. The bastard likes to keep his secret close to his chest. He also has the added complication of his best friend being his business partner. It's his life, so I'll leave him to it. If he wants to stay miserable, then so be it.

I'm probably more like Remi than Stirling. We are free-spirited guys who love women. Neither one of us is ready to settle down. I'm too selfish when it comes to my career to devote time to any one person. Medicine is my first love. Plus, I've literally spent half my life studying. I'm not about to give it up for anyone. Recently, I've finished my residency and I'm a full-fledged ER doctor now. It's taken me over a decade to get here and I still have years to go to be any kind of contender for promotions, especially after I messed up recently. Kind of got involved with another doctor from my ward. She was the closest thing to a girlfriend I've had in years. I'll admit I was falling for her. She crept through my defenses, but unfortunately for me, she was also sleeping with my boss to secure the promotion we were both going for. Then, to my surprise, my brother Remi too. Wasn't his fault, he didn't know the girl he picked up at the club was mine, he also didn't know she'd never been to my apartment before. When I walked in on the two of them fucking on my couch after I found out she had betrayed me with my boss, I kind of lost my shit with my brother. We were strained there for a little while, but we got back on track again.

"Fine, I'll be ready in ten," I tell my brother.

"All good, these lovely ladies will keep me company, won't you?" Remi asks the nurses, who give him a giggle as an answer.

Rolling my eyes, I head on out the back to clock out and get changed in the locker room. Luckily, I have some dressy clothes in my locker. Ten minutes later, I'm strolling out and dragging my brother from the nurses' station and heading toward the exit of the hospital.

"Tell me you haven't slept with those two beauties? Otherwise, I'm going to have to delete the numbers they gave me," Remi asks.

"Seriously?"

"Um, yeah. I know you, brother, you're more of a player than I am," Remi jokes, nudging my shoulder with his own.

"I'm not that bad," I reply, insulted by his assumption. Remi raises a brow, questioning me. "Fine, yes I have hooked up with those two nurses before," I answer with a huff, which has Remi cackling beside me as we exit the lift out onto the street. "I'm not a bad guy."

"I know you're not." Remi chuckles. "You like women a little too much is all."

"And you don't?" I question him.

"Of course, I love women. Difference is I don't pretend I'm a saint," Remi tells me, giving me a pointed look.

"I'm not pretending anything. I don't advertise my love life like you do, that's all." I shove my hands in my pockets, getting annoyed with my brother and his assumptions.

"Whatever, come on we're running late, and Mom is going to be upset with you if we don't hurry," Remi tells me as he hails a cab.

We were thirty minutes late by the time we arrived at the restaurant. As soon as we entered, I could see Stirling sitting with our parents.

"We finally made it," Remi announces to the table. Mom looks up with a wide smile on her face as Remi kisses her cheeks. Then I follow, doing the same.

"You're late," Dad grumbles as we greet him too before slapping our other brother on the back with love.

"Doesn't matter, Leon. Remi was able to get Miles here, and that's all that matters," Mom explains to our father.

"Hey, I was on time," Stirling adds.

"I know you were, sweetie, thank you. But with Miles, a person dying could have stopped him as he was leaving," Mom explains to my brother. Probably wouldn't happen, but if there are multiple fatalities from one scene, it can cut short your plans real quick. Hence why I don't do relationships. Women don't like it when you stand them up at a restaurant because an emergency came in and you didn't have time to let them know.

Remi swipes Stirling's drink and knocks it back. "Hey." He curses, glaring at our younger brother, who gives him a wide smile.

"I needed it after trying to deal with him on the cab ride over," Remi jokes.

My brothers are so annoying. It's the reason we never get together. I have to put up with their bullshit.

"I'm starved, let's eat," Dad states firmly.

We fall into a familiar pattern of ribbing each other while Mom looks on with a smile on her face and Dad grumbles into his wine.

"Stirling, how's the apartment search for Audrey going?" Mom asks my brother.

"We've seen some, but she's particular about what she wants," Stirling explains to Mom.

"I follow her online; she's grown into such a beautiful young lady," she gushes. "Remi, introduce her to some of your polo friends." Mom turns and looks over at my brother. Stirling stiffens at our mother's suggestion, which makes me grin. Remi turns and looks over at Stirling, who ignores our younger brother's laughter. "I follow Nell online too. I will never understand how the two of you became nothing more than friends. I thought you would end up together." Remi chokes on his drink.

"Your mother had planned out your wedding," Dad adds with a huff.

"Leon, hush," Mom chastises our father, who shrugs his shoulders at her and takes a large sip of wine as a smile dances across his lips.

"Nell and I are friends," Remi explains to Mom, letting her dream of the two of them getting married disappear. Stirling huffs beside Remi, who hits him in his stomach under the table. Interesting, what's that about? "Mom, I'm too young to be thinking about marriage. Plus, my life doesn't suit a relationship."

"You sound like Miles," Dad adds, raising a brow at me.

What is going on tonight?

"Miles is going to be a bachelor until he's fifty," Remi makes fun of me.

I shake my head at him. Look, do I want a family one day? Yes. Do I want it all now, no.

"Your mother wants grandchildren. She needs a project." Dad looks at the three of us as if the lack of grandchildren is a problem.

"How about a dog?" Remi adds.

"Yeah, sounds like a good idea," I say, agreeing with my brother.

"No. Your mother will want one of those fluffy, yappy things." Dad groans. Which makes all of us laugh. Maybe we should buy Mom a little dog to irritate Dad.

"Please, you will end up loving the dog more than I will." Mom smiles, leaning over and kissing Dad's cheek. "What about you, sweetheart, met anyone nice recently?" Mom asks, turning her questioning to me.

"If you mean sleeping with most of the nurses in his ward meeting, then yeah, he has been getting out there," Remi answers for me.

Fucker. I punch him in the arm for throwing me under the bus.

"Miles, I sure hope you're not. I thought you would have learned your lesson last time," Mom whispers.

I cringe at her comment, feeling like the biggest dick for my lapse in judgment.

"To be fair, she was the closest a woman has ever come to locking him down," Remi says, sticking up for me.

"Until you slept with her, Rem," Stirling mumbles.

Mom gasps, and Dad glares at Remi while my brother and I cuss Stirling out. Mom and Dad knew the story about Tracey. They didn't know Remi was the person I found her with. Thanks, Stirling.

The night didn't last long. With all of us arguing back and

forth, Dad had eventually had enough. He told us dinner was on us and grabbed Mom's hand and hauled her out of the restaurant without a backward glance.

"You're such a dick, Stirling," Remi growls at our brother. "Thanks for ruining the night."

"Hey, I was mucking around," he tries to defend himself.

"Still a dick move," I tell him.

"I know."

"Dinner's on you, then?" Remi adds.

Stirling looks up at our brother and shakes his head. "Fine, dinner's on me."

5

PORTIA

"Portia, sweetheart," Carrie Hartford greets me warmly. "It's been such a long time since I've seen you," she tells me, as her green eyes look me up and down. "And you're in college now?"

"Yes. Who knew college would be so hard?" I explain to her, which has her chuckling at my comment.

"You may not know this, but your teacher Andre used to work for me. I trained him up to be who he is today," Carrie tells me. "And when he saw you had an internship with me, which, as you know, I stopped doing a long time ago, he had to call me for a chat. He's very impressed with you."

Oh wow, I did not know.

"I told him you were my goddaughter after he raved about you," Carrie says before giving me a wink. "I'm so proud of you, sweetheart." She squeezes me tightly again.

"Did I hear Portia is here?" Leon calls out as he steps into Carrie's office.

"Hey, Uncle Leon," I greet him. He picks me up and gives me a big hug. Technically, he's not my uncle, but it's what my parents called him and so it stuck.

"Look at you, wow. You have grown up into a beautiful young woman," he tells me, giving me a big smile. Leon is known as a grump most of the time, but I find his grumpiness endearing. I now see where Stirling gets it from. "We are so excited you're working with us. I mean, we are the best, still you could have had your pick of anyone in the city." Leon states proudly.

"She's here now, sweetheart. Let's get her started then. Portia, I'm going to get you to shadow me for this first week. Sit in on phone calls, meetings, design consultations, and even some site visits. That way, you can see what happens on a day-to-day basis in this company. Then next week we can get you working on solo projects," Carrie explains to me excitedly.

I can't wait to start.

"Afternoon, Deidre, I'm here to take my mom to lunch," I hear a male voice state to Carrie's assistant.

"Sure, go on through. She's expecting you," Deidre tells him.

The door to Carrie's office opens and the last person I was expecting to see is Miles Hartford. Isn't he busy saving lives or something? Who knew he had time to drop in and have lunch with his mom, who's not here at the moment. His green eyes widen in surprise as he stares at me sitting in his mother's seat.

"Nell?" he questions me with a frown on his face. He thinks I'm my sister.

"No. It's Portia," I say, correcting him.

"Portia?" he says as his voice raises. "Last time I saw you was years ago. You didn't look so grown up." He frowns as if he can't believe I've grown.

"Last year of college, actually."

"No way," he says, not believing me it seems.

"Yep. Your mom offered me an internship for my last year working with her. Started this week," I explain to him proudly.

"That's fantastic," he says, shaking his head as he can't quite believe I'm standing here in front of him as a fully grown adult. "Swear last time I saw you, you were in diapers." Gee, thanks. That's what a girl wants to hear from a hot guy. Yes, Miles Hartford is hot. All the Hartford brothers are. Being the youngest of everyone by a lot, I never looked at them any other way than family friends, but now, as an adult, I appreciate their aesthetics.

"You didn't just say that to this beautiful woman." Miles's mom interrupts our walk down memory lane.

"Mom," Miles says before giving her a kiss on the cheek and a hug. "I wasn't meaning to be rude, just shocked at how grown up she was. I thought she was Nell when I first came in." He shakes his head.

"They could be twins, right?" Carrie states as she stares at me.

Yes, my sister and I look like twins even though we are four years apart.

"Well, I'll leave you both to it. It's been nice seeing you again, Miles," I say to him as I gather my things from Carrie's desk.

"Why don't you come to lunch?" Carrie asks.

"I've made plans to meet my girlfriends for lunch, sorry."

"Of course. Go, have fun and I'll see you later this afternoon."

I give them both a wave and head out the door.

By the end of the week, I'm exhausted. My brain hurts and all I want to do is crawl into bed and sleep. Who knew working for money would be so exhausting?

"Portia, you down to test out a new bar tonight?" Rachel, one of the office girls, calls out to me. Sucking in a deep breath, I turn around and give her a warm smile. I love the fact they are inviting me out already. The office has been wonderful. Everyone's so nice here.

"Sounds good. I must run home first and get changed. I spilled coffee down my shirt this morning. Do you mind if I bring my besties?" I ask her.

"More the merrier," Rachel says.

I give her the thumbs up and Rachel texts me the information and I head out of the office like a real working person. I jump on the subway and commute uptown, where my apartment is with all the other working people. I feel like such an independent woman. I've got this.

"Hunnies, I'm home," I call out into the apartment as I enter. Cora is lazing on the couch watching the Gossip Girl reboot and Hannah is scrolling on her phone. I'm surprised the girls are home. Cora is working the summer at her mother's company. She runs a multi-billion-dollar luxury brand; her mother's family acquires luxury brands such as fashion, beauty, alcohol, and anything that is a hot commodity in the world of luxury.

Hannah has been a huge sports fan, especially football, as she idolized her big brother Walker all his career until he messed up a couple of years ago. She still follows her other brothers, Jayden and Brooks, who are both football players too. As the only girl in the family, she wasn't given the option to play professionally, so she turned to the highly competitive career of sports reporting. Walker was able to secure her a summer internship at the network he works for. I think he did it to help repair his relationship with her, which has been strained for years. But she knows her stuff better than anyone else. She grew up in a famous football family; her dad played and her mom was a cheerleader, which is how they met. It's in her blood but seeing as she's a woman in a mostly male-dominated work environment, she must work harder than the others to be taken seriously, especially since she looks like a supermodel. Her male work colleagues don't think she can be beautiful and smart.

"Yay, you're home!" Cora calls out, turning her head.

"You survived your first week?" Hannah asks.

"Sure did. You girls up for a night out?" I ask, wiggling my brows at them.

"Sorry, I have a date." Cora grins.

"I'm working the night shift this weekend at the studio." Hannah makes a face.

"Boo. Some people from work have invited me to check out a new bar with them," I explain.

"That's awesome. Text me the details. If my date sucks, I'll meet you there," Cora tells me.

"Have a drink for me. I'm off to grab a double shot espresso to make it through till the morning. Wish me luck." Hannah moans as she heads toward her bedroom to get ready for work.

"So, who's the date with?" I ask Cora.

"Not sure. Mom has organized it." She cringes, which makes me chuckle.

"Guess I'll be seeing you tonight then?" I say, sending her a wink.

"Probably."

"Okay, well, I've got to go. Text me if you need me," I tell her. Cora waves me off and I head toward my bedroom to get ready.

I'm heading downtown and realize my phone is on silent when I look at it with a million missed calls and text messages from my sister since I'm running late meeting up with her. She was out earlier celebrating her internship in Paris working for famous designer, Yvette Sanchez. I'm proud of her stepping out on her own. I know she has wanted to work with Mom on her equestrian label, but Mom's designs are more working gear not party gear, plus she's stuck in her ways. I know Mom's tough love treatment hurt Nell, but it has made her think about what she wants to do with her life. The girl gets paid a ridiculous amount of money to be an influencer. She's roped me into doing some work with her. She signed me to the same agency as she is with, and slowly I've been building up my brand. Nell is more into the fashion side of influencing whereas I'm into architecture and design.

I pay the cab driver and get out right in front of the bar when my phone rings again. This time I hear it and pick it up.

"Where the hell are you, Portia?" Nell hisses down the phone, a slight slur to her words. Oh dear, Nellie's trashed and cranky. I grab my ID and realize it's not in the back of my phone. Where the hell is it? I search around the ground, thinking it's fallen out somewhere. I can hear Nell huffing on the end of the phone, getting agitated with me. No, I remember pulling my cards and stuff out of my wallet and stuffing them into my phone case so I didn't have to bring my bag. I must have pulled my ID out and left it at home. Shit.

"Chill. I'm outside. I forgot my ID. Can you lend me yours?" I ask her, seeing as we look so similar.

"Fine. I'll be out in a sec." She curses and hangs up on me.

Nell's acting weird tonight. I wonder if it's got to do with Remi. He usually causes her to lose her mind. I don't understand why she is fighting the attraction the two of them have. They have been back and forth with each other most of my life. Remi's hot. His billboard in Times Square is a work of art; I mean, who doesn't love a ten-foot dick. Maybe I need to date older men. Because after the disaster which was my relationship with Axton, the immature fuck, I should date men, not boys. He still stalks my socials. He still likes my photos. What did I ever see in him? *The six-pack and big dick.* That will usually do it. It's a shame the big dick was wasted on someone like him who didn't know how to use it.

I see Nell exit the club and she doesn't look happy at all, especially as I realize we are both wearing the same dress. She's in black and I'm in red. Could be the reason her face looks like thunder. Hey, not my fault, we have great taste in fashion.

"Here." She hands me her ID. "Where are your friends?"

"They're stuck in traffic," I tell her.

Rachel messaged me while I waited. They stopped somewhere else first and lost track of time and now are stuck in traffic trying to get across town.

"Right, well, Miles Hartford is inside. He was helping me celebrate my move to Paris. He's drunk. Nothing happened," my sister says quickly, which means *lie.* Nell has had a crush on Miles forever, which I think is stupid because Remi is the right guy for her. Nell's too stubborn to let herself fall for Remi again because he's hurt her in the past, *which I get.* You don't see me giving Axton a second chance. No way in hell, but Remi is a good guy underneath all his ego. Axton isn't. "Make sure you keep an eye on him," Nell tells me pointedly. He must be extremely drunk if she's asking me. Poor Doc partied too hard for an old man.

"Sure thing. Why aren't you staying?" I ask her because leaving me with Miles is plain weird.

"Champagne headache," she says before dashing off toward a cab and leaving me there, staring at her back in confusion.

I hand my ID to the bouncer who looks at it and gives me a wink before letting me in past the red velvet rope. Where the hell is Miles? As I look around the bustling bar area, this is going to be like finding a needle in a haystack. Pushing my way through the crowd, I see Miles standing in the corner, swaying to the music, and sipping on a drink. His cheeks are bright red. Oh boy, he's gone.

"Hey, watch it," a man sneers at me as I accidentally bump his arm, which sloshes his drink down my side. Oops. When I look up to apologize to the guy, familiar blue eyes stare back at me. "Portia?" Axton asks, looking as surprised at me standing there as I am at him. What the hell is he doing here? I stare at him for way too long before pulling myself together.

"Sorry, didn't see you there," I tell him as I try to move away from him, but he grabs my arm instead.

"Are you stalking me?" he asks.

I don't mean to burst out laughing, but I do. Unfortunately, this captures the attention of his friends who look over at us curiously, especially Raylene, whose eyes bug out when she sees me standing there talking to Axton.

"Ew. No. I'm meeting someone," I tell him as Raylene slithers up and wraps herself around Axton's arm. He tenses for the slightest of moments, but those blue eyes narrow on me, and he pulls her tighter into his side. Whatever, good luck with all that, Raylene, you're going to need it.

"Who?" Axton asks, not believing me.

"The man over there," I point in Miles's direction, and by a stroke of luck, he looks my way. His face lights up and he waves at me. Thank goodness he remembers me. Axton's eyes darken as he spies Miles, and Raylene's eyes widen in appreciation. Miles is a damn supermodel compared to Axton. "This walk down memory lane has been fun, but I have a man waiting for me." And with that, I push my way through the crowd, feeling Axton's angry eyes on my back the entire way.

"Just go with it," I say quickly. I don't give Miles time to say anything before I grab his face and kiss him.

Holy shit, this was a bad idea. Especially when Miles takes charge and kisses the ever-loving hell out of me. His tongue sweeps across my mouth as thick lips press against my own. Strong hands wrap themselves around me as large palms grip my ass and pull me toward him, feeling his hard package against my stomach. Oh wow, the Doc is packing.

"I thought I overstepped earlier when I tried to kiss you, Nell," Miles confesses as he holds my face with his palm. My lips tingling. I've never been kissed so savagely before and I kind of want more. "I know I don't compare to Remi, but..."

That's why Nell was running like a bat out of hell to get away from Miles—because he kissed her. I bet she realized she's in love with Remi, not Miles, and it hit her like a ton of bricks. A smile falls across my lips at the crazy feelings my sister is probably dealing with at this moment. I should tell Miles I'm Portia, not Nell. I should, but Miles leans in and kisses me again and the entire world fades to black. Especially when he picks me up and pushes me up against the wall and I can feel every hard plane of his body, every divot of muscle, every throb of his thickening length against my stomach. Shit. This man is dangerous, especially when I kiss him back with as much furiousness. I know this is wrong, but five more minutes of this and I'll stop.

Promise.

Then Miles moves his thigh between my legs, and I unashamedly rub myself against his thigh and my entire body lights on fire. I'm not so sure I can keep my promise.

Five more minutes, then I'll push him away. I promise.

6

MILES

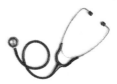

"Oi, get up dickhead." Someone curses as they shove me hard. What the hell? I was having a pleasant sleep dreaming about all the things I want to do to... I turn over as I try to focus on the person talking to me. "Fucking hell, man, put some clothes on." The voice groans as I realize I'm still nude from the night before. I pull my sheet across, covering me, and then reality hits me. Shit, I look over beside me expecting to see her lying there naked, but when I focus my eyes, she's not there.

"Looks like you had a good night last night," Remi teases me as I stare at the crumpled sheets around me. Remi. Shit. I frantically look around the room for her, but she's not here. He is going to kill me when he finds out what I have done. Why the hell did I bring her home when I knew I had brunch with Remi this morning? Am I an idiot?

"Um, yeah, something like that. I might have a shower." I get up and rush to the bathroom and slam the door shut. My head hurts like it's about to split into pieces. My stomach turns as if every remnant from last night wants to be expelled. I switch the shower on and jump in, letting the freezing needle-like jets of water hit my body, praying it will sober me up. I must tell Remi what I did last night. *No, don't, it will hurt him.* But he feels something for her. And you thought with your dick as per usual, didn't care about the consequences of your actions all because you felt good in the moment. *She felt good, oh so good.* She was practically tearing my clothes off at the club, in the cab, and in my foyer as I tried to get my keys.

"I need you, now," she purrs, unable to unhook herself from my lips long enough for me to turn the key in the slot.

"Soon, baby, I promise," I tell her as the lock clicks and the door swings open with the two of us stumbling in. Her lips are back on mine as she drops her things to the floor. I trip over them and end up kicking them sideways. I'll worry about them in the morning. Her hands are on my belt buckle. Undoing it quickly, she pulls the leather from its straps and gives it a crack like a whip. I still at the sound and pull away from her ever so slowly. She quirks a brow at me, a mischievous smile falling across her lips.

"Do you like to be spanked, doctor?" she questions me seductively. Oh shit, that's hot. I... crap, my brain seems to have malfunctioned at her words. And the way she used the word doctor in that tone sends shivers running down my spine. Look, I'm up for a bit of role play, but usually most of my liaisons are quickies as neither one of us has the time. But now she's asking me for something I didn't know I needed. I did not know she was kinky. Is that why she is so far under Remi's skin?

"Things just got interesting," she says, grinning as she takes a couple of steps back from me, her brown eyes flaring with flecks of lust filled gold as she looks over me hungrily. "Shirt off, doctor," she commands, and I do as I am told. I've been with assertive women before, but usually in the end they like it when I take control, but this seems different. I want to submit to her; see how far she is taking this little scenario. My dick throbs at the prospect of this happening. "Now your pants." Her voice is

serious as her eyes trail over me. I kick off my shoes, then toe off my socks before I swiftly, in one move, pull down my pants and underwear, leaving me naked in front of her. I watch as her eyes widen with need as she focuses on my cock. Yes, I've been blessed in the pants department. It's why I have such a reputation with the nurses. They all want a ride of my anaconda. "Impressive, doc." She grins. Her cheeks are flushed with need, transfixed by my dick. Then the crack of the leather belt flicks again in her skillful hand. She grew up around horses, so I'm sure she knows her way around a whip or two. My dick twitches at the thought and bobs around in front of me. She notices and a smile forms on her lips. "Hands on the couch, doc," she demands, and I do as I'm told, reaching out, placing my hands on the edge of the couch, my fingers gripping the fabric as I try to still my beating heart which is running a mile a minute with anticipation.

"Arch your back for me," she whispers against my ear as her fingers run down my spine, giving me goosebumps along their trail. "Open your legs a little more." She taps my thighs, making me spread myself open for her. I've never put myself in a such a vulnerable situation before. Her hands then run along my ass cheek and she gives the taunt skin a pinch, making me grunt in appreciation, which pulls a giggle from her lips. "What are your thoughts on ass play, doc?" she questions me as her thumb runs along the crease of my ass, making me flinch ever so slightly till a thumb passes my hole and the tiniest bit of pressure is pushed against it. A low moan falls from my lips at the feeling. No woman has pushed the boundary like this before, but I think I like it. Her finger then runs along my taint before cupping my balls. Shit. Who the hell is this woman? She pulls a grunt from me as she cups my aching balls in her palm. "They feel heavy with need, doc," she purrs behind me. Damn right they are heavy with need. This woman has worked me up into a frenzy. If she doesn't hurry up and fuck me, I'm going to embarrass myself tonight and probably come all over my couch. Worth it for sure.

Then her warm hand moves from my balls to my dick and tries to wrap around me. Like I said, I'm known for my dick, it has impressive girth. Her hand hardly wraps around it, but she gives it a good go, sliding my pre-cum over my dick. Damn, this is hot. She continues stroking me, building me up. I'm lost in her rhythmic strokes until a crack hits my bare ass, surprising me, but her hand continues to slide up and down my shaft which takes the sting away from the bite of leather across my ass. Wow. I'm very confused over what I am feeling in this moment until she does it again, not too hard, just enough of a bite to sting nicely while she continues to stroke me. She does this two more times and I swear I'm moments away from dumping a load all over the couch. Next thing I know, she is dropping to her knees and her lips are wrapping around my dick as she tries to take me down her throat. The moment I feel the back of her throat I'm done for. My fingers move from the edge of the couch to her hair as I hold her in place and fuck her face until my balls tingle, and I know I'm moments away from blowing my load down her throat.

"I'm about to come." I gently tug on her hair, giving her the option to move or not. She looks up at me with those molten brown eyes and smirks around my dick. Fuck, that's the hottest thing I've ever seen. She tries to take me further down her throat and I'm done for. A couple more pumps past her lips and I'm coming down her throat and she's swallowing me up like a good little girl. Fuck. Yes. She falls from my dick panting and I need a moment to catch my breath because it was so much more than I ever expected.

"I've never done that before," she confesses quietly from her knees. I stare down at her, still fully dressed. Her mascara has run from tears when I choked her with my dick, her cheeks are flushed from my orgasm, and those innocent brown eyes stare up at me.

This woman is perfection.

"Never sucked an enormous cock before?" I question her. She smiles and shakes her head.

"Spanked no one before either," she adds, surprising me because of the way she wielded that thing and how confident she was, I thought otherwise.

"But you've thought about it before, haven't you?" I ask, cupping her face. She nods and smiles. My dick twitches back to life, but I need more. She's unsettled me since the moment we walked through my door. I pick her up from her knees and throw her over my shoulder before I storm down the hallway toward my bedroom. Kicking open my door, I throw her on the bed and launch myself at her.

My mind wanders back to reality, even though my dick is now thinking about the best sex of its life with someone I shouldn't have had it with. Let me get through this brunch with my brother and when I come home, I can sort out what the hell is going on in my head.

Stepping out of the shower, I grab my towel and dry myself off before heading into my bedroom. I grab a pair of jeans off the floor and a T-shirt before stepping out into the hallway and bust my brother raiding my fridge.

"Shit, sorry, man." Remi jumps as he drops the ceramic plate on the floor, shattering it after I find him devouring a brownie I've been saving for later. Guess it's the least I can do after last night.

"Don't worry about it," I tell him.

Remi gives me a strange look because I'm a clean freak. Must be at the hospital and my brothers come into my home and mess shit up, and it annoys me, which usually makes them do it even more. Me telling Remi to forget about breaking a plate and eating my brownies is a little off.

"Let me clean up and we can go," he tells me as he searches in cupboards for the dustpan and brush. He stills for a moment, lost in a thought before standing up with something in his hand.

It's an ID. How the hell did that get there? Then my stomach sinks as Remi's eyes narrow on the photo and he turns slowly and glares at me. Shit. My entire body stiffens. This is the moment my brother kills me. I can see it on his face. He's confused and angry.

"Look, I can explain, Remi," I tell him, holding up my hands.

"You can explain?" he growls at me.

"We were both extremely drunk." As soon as the words leave my mouth, I know it's a pathetic excuse. There is no excuse. Nothing I can say can make up for what I've done.

"When you say we, you mean, you and Nell?" he snarls through clenched teeth.

"Remi, please. It just happened," I explain to him, trying to defuse the situation.

"It just happened. It just fucking happened!" he screams at me before punching a hole in my wall. Shit. His hand. That's his livelihood, I can't destroy it too.

"Remi, stop, you're going to break your hand!" I scream at him.

"You motherfucking bastard." Remi runs at me, his hand grips me by the collar as he pins me to the wall. Hit me. I can take it. I deserve it. "You could have any woman in New York and yet you fucked the woman that I love!" he screams in my face. Shit, he actually loves her. I thought it was more that I had her first. She's mine, don't touch, but this is bone deep to the core love I can see written on his face. Fuck. I'm the worst brother in the world, that's for sure. He's never going to forgive me for this.

Pushing him away. "I had no idea you were in love with her. Fuck, Rem. I thought you were just friends. That's all you've ever told me you were. I did not know you were in fucking love with her. Shit. Fuck, I'm an asshole. I didn't know. She said nothing," I pace. Why the hell did Nell not say something, she could have stopped it. Warned me.

"I never want to speak to you again," Remi tells me through gritted teeth and unbridled rage.

"Remi, come on. I'm your brother."

"Exactly. My fucking brother." He points at my face.

"Remi. I didn't know!" I scream at him as he turns on his heel and disappears through the door.

What the hell am I going to do?

PORTIA

"What the hell time do you call this?" Hannah asks, popping her head over the couch in the living room as she watches football highlights.

"I've fucked up, Hannah," I tell her, taking a seat beside her on the couch. Hannah raises her brows at me but doesn't push for more. She waits me out. "I can't tell you. I'm embarrassed."

"Babe, we've all been there. Gone home with someone who we thought was hot and then woke up and realized who the hell is this?" She tries to calm me.

"Oh no. The guy was hot. And big, oh so big, but…"

Hannah stares at me, confused I'd be upset over the combination and ordinarily I wouldn't be this upset, but Miles is different.

"Then what's the problem?" she asks.

"If I tell you, swear this goes no further even to Cora?" I ask her.

Hannah glares at me before frowning, but ultimately, she agrees. I hate keeping secrets from Cora, but I need someone to talk to about this and until I've worked through it, I don't want anyone to know.

I explain to her what happened last night, about Nell and running into Axton and then using Miles Hartford as my personal scratchboard even though he was very drunk and thought I was my sister for most of the night. Hannah stares at me, processing everything I dumped into her lap.

"I thought doctors were smart?" she asks, catching me off guard with her question. "How the hell did he not realize he was with two different girls?"

"He was drunk," I explain to her.

"But not too drunk to have sex?" she questions me.

"He had stamina," I add. We both look at each other and burst out laughing, which was exactly what I needed.

"Still weird he thought you were your sister. Was it some kind of kink the doctor was interested in?" Hannah asks.

"Looking back on what happened, yes I can see how it would seem strange not to realize at some point who I was but, in the moment, we sort of went for it. There wasn't a lot of talking."

"It's because the doc's giant dick kept your mouth shut?" Hannah asks, cracking up laughing at her crude joke.

"Screw you. But yes. His dick was huge but not unusable if you know what I mean," I tell her, wiggling my brows at her.

"You're such a bitch. I can still smell sex on you. Go have a shower and wash your filthy sins away. But don't stress too much. Chalk it up as an experience which will never be repeated. And if he was as drunk as you say he was, he probably won't remember a thing." This is true. It's going into my spank bank never to be repeated. "Plus, your sister isn't interested in him, anyway. You didn't break girl code," Hannah reassures me.

I let out a heavy sigh and make my way to my bathroom and undress after my walk of shame. I get into the shower and let the warm water run over my aching muscles. Why does it feel like I've run a marathon? Who knew you could pull muscles from sex?

"Open those legs, woman, and let me feast," Miles growls as

I lay back on the bed. I think I've lost my mind because what I did to him earlier, um, yeah, was totally out of the box for me. Spanking? Pretending I'm some confident dominatrix, who the hell am I in this moment? The first swipe of his tongue along me has me arching off his bed, and he hasn't even bothered to take my underwear off. Not like it's anything more than a piece of string anyway, but he's moved it to the side and is currently eating me out like a starving man. I bet because he's a doctor and knows anatomy and stuff, he knows exactly how to find the G-spot and the clit. As those thoughts enter my mind, the good doctor does exactly that. Long, thick fingers disappear inside of me, stretching me, finding my delicate core, and caressing the sensitive nerves right inside of me, and have me panting and thrashing against his face. Yes. He continues to work me into a frenzy, pulling me closer and closer to the edge until he stops as I'm about to reach the precipice. What the hell? No. Why? Then the next thing I know, my underwear is being pulled off me. He then flips me over onto my stomach and tells me to get on all fours, which I do. He unzips my dress and pulls it off me. My bra goes along with it. Then his fingers grab my hips, picking me up and resting me back over his face. Oh, my goodness, I'm going to suffocate him doing this.

"Stop moving, would you, and let me finish what I started," he mumbles against my pussy. *This is a first for me. Most guys I've been with, it's a mission and a half to get them to go down on me, let alone letting me sit on their face. Seems like a lot of firsts tonight. Just go with it, Portia. It's one night of passion and fun. His expert tongue does its divine dance across my pussy until I'm squirming again, until my hands are gripping the headboard and I'm moaning his name across my lips till his teeth nip my clit and push me over the edge into oblivion. My legs shake, my body convulses; I swear I see stars and I sag forward, trying to catch my breath. "Fuck, you taste amazing, Nell." I still at the*

use of my sister's name in the moment, and it quickly takes the shine off my euphoria.

"It's Portia," I mumble to myself, knowing I should correct him properly, but I know if I do, he will not fuck me. His anaconda dick is going to get tucked away, and I'm going to be sent home in the closest Uber. We've come this far, might as well keep going. He's going to be upset when he finds out, so might as well get my happy ending in first.

Miles lifts my hips up a bit and moves from beneath me, the crinkle sound of wrapping being torn fills the room. Then I feel two hands grab my ass and grip it tightly. He spreads my cheeks and nudges my entrance with the tip of his dick.

"I'll go slow at first, sweetheart," he mumbles as he tests my entrance with the tip, teasing me mercilessly, until I push back against him and feel the delicious burn of him stretching me. Damn, he's big.

"Shit." Miles groans as I stretch around him. His fingers dig into my hips as he tries to control himself. He eases himself out ever so gently before pushing himself back in, hitting every delicate nerve ending, and then I'm done for. He doesn't give me any more chances to get used to his size as he begins pistoning into me at a rapid rate. Animalistic grunts fill the room as he takes what he wants from me, and I'm powerless to do anything but enjoy the ride. I'm going to be sore in the morning. Without breaking his rhythm, Miles reaches around, and his expert fingers strum my clit as if he has done so for years. The sensations are all too much and I come on a scream probably waking up his neighbors, but I don't care because it was one hell of an intense orgasm and I swear I've died and gone to heaven because I'm seeing nothing but stars. Miles doesn't stop. He keeps pushing through my quaking and continues to fuck the hell out of me. His fingers strum again and what on earth is happening? How the hell is he pulling another orgasm from me so quickly, I don't have time to *brace myself as I'm pushed so far off the edge where I'll never to be found again. The only reason I don't collapse fully is his strong fingers holding my hips. There will probably be bruises in the morning, but I don't care. Then his fingers dig into me harder and his thrusting increases until Miles growls his release so loud we have well and truly woken up his neighbors. A slew of curses fall from his lips as he continues to buck into me. Then I feel something sticky inside, and I freeze. Miles must feel it too as he pulls himself immediately from me, and I hate I feel his sudden loss.*

"Shit, the condom broke." Miles curses. "Please say you're on birth control?" he asks, panic lacing his words.

I roll over and stare at his handsome face. "Yeah, I'm on birth control."

"Thank fuck. I've never had a condom break before," he states as he shakes his head in bewilderment.

"We were kind of rough," I say with a smile, feeling the delicious ache between my legs from him.

"Did I hurt you?" he asks, concerned.

"Gosh no. It was the perfect amount of rough," I say, giving him a wink, which relaxes him.

"Right, let's get cleaned up then and maybe we can rough ourselves up again."

Oh, hell yeah. I like the sound of that.

The hot water brings me back to reality as I scrub myself clean, because the dirty thoughts swirling around my head have me all hot and bothered again. I don't understand how I could be raring to go again after an insane number of orgasms. Is it even possible to come that much in one night? How am I ever going to go back to dating normal guys after Miles Hartford's magical dick? *You must, because there is no way in hell he is going to want to see you again after he knows you pretended to be someone else for the night. Not my fault he was stupid and didn't realize I wasn't my sister.* A little voice inside my head states the obvious. He's going to be kept as your dirty little secret and his magical dick is going to have to stay in your spank bank vault, never to see the light of day ever again.

Stepping out of the shower feeling more human than I did jumping in, I wrap my towel around me and walk into my bedroom and grab my phone. I've missed a call from Nell and have some text messages from her.

Nell: Wake up. I need my ID back. I'm packing for Paris.

Nell: Answer your phone. What happened last night?

Nell: Where the hell are you? Call me as soon as you can.

Hitting the call button, I wait for my sister to pick up the phone.

"Finally, where the hell have you been?" Nell questions me.

"Sorry, not all of us went home early like a grandma," I tell her.

"Hey, I was day drinking and you know it hits differently," she declares. "How was your night? Did Miles get home okay?"

Oh yeah, Miles got home fine. "Miles left not long after you. Guess he doesn't have the stamina like he used to," I say, cracking a joke which makes my sister grumble.

"Did he say anything about me?" she asks. I can hear the undertone of her panic in her words.

"No. Why did something happen?" I ask, wondering if she will tell me what happened between them.

"Oh no. Nothing at all. He's like a brother. Ew," she answers quickly.

"Haven't you had a crush on Miles for like years?"

"I've had no actual feelings for Miles," she explains to me.

"Because of Remi?"

"Yeah. But you know it's complicated. Doesn't even matter now I'm off to Paris. I need to concentrate on my career, not men."

Sounds like a solid plan. Maybe I should take a leaf out of my sister's book. Forget Miles Hartford because nothing can happen with him. And concentrate on this internship and making a great impression so once I've graduated, I can get a full-time job there. Oh, no. Realization hits me that I work with Miles's family. How am I going to look Carrie in the eye on Monday knowing exactly what I did with her son on the weekend?

"So, can I come over and grab my ID?" Nell asks again.

"Sure. I guess," I answer Nell before hanging up.

I flip my phone over and pull the cards from my phone and freeze. The ID isn't there. What the hell? I frantically turn my bedroom upside down looking for the little slip of plastic, but it's not here. I sit on my bed and try to think back to where I might have lost it. Then it hits me. No. I've left it at Miles's place. I dropped my phone, and the contents spilled over the floor when I was dry humping him in the doorway. This morning when I was rushing out of his apartment, I grabbed what I could find and shoved it into my phone case. I'd completely forgotten about the ID. I can't go back to Miles and ask him for it. There's only one thing to do. I look down at my phone and text my sister back.

Portia: Sorry, babe, looks like I've lost your ID while out last night.

Nell: Are you fucking serious?

My sister writes back instantly.

Nell: I need it for Paris. Thanks, now I have to add getting a new ID to the long list of things I need to do before moving to Paris. You're so annoying.

I'm happy to take my sister's wrath over losing the ID than her finding out I went home with Miles.

No one can ever know.

8

MILES

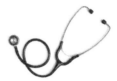

I 've joined some buddies for drinks at our local sports bar, hoping a night out with them will give me clarity on the whole Remi situation. I fucked up big time. I'm worried I've done irrefutable damage to our relationship because of my dick. I know how angry I was when I caught him and Tracey together and I wasn't in love with her. Yes, I felt something, but love? Hell no.

He loves Nell.

"Hey," Smith Johnson says. He's one of my closest and oldest friends. He's a detective in the NYPD and is the first person to arrive on time. I give him a nod as I take a seat in our favorite booth. I try to catch the eye of the owner and one of our close friends, Dylan King. The crazy Australian, he owns our local bar, The Antipodean, which is a weird mix of Australian and Americana. One television will play baseball while the other is playing a weird ass game called cricket, then another might have football on it while Australian Rules Football is playing. Dylan owns the bar with his brother Liam and their cousin Owen King. It's a good night in here, a place where I can switch off from the stressors of the emergency room. It's the same with

Smith too. Both of us dealing with death daily sometimes need to be surrounded by stuffed koalas and watching *The Crocodile Hunter* on loop to decompress.

Dylan eventually spies me and gives me a wave and nod to let me know he'll be bringing over my drink.

"You look like shit," Smith states bluntly as his eyes look me over intensely.

"That's because I fucked up, man," I tell him seriously. The detective raises an inquisitive eyebrow in my direction.

"If it's illegal, you know you're putting me in a precarious situation, Miles," he warns me before lifting his beer bottle to his lips and taking a long drag of his beer.

"Nothing like that, but I may have broken the bro code," I explain to him, letting out a heavy sigh.

"Shit, sorry I'm late. The babysitter was stuck in traffic," Lane Campbell states, rushing into the booth looking exhausted. Which he probably is. The guy's a single dad and runs his own media company, doing high profile advertising for luxury brands and is juggling the two. "What did I miss?" he asks, looking between Smith and me.

"Miles has broken bro code, and he's freaking out," Smith fills him in. Lane stares at me, trying to work out what's going on, but I'm interrupted when Dylan comes over with a tray of beers.

"Here you go, fellas, get 'em in ya," he says with an Aussie twang.

I grab mine and throw it back, almost finishing it in one gulp when I place the bottle back. My friends are all staring at me like I've lost my mind and maybe I have.

"Spill," Smith commands using his detective voice, and so I do.

I would totally crack under his interrogation. He's a scary guy. I tell them all about my night with Nell and how Remi found her ID and how he had a massive blow up and now he's blocked me. They are sitting in silence, staring at me, slowly blinking.

"Mate, come on, that's a dick thing to do," Dylan says as he stares at me with a frown on his face.

"I know. I was so drunk I had no idea what I was doing," I try to explain.

"But you kind of did though," Smith tells me honestly. "Except you didn't care."

Look, I appreciate my friends being honest with me, but maybe not this honest. I feel like the worst person in the world.

"She also could have said no. So, it's not all Miles's fault," Lane adds.

"True, but his loyalty was to his brother, not this chick," Smith argues.

"Was it at least good?" Dylan asks with a grin on his face as he sips his beer.

"Come on," I say to my friends, shaking my head.

"I'll take that answer as it was." Dylan smirks.

"Would you do it again?" Smith asks.

I hesitate for the briefest of moments, and it's enough for my boys to call me out. They all start yelling at me, cursing me out while ribbing me. Of course, I wouldn't do it again, especially seeing Remi's face, but the sex was unforgettable and as bad as it sounds, it's going to stay in my spank bank for a long time.

"Least we know not to bring any women around this dickhead," Dylan teases and my asshole friends agree.

"Hey, come on, guys. I'm not that bad. I put myself in a fucked-up situation, let my dick do the thinking and now I've fucked everything up."

"Least Remi will be in Europe for the summer. Give you two time to work out your shit," Smith adds.

"He's blocked me. Don't think we are going to resolve anything that way," I mumble as I rip the label off my beer bottle.

"Time is the only healer," Lane tells me.

Man, I feel like a dick complaining about my problem when it's been two years since Lane's wife died and left him and his son alone. Yes, the way she died was pretty messed up. She was sleeping with his business partner, and they died when a drunk driver ran them off the road. Lane lost it there for a while with every new revelation coming out.

"How are you doing?" I ask Lane, changing the subject of the disaster that is my life.

"How was your date with that chick... um, what was her name?" Dylan asks.

"Britney." Lane looks up at Dylan and from the face he is pulling, it doesn't sound good.

"Yeah. She was hot," Dylan says with a grin.

"It was like talking to a cardboard cutout. She spent all her time taking photos of her meal, then herself." Lane cringes as he tells the story.

We've been setting Lane up with people helping him get out there again, otherwise he would go from his office to home and back again without going outside, and that's not healthy.

"Wasn't thinking about her conversation skills when I set you up," Dylan states with a deep rumble of a laugh as he slams his hand on the table.

"Unlike you, I need more than a great rack to get my dick going," Lane grumbles.

"Least you noticed she had a great rack. We're making progress," Dylan teases while Lane shakes his head.

"The guy's damaged, not dead, Dylan," Smith adds bluntly, making us all wince at his choice of words.

"Thanks, I think?" Lane mumbles while taking a gulp of his beer.

After a couple more beers, the drama of my life is forgotten.

"It's going to be all right," Smith mumbles to me as we

slump in the booth, way past closing time. "It may not happen overnight, but Remi will eventually forgive you."

"He loves her, Smith. Like deep to the core," I explain to him.

"Maybe so, but it's not all on you. Yes, he's your brother, but she too, has or had a relationship with Remi for as long as you have. Your families are close," Smith says.

"This is true, but I still should have known better. I need to stop thinking about my dick so much. I should probably grow up and stop thinking I'm still in my twenties," I say, turning the beer bottle in my hand around.

"How you act after this will define your relationship with your brother," Smith says, advising me. "You going to still have contact with the girl?" I shake my head. It doesn't matter how amazing the sex was, there's a hundred other girls in New York that could give me what I want. *Being tied up again?* Yeah. Maybe. Probably. I enjoyed it. Man, I'm losing my mind. "If you stay away from her then you and Remi can work on your broken relationship."

"What happens if they end up together?" I ask him.

"Then it's on them. It has nothing to do with you," Smith explains.

Will I be able to sit across from her at family functions and not remember the way she blew my mind?

"Miles, it has nothing to do with you," Smith says, reiterating his words.

"Yeah, yeah I know," I tell him, unconvincingly.

9

PORTIA

I t's been a month since that fateful night with Miles and I may have spent my time stalking him on his socials. Never knew I needed hot doctor thirst trap photos but here I am staring at Miles in his light blue scrubs leaving nothing to the imagination, the whore. Showing off his anaconda's imprint against the thin material with a sly smirk on his face. He knows exactly what he is doing and is loving it. I'm one of the millions panting over the images, only thing is I know exactly how the dick print feels.

"Ah," I scream, dropping my phone on the bed.

"What is it?" Cora says, rushing into my room, her eyes widen with panic.

"I accidentally liked Miles's photo," I say, staring at my phone. My heart racing a million miles a minute as I try to work out how to come back from a rookie error.

"Did you unlike it?" Cora asks.

"I didn't know I liked it until he sent me a DM," I explain to her.

Cora stares at me, her eyes wide, as her long lashes blink slowly. "He DM'd you?" I nod. "What was the photo?" she asks.

I'm not proud of myself for looking, but it's his fault for putting thirst trap pictures all over his socials. I pick up my phone and turn it to her, showing her the photo of his glistening, chiseled chest as he pushed himself out of the water. Thank goodness it wasn't one of the doctor scrubs photos with his obvious dick imprint, at least this could be explained away innocently. I was liking one of his holiday snaps.

"Oh," is all Cora can say.

"See, this is a problem," I tell her.

"Not really. What does his DM say?" she asks.

"I haven't read it yet. I freaked out when I saw it pop up," I explain to her. She raises a brow at me and urges me to see what it says. With my heart thumping wildly in my chest, I open my messages to see what he says.

Miles: Hey there. Hope you're well. Damn, I miss Mexico. I need another holiday stat. Been working too hard.

I read out the message to Cora.

"That isn't that bad. He's opened the door for you to reply," she says.

"You think he wants to have a conversation with me?" I ask her.

"Well, you liked his photo, and he noticed, so I'm assuming so. Has he liked any of yours then?"

I stare back down at my phone and scroll through my notifications and sure enough; he has liked some of my photos. He's liked a heap of not so innocent photos. I turn my phone back around to Cora and show her the photos. Most of them were after my breakup, where I went a little crazy with the half-naked photos in Mexico.

"Guess he's interested," Cora adds.

"Interested in me?" I question her.

"Why else would he like all your bikini photos?"

"Because they were in Mexico, which is where his photo was

taken." Trying to explain logic other than he likes me to her. "You don't think he remembers, do you?"

"If he does, then he wants more," Cora teases me.

I eventually caved one night after too many cocktails and explained the whole sordid night to Cora. It's hard keeping things from your besties. Still, I'm not sure how I feel about the chances of him remembering that night and wanting more. Yes, it was the best sex of my life, but I work for his mom. Our families are close. Pretty sure my dad would kill him if he knew about what we have done. No. He was being nice, liking some photos back of mine. Maybe I should follow him. It would be weird not to, especially after liking his stuff. I mean, how else would I have seen him if he didn't show up on my feed. *You stalked him.* Exactly, and that seems way worse. I click the follow button quickly and pray he doesn't notice.

"What are you going to say back to him?" Cora asks, pulling me from my internal freak out.

"Nothing."

"You have to message him back, otherwise it will make things weird," she tells me. Maybe she's right. I do work with his mom.

"Fine. I'll think of something non flirty to say."

"Good girl," Cora says, giving me a smile as she walks back out of my room.

I slump on my bed and stare at the screen, wondering what on earth I should write?

Portia: Love Mexico. It's one of my fave places but last time I was there, my boyfriend dumped me to go hook up with a friend.

There, friendly enough, isn't it? He can't read anything into that at all, can he?

Miles: That fucking sucks. What a dick thing to do. Are you talking about that football douche?

I stare at the screen in shock. How does he know about Axton?

Miles: He totally downgraded. She's pretty, but…

Portia: How do you know about them?

Miles: Mom told us about the breakup at dinner one night. You're better off without him anyway, his photos are douchey. I may have done some stalking of his profile earlier wondering who the hell would dump a girl like you.

How am I supposed to respond to that? Is he flirting with me or being nice?

Portia: Guess I dodged a bullet there.

Miles: Sure did. You're young and beautiful. There will be plenty of men vying for your attention.

He thinks I'm beautiful. I'm still confused by this entire conversation.

Portia: I'm focusing on my career. It's my last year of college.

Miles: Good plan. There will be plenty of other guys out there for you.

Guess that means no round two from him ever happening again.

Portia: Well, thanks for the chat. I've got to go, college stuff to finish.

Miles: Sure, totally understand. Don't be a stranger. I'll see you around. And good luck with everything.

Ugh. I throw my phone onto the bed beside me and scream into the pillow. I'm a fool for ever thinking he would look at me any other way. Portia, you need to forget about Miles Hartford, he's not into you. My phone rings, which catches me off guard. I grab my phone and stare down at the screen and see Miles's name. Why the hell would he be calling me? I slide the green button to answer. "Hello," I say, quietly, confused. But all I hear are muffled sounds on the other end. Did he accidentally butt dial me? I press my ear against the screen as I strain to hear what is going on, on the other side of the phone. Then a hear a groan. Everything in me pauses. I know that sound. Heat rushes across my skin, prickling every nerve ending. I strain my ears again and hear skin sliding against skin. Is he? No. Not after we've had a conversation. Is he thinking about my photos while he touches himself? Heat blooms across my chest. Tingles lace my body as I'm unable to pull myself away from the phone. If Cora wasn't walking around, then I might join him in the art of self-pleasuring. The guttural grunts fill my ears as I listen to him in his moment of solitude. It's hot. He must be getting closer as his groan vibrates through my chest. I'm lost for words as he loses himself to the feeling until he pushes himself over the edge and I hear him shudder. I feel like I've run a marathon listening to him.

"Shit. Fuck. Portia?" he curses from the other end of the phone. Oh no, I think he's realized he pocket dialed me. Panicking, I hang up the phone and throw it across the room as if it might catch on fire. My body sure as hell feels like it's about to catch on fire after listening to Miles pleasuring himself, hopefully to my pictures. I get up off my bed and head into my bathroom to have a cold shower.

My phone rings pulling me from my sleep. "Hey, Cora," I say, answering the phone.

"Did I wake you?" she asks, noticing my sleepy voice.

I needed a nap when I got home tonight and fell asleep, which is rather strange. But I've heard adults say when they get home from work, they need a nap. Guess when you work hard all week, sleep feels pretty good. *I get it now.*

"Yeah, I'm not feeling a hundred percent. I must have fallen asleep," I tell her, looking down at the clothes I'm still wearing.

"Oh, that's not good. You have been working long hours.

Guess you're not up for being my plus one for a work thing?" she asks.

Internally I groan because the last thing I want to do is go out, but as I turn and look at the clock on my wall, it's only eight on a Friday night. It's ridiculous for a twenty-one-year-old to be in bed this early on a Friday night.

"No, no. I can come. I feel better now after my power nap," I lie.

"Fantastic. I owe you. Wear your sexiest outfit from one of mom's brands, if that's okay?"

"Yah sure."

"I'll text you the details. Your name will at the door. Thanks again. See you soon babe got to run." And with that, Cora is gone.

Guess I better get my butt into gear and try for my friend.

An hour later, I'm standing outside one of her family's luxury brand stores getting my photo taken by the paparazzi as I walk the red carpet. I followed Cora's brief and chose a red shimmery mini dress fitted at the top, then a flared skirt on the bottom. It barely covers my ass, but thanks to the flare, it covers me.

"Thank you so much for coming," Cora greets me at the front door. We pose for a couple more photos before grabbing a glass of champagne from a passing tray and handing it to me, then throwing her glass back almost in one large gulp.

"Are you okay?" I ask her, staring at the now empty glass before handing her my untouched glass.

"I'm nervous. They put me in charge of tonight's event, and I want to do a good job for my mom." Cora gives me a small smile.

"Oh, babe. You've got this. It already looks amazing. Everyone seems to be having a good time. You've organized a million and one parties before. You're the queen of entertaining," I tell her.

"I know, but it's different from some sorority event," she says, waving her hand dismissing herself.

"Don't sell yourself short, Cora. No one could have rounded up fifty college girls at 6am to go feed the homeless on Thanksgiving like you could." My best friend gives me an appreciative smile. "Now show me your work so I can admire it," I say.

The party was awesome. Cora did a brilliant job, and I wanted to be there for her, but my stomach was playing up. I didn't feel well. I didn't even have a sip of champagne. Looking at it made me nauseous. I've stuck close to Cora as she introduced me to her work colleagues, designers, influencers, as she made her way around the party. I forced a wide smile, even though I felt like shit.

"Nell, is that you?" a male voice asks behind me. It's not the first time I've been mistaken for my sister. "I thought you were in Paris?" I turn around and the contents of my stomach almost end up in my mouth as I see Miles Hartford standing right in front of me, dressed in a navy suit which is molded to every muscle of his body with a white business shirt underneath unbuttoned enough to expose a little tanned chest. I don't answer Miles because I've lost the ability to speak. He looks so good. We've been chatting on and off for the past month since that fateful day I liked his photo.

"Portia?" he says my name, realizing it's me standing in front of him. I notice a tall, blond man beside him but register nothing else, not when Miles's intense green eyes are taking me in.

10

MILES

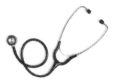

A while ago, I noticed little Portia Garcia liking one of my photos. It was one I took to add to my online dating profile while I was with the boys in Mexico. It surprised me seeing the notification pop up with her name on it, not like I haven't checked out her socials recently after seeing her again all these years later. Not sure why I did it, but I sent her a DM saying hi. There's nothing wrong with chatting to her online. I mean, our families are friends. Then after we had a friendly conversation, my dick was throbbing from talking to her, probably didn't help as I was talking to her, I was scrolling through her bikini photos. Little Portia Garcia is most definitely all grown up. Still, I'm a dick for jerking off over her. Even more of a dick when I realized I had pocket dialed her. I sent her a text saying sorry to pocket dialing her. She said she hung up when I didn't answer, so for the love of God; I am hoping she didn't listen to me jerking off over her.

"You promised me beer and models," I say to my friend Lane, who has dragged me to an industry event put on by his client. Everyone else was busy, and I was his last resort, plus who could say no to models and beer.

"Let me work the room first, then you can go off and pick up whoever the hell you need to, to take back home to your den of depravity." He chuckles at his lame joke.

"Don't knock it till you try it," I tell him, raising my beer at him. He chuckles and shakes his head at me.

We make the rounds of the party until a familiar blonde catches my attention from across the room. Shit. As I make my way through the crowd, Lane is right behind me.

"Nell, is that you? I thought you were in Paris?" I call out to the woman. She turns around and I still when I notice it's not Nell at all, it's… "Portia?" I take her in before me. She's dressed in a sinful red dress that barely covers her ass. She looks gorgeous. I shouldn't be looking at her how I am, but I can't help it. We stare at each other in silence for longer than we should. Thankfully Portia's friend breaks the awkwardness between us.

"Hi, I'm Cora. Welcome to my party." She holds out her hand for both of us to shake.

"Cora Jeffries?" Lane asks.

"Yes," the beautiful blonde answers him.

"It's so nice to meet you. I'm Lane Campbell. I own the Campbell Company."

Her face lights up at Lane's introduction. "That's right. Mom has worked with your company before. Brilliant work." Cora smiles excitedly.

"And we're about to start on a new campaign next week," he adds.

Cora and Lane chat about work, ignoring Portia and me.

"I'm sorry about earlier, thinking you were your sister," I tell her.

"It's fine. I'm used to it," she states, waving away my apology.

"I know, but I should know the difference between the two of you."

Portia stills. Her brown eyes look up and over her glass of

champagne as she stares at me for a couple of moments as if she's about to say something before shaking her head and changing her mind.

"I see Remi's doing well in France in the rankings. I sent him a text the other day congratulating him on his win," she tells me, changing the subject. I stiffen slightly at the mention of my brother's name.

"He's been doing great. So proud of him," I answer awkwardly. "How's Nell getting on in France?"

"Really well. She's loving it. Living her best life. How weird is it they are both there together but not together?"

Would be weird if I didn't know the reason. It's all because of me.

"Have you spoken to her since she's left?" she asks.

Why would she ask that? Did Nell say something? Of course, she would say something: they are sisters. I have said nothing to Stirling. *Because you are ashamed of what you did. And you don't want to hear him rant.* I don't want Portia to think any less of me. *Are you worried she will find out and not sleep with you?* A little voice inside of me questions me. No. I don't want to sleep with Portia Garcia. *Liar.* My dick does because she's a beautiful woman, but I don't because it would be wrong. Very wrong. *But would it though?* Yes. It would, I tell my subconscious. I might need to cut back on the beer. It's making me think things I shouldn't.

"No. Not at all," I tell her.

We both stand there awkwardly for a couple of moments, the conversation turning in a direction I'm guessing neither one of us wanted to go to.

"I need to apologize," I tell her.

"What for?" she asks with a frown on her face.

"About that pocket call," I say, hoping to God she heard nothing that went on the other end. I watch as her cheeks get the tiniest hint of pink across it. Shit. She heard. How the hell am I going to face her parents, knowing little Portia Garcia heard me jerking off over the phone while looking at her photos. That last bit she doesn't need to know about. Then silence falls between us.

"Certainly was interesting," she says, surprising me with her forthcoming comment. Portia looks at me over the rim of her glass and gives me a small smile. I take a step forward closer to her so Lane and her friend Cora do not hear our conversation. If Lane finds out he'll tell the boys and I'll never live it down.

"It's not what you think," I explain to her.

"So those sounds weren't what I thought they were?" she asks me, looking innocent as fuck, which makes my dick twitch. No. What the hell is he doing?

"What did you think they were?" I ask, my voice dropping deep and low. Shit. Abort flirtation. Abort now, Miles.

"The sound of your hand on your dick coming to photos you were looking at on the internet?" She raises a suspicious eyebrow at me.

I choke on my drink at her words. They were the last thing I ever expected to fall from her lips. She is not the shy wallflower I thought she was.

"I'm interested to know what exactly got you worked up?" she asks in a flirtatious tone.

"You are?" The question falling from my lips before I realize what I'm asking. "Why?" Would you stop flirting? What is it with you and the Garcia girls? When you are around them, you lose all sense of decency.

"Because you liked a fair few of my bikini pictures," she says, licking her lips at me. Who is this girl? My brain and dick are so confused because this woman is saying the sexiest things, yet my brain remembers when she used to play with Barbies.

"I did."

"Curious if I should post more? Seeing as you liked them so much. Have to give the people what they want," she says, giving me a wicked smile. Not sure how I feel about this. On the one hand, I want more and yet on the other I don't want sleezy guys ogling her. "Let me know what you want," she says, patting my chest with her hand as she moves away from me and walks back off into the party with her friend.

"That was Portia?" Lane asks me as he stares off after her.

"Yep and I shouldn't be looking at her the way I am," I tell him.

His eyes widen at my confession before he shakes his head.

As the night progresses, my eyes never leave where Portia is standing talking to people. Men, no boys, swarm around her and her friend like bees to honey. It irks me. Which it shouldn't, but it does, and I don't like the feeling. Eventually, Portia excuses herself, but I notice something seems wrong. Her face was glowing pink earlier but has now turned gray.

"Are you okay?" I ask as I rush toward her, wrapping my arms around her shoulders and pulling her to me. She stumbles a little but thankfully I have her in my arms, holding her up. I find a chair near the bathrooms and walk her over to it.

"Thank you," Portia says quietly. "How did you know?"

"I'm a doctor. Of course, I noticed something wasn't right. Plus, I haven't been able to keep my eyes off you," I confess.

She turns and stares up at me, those chocolate eyes so much darker than her sisters, more molten, liquid pools of the finest cocoa I'd willingly drown in.

"I felt a little dizzy. Never had that before. I think I ate something today that didn't agree with me. I've been feeling off," she tells me.

"Did you have any champagne?" I ask her. Maybe she's a little tipsy. But she shakes her head, indicating no. "Maybe you ate something then. Food poisoning can happen hours after," I explain to her.

"Oh, my goodness, babe, are you okay?" Cora asks as she rushes over, Lane not far behind her.

"A dizzy spell, that's all," Portia tells her friend, waving her concern away.

"You've been feeling off all week." Cora adds.

I turn and look over at Portia.

"I've been working hard. This princess isn't used to hard work," Portia says, cracking a joke. I'm not convinced.

"This could be the start of it. Drink some Gatorade when you get home and have a bucket on standby. Nibble some saltines if you feel nauseous and hopefully have a good rest and you will be back to normal in the morning," I explain to her.

"Thanks, doc." She gives me a chuckle.

I still and stare at her for a couple of beats. The way she said doc seems so familiar.

"Come on, babe, let's get you home to bed," Cora tells her. Portia nods, and I help her out of her seat.

"Let me see you to a cab," I tell her. She nods and links her arm with mine as I escort her out of the party and toward the taxi area. I help her into a waiting cab. "Call me if you need anything, okay?"

"Sure will, doc," she states, giving me a weak smile.

I slam the taxi door shut and watch it disappear into traffic.

"You, okay?" Lane asks.

"Yeah. Had a weird sense of deja vu just then," I tell him.

"Good or bad?" he questions.

"I'm not sure."

11

MILES

"I can't believe how much she looks like her sister," Lane says. As we walk back into the event. "If only you had taken her home instead of Nell, it would make things with your brother better."

I still at his comment as shivers run up my spine as a memory hit me of Nell saying her sister was meeting up with us with her friends, but she was running late. Did Portia come out with us that night? No. I would have noticed, wouldn't I?

"But don't do it," Lane adds, warning me.

"She's twenty-one; as if I would." *Didn't stop you flirting with her, though?*

"A beautiful twenty-one-year-old." Lane smirks at me.

"As was her friend." I raise a questioning brow in his direction.

"Hey, unlike you, I don't mix business and pleasure. She's a client. An extremely big one too."

As I am too. "I'm concerned about Portia's welfare. The dizzy spell has me worried."

Lane glares at me. "Lucky you're a doctor, hey?" he jokes

before he stills and looks over at me. "You're going to find a way to see that girl again, aren't you? It's a terrible idea."

Maybe, but he doesn't need to know how badly. "She's a family friend. Mom would kill me if I didn't check up on her tomorrow."

Lane shakes his head. "You're your own worst enemy sometimes, Miles. Why would you even be considering pursuing Portia after Nell?"

"I'm not. She's like a little sister to me. I'm worried because at her age she shouldn't have an episode like that. There could be serious underlying health issues. I feel responsible for her. Yes, she has grown into a beautiful woman, but she's still in college."

"You've been with college chicks before."

"She's different though."

Lane shakes his head again at me. "I know you're going to get yourself mixed up with something you shouldn't. You always have, always will."

I don't think I'm that bad.

Later that night, I scroll online, looking over Portia's profile again when my fingers tingle with the urge to message her. It's the right thing to do, to see if she got home okay.

Miles: Hope you made it home safely.

Portia: I did thanks. Feel better now I'm in bed nibbling on saltines.

Miles: Rest up. Message me if you need anything.

Portia: Will do. Night.

Just talking to her has my dick throbbing. I need to get laid. I haven't been laid since…that night. My hand slips underneath the elastic of my pajama bottoms as I run my hand over my aching dick. Fuck it. I need a release. I push the material down and let my dick free. I wrap my hand around myself and run my hand up and down my length as I flick through the photos of Portia again. *I'm going to hell for this.* A recent photo of her in her bikini has my balls tingling as I focus on every dip of her curves. My mind wanders to all the things I would love to do to that ripe little ass peeking out of the barely-there bottoms. My hand tightens around me as the first beads of pre-cum glisten from the tip. My hand rubs over the top and slides down my length easily. I study every inch of her committing her to my brain, but the more time I spend looking at her photos, the more I feel like she seems so familiar. Maybe it's some Freudian shit and I'm projecting my night with Nell onto her. Wishing it was with her instead and I wouldn't have hurt my brother so much. I shut my eyes and let the muscle memory of my hand take over, doing what it needs to do to push me over the edge. My mind never stops thinking about the things I would do to Portia if she was the one I brought home that night. It's not long till the visuals have me blowing my load in a matter of moments. Yeah. I'm going to hell, but gee it was a hell of a ride.

After cleaning myself up, it doesn't take long till I'm asleep and my mind is returning to my night with Nell, but instead of Nell looking down at me, it's Portia.

"I bet you don't let anyone take charge of you, do you, Miles?" she asks me as she ties my hands to the bedhead with my belt. *"Always the boss. Taking charge. Having people's lives in your hands as if you were God himself,"* she tells me as her breasts press against me. My mouth opens as my teeth bite ever so carefully over her nipple, which makes her moan. My tongue laves her nipple as she continues to tie me up. I move to the other breast and do the same. My dick is hard again. He's ready and willing for round what is it now, four or five. I've lost count. I don't remember the last time I had this much sex in one night. Probably when I was younger, I still have the stamina it's that I know what I'm doing, so don't need endless rounds of sex

like I used to for the same results. But with Portia, I can't seem to get enough.

"Let me take care of you tonight, Miles. Let yourself go. I promise I'll make it worth your while," she purrs as her naked body moves down my chest after she secures me. I've never let anyone tie me up before, but I trust her. Portia moves along my body toward my dick. She has a predatory gleam in her eye as her hands begin to run up and down my length. I thrust my hips as I arch off the bed and all I want to do is run my hands into her hair and push her pouty mouth over my dick, but I can't. Oops. Didn't think this through. Her fingernail runs along the thick vein along my dick and the gentle scrape has me seeing stars, this girl is going to be the death of me. Animalistic sounds fall from my lips, sounds I've never made in my life before vibrating through my body. She kicks my legs apart to nestle between them as her tongue dances across the tip of my dick, collecting the tiny beads of pre-cum from it. She licks her lips and gives me a devilish grin and I'm gone for. Her mouth wraps around the thick head, and I watch as her jaw stretches to accommodate me. Yes. Like that. I pull against my restraints, but once I settle into the fact I have no control over what happens, the sensations happening to my body are heightened as I close my eyes and enjoy whatever the hell Portia wants to do to me. She continues to choke on my dick progressively as the night goes on. She's able to take more of it down her throat. Next thing I know, she is climbing on top of me again, this time placing her pussy over my mouth, while she continues to suck down my cock. Yes. My tongue hits her wetness, and my balls tighten as her scent washes over me. My tongue works on overdrive as her throat hums to vibrate up my dick when I hit the right spots on her pussy. As I'm unable to touch her, I must concentrate on her nonverbal cues so much more. The way her pussy presses down against my tongue when I hit the spot, a deep throat hum when I lick her clit shoots sparks up my balls. I could stay buried here

forever. Closer and closer I bring her to the brink until one perfectly timed suck on her clit has her coming all over my face. I don't care if I suffocate in this moment. What a way to go. I must concentrate to not blow my load down her throat because I want her to come again all over my dick. Once she's come down from her high, she shuffles down my body and flips over. She grabs a condom from the side table and sheaths me. Yes. Then, moments later, she is sinking down on my dick, arching her back away from me as she leans back and cups my balls as she rides me. Shit. Fuck. Damn. My balls tingle and I swear I see stars because that move nearly has me blowing my load way too soon. Portia giggles at my groans. My hips shift and hit her right in the spot, and she falls forward on a moan. Her hands fall on my chest and her cunt squeezes me as if to tell me to stop. I'm in charge. You'll go at my pace as she slows me down. Once I slow my rhythm to the speed Portia desires, she takes over again and this time she's in control, using me as her own personal sex toy. I don't care. I'm not mad. She can use and abuse me any time she wants. Her pussy continues to swallow my dick whole as she shifts her direction, which hits her g-spot. I don't move at all even though it's the hardest thing in the world not to do, but she continues to ride. She's lost in the sensations, as her legs quiver, her pussy constricts around me and now I know is the time to take back a little control and I thrust deep inside of her, it makes her explode but I don't let up, as I chase my release. My hips have a mind of their own as they move in a steady beat, all the while Portia is hanging on for dear life because I've pushed her far over the edge. Then her hands fumble with the belt and seconds later she has my hands free, and they go straight to her hips, holding her against me while I fuck her. She crumples forward as I chase another orgasm from her sated body, and we come together in a sweaty, heated mess.

Fuck.

I'm going to hell.

12

PORTIA

A s soon as I open my eyes, I jump out of bed and head directly to the toilet and throw up. What is happening to me? What the hell did I eat?

"Portia, are you okay?" Cora asks. As she knocks on my bathroom door.

A groan falls from my lips as I continue to heave up everything I've ever eaten. Why do I feel like I'm dying?

"Do we need to call a doctor?" Hannah says.

"No. I'm fine. It's just food poisoning," I say, grumbling from the tiled floor of my bathroom. "I'll be fine in a minute." Eventually, I'm able to peel myself from the floor of the bathroom and get into bed.

"Here, drink this." Hannah offers me a ginger ale.

I take a sip and instantly it settles my stomach. "What did I eat? I've never felt this sick before," I groan as I sip slowly on the drink.

"I don't know what could have made you so sick. None of us are sick and we all ate the same things," Cora adds.

"You're not pregnant, are you?" Hannah asks with a chuckle.

"Oh, hell no," I answer quickly. "Could you imagine?" My stomach rolls at the ludicrous thought.

"You threw up in the morning," Cora says.

"How many times have you thrown up in the morning after a night out?" Hannah asks Cora.

"Portia wasn't drinking last night," Cora adds.

Hannah's eyes widen as she turns from Cora to me. "Who was the last person you slept with and when?"

I glare at my friend. She knows exactly who the last person I slept with was. "It was Miles." The room falls silent. "No. Do not even think like that." I look at my two friends. "I'm on birth control. We used protection." As my mind wanders back to that night. My stomach sinks as a memory filters through where we realized the condom broke. No. There's no way. I'm on birth control.

"Do you think you should do a test?" Cora asks.

"No. No way in the world I'm pregnant. I practice safe sex. I do everything right. I've eaten something or caught a bug."

The buzzer to our door rings, breaking the tension of the room.

"I'll get it," Hannah says, walking out of my room.

"Look, I'm sure it's nothing serious, but why don't you do one. Put your mind at ease," Cora says.

"I'm not pregnant," I tell her, pulling the covers up over my chest.

"Okay, I believe you."

"Heads up, Miles is on his way," Hannah says, bursting through the doorway.

"What? Miles is coming up?" I question my friend.

"Yep. He wanted to check in on you," Hannah says with a grin.

"I look like shit."

"Pretty sure he doesn't care," Hannah adds.

"No. I don't want to see him," I tell them both, shaking my head as my stomach does the loop de loop.

"Too late, he's here." Hannah squeals, answering the knock on our front door.

I look over at Cora, who gives me a small smile. "That's sweet of him to check in on you. I'm sure Miles will help you work out what's wrong."

"How's the patient?" Miles steps into my room with a warm smile on his face. He's dressed in jeans and a blue t-shirt that hugs his enormous frame. Then I inhale his delicious scent and as soon as the musky scent hits my nose, I recoil and scramble quickly out of my bed and toward the toilet and throw up.

"She's still not feeling so great," Cora explains to Miles.

"We might leave you to it." I hear Hannah tell him.

"Are you okay?" Miles asks, popping his head into my bathroom.

"I'm fine." I wave his concern away.

"Have you been throwing up a lot?" he asks. I can hear the concern in his voice.

"A little. I'm sure I'll be better tomorrow," I tell him through gritted teeth. Can he go away now because I don't need him seeing me like this on the bathroom floor? "You don't have to stay, I'll be fine."

"My mom will kill me if I don't check up on you." He chuckles.

"You have. I'm fine. Please go."

"I'll wait outside for you then," he says, ignoring me.

Ugh. He's so annoying.

Once my stomach has settled down enough for me to get up, I head out of the bathroom and jump straight into bed. Miles is sitting on the chair beside it, flipping through a magazine. Why is he still here?

"There is fresh water, ginger ale, and a banana for you." He points to my side table.

My stomach grumbles and I grab the banana and eat it.

"Can I ask you a personal question?"

"Sure," I mumble around my banana.

"Is there a chance you might be pregnant?" he asks.

I choke on my banana. Oh, shit. My entire body freezes. Does he know? No.

"Your symptoms seem like early pregnancy. I'm not judging you. I'm here to help," he says, giving me his doctor's voice. "When was the last time you had sex?"

I am not talking about this with him, especially not when the last man I had sex with a couple of months ago was him and he has no idea.

"You can trust me, Portia. I'm here for you," he says, placing a reassuring hand on mine.

Tears well in my eyes as I raise my voice at Miles. "I appreciate you coming down here, Miles, trying to help. But I can assure you I'm not some stupid girl who got herself knocked up because she wasn't careful. I am diligent in my birth control. I have food poisoning. I know I don't have a medical degree like you, but I have a degree in Portia."

"I'm sorry. I didn't mean to upset you. I put my doctor hat on and forgot you're a friend." Miles gives me a small smile. "Please don't cry." He reaches out and brushes away my tears.

Why am I so emotional? "I know you're trying to help."

"How about I let you rest," he says, getting up off the bed. "Call me anytime day or night if you need anything, okay." Miles gives me a bright smile.

I nod, letting him know I will, and he leaves my room. Moments later, I hear the door to our apartment close and my two best friends rush into my room.

"What the hell?" Hannah says.

"Told you I think he's interested," Cora adds.

"He's a doctor. I was sick. He took an oath to look after people, that's all."

"Still," Cora adds.

"He's too old for me, anyway," I say, curling up into my pillow a little more.

"The more you see him, the more I think you need to tell him about that night. You can't keep letting him think it was your sister he went home with," Cora tells me.

"How does he still not know he went home with you?" Hannah says questioningly.

"Who knows? But Miles will never find out it was me that night."

"Do you think that's fair to your sister though?" Cora questions me.

"She doesn't know I went home with him. She never needs to know."

"Secrets eventually come out," Cora warns me.

"Not today though," I tell her. I get Cora is being a friend and warning me, but if I tell Miles or Nell the truth, it's going to ruin things between us all.

13

PORTIA

"Call us if you need anything," Cora tells me as she and Hannah leave for work.

I'm still crumpled in bed after throwing up again this morning. I messaged Carrie Hartford this morning that I was still sick from food poisoning from the weekend. She told me to rest up and get better. Which was nice of her, but I feel bad letting her down like I have. I don't know why I am so sick, but it sucks.

I must have fallen back asleep at some point because I'm woken up by my phone ringing. I pick it up and answer without looking to see who it is.

"Hello," I answer groggily.

"Portia, are you okay? Mom said you called in sick to work today," Miles says.

I sit up quickly in my bed and my stomach rolls, but I'm able to keep the contents in check. What the hell is he doing calling me?

"I'm fine, Miles. Seriously, you don't need to worry about me."

"It's the doctor in me. I can't turn it off," he says lightly.

I feel like a cranky bitch now, and I know he's concerned, and I would be too if my life's work was to help sick people and someone you know is sick but won't listen to you.

"Thank you for checking in on me."

"It's all good. Look, I know you will not like it, but I'll pop over tonight after my shift, should be around nine, and I'll check in on you."

"Miles, it's okay." I try to dissuade him from coming over.

"I don't have a choice. My mom has already spoken to your mom, so expect a call from her checking up on you. And if I, as the doctor in the family, do not go over and check on you again, then my mom is going to have my balls," he says, with a chuckle.

He's right, now Mom knows I'm sick too, they are going to be relentless until I've been looked after.

"Fine. I hate being a burden to you."

"You're not. I promise."

"Guess I'll see you at nine then."

"I won't stay long, I promise. Rest up. Look after yourself and I'll see you tonight."

And with that, he's gone, and I flop back against my bed, exhausted by the conversation.

Once I wake up again, I call Mom and have a big conversation about what foods could make me so sick and how I should be looking after myself and maybe she needs to send Rhonda around to my apartment now Nell isn't there to come look after us. Why is this becoming such a big thing? Eventually Mom lets me go and I potter around the house. I'm so hungry, and it must mean I'm getting better if I need to eat.

I sit down and watch some TV while eating popcorn in the middle of the day and as the movie continues my stomach sinks as the girl on TV has the same symptoms as I do. Eventually she takes a pregnancy test, and it's positive. Dread fills me. What happens if the girls are right? I might be pregnant? I can't be. There's no way in the world I am, not when I use birth control. But maybe I should do a stupid test. Then I can tell people when they question me again I'm not because I did a test, and it told me I'm not pregnant. I grab my phone and do an online order at the local pharmacy, and it says it will be here within the hour. Until then I need to relax and have positive thoughts.

My hands shake as I take the test out of its box and look down at the stick. *Hurry and pee on it, get the results and then you can put this all behind you.* I do what I need to do and place the offending piece of plastic on the bathroom counter and wait the two minutes it needs to determine this life altering situation. I pray the little screen says not pregnant because the thought I could be pregnant scares me. Even worse, who the baby daddy will be. Oh shit, Miles is coming over tonight and if the worst case happens, then I'm going to have to tell him. How the hell am I going to tell him, "by the way you got me pregnant" when he does not know we have even had sex. This is a cluster fuck of epic portions. I continue to pace around my room until the timer on my phone goes. Must have been the longest two minutes in history. Gingerly, I walk into my bathroom, my heart thundering in my chest the closer I get to the bit of plastic. My hand shakes as I reach out and grab the stick before closing my eyes, not wanting to see the result because once I look down, it's going to be life changing. Willing my eyes open, I stare down at the stick and my stomach drops.

Pregnant

The word is as clear as day on the little stick. No. No. Tears well in my eyes as my legs give out from under me and I collapse against the tiled floor of my bathroom, clutching the stick to my chest as my entire world crashes down around me. This can't be happening. It has to be a lie. A prank. I cannot be pregnant with Miles Hartford's baby. A man that has no memory of sleeping with me.

Pulling myself up off the floor, I grab my phone and call the one person who can help me in this moment, my sister.

"Hey, babe, how are you?" she says, answering the phone groggily.

I have no idea what time it is in Paris, but it must be late.

"Nell. I fucked up," I cry down the phone.

"Portia, are you okay? What's going on?" Nell asks. I can hear the panic in her voice.

"Mom and Dad are going to kill him. Oh my god, Dom is going to kill him too," I say, as the realization of what has happened hits me, as a panic attack consumes me.

"Babe, please, you're scaring me. Tell me what's going on so I can fix it," Nell asks me.

Rip it off like a Band-Aid. "I'm pregnant," I confess.

There's silence on her end of the phone, which I don't blame her for. I dropped the mother of all secrets in her lap.

"I'm here for you. Okay. How far along are you?"

"I just found out," I tell her. Then my mind filters back, trying to calculate how far I am along. "I'm like ten weeks." Shit, feels like that might be far along.

"And what about the father? Does he know?" Nell asks gently.

"Um. No, not yet. I just took a test a couple of minutes ago."

"I'm glad you called me, Portia. I wish I was closer so I could hug you and tell you everything is going to be okay."

I wish she was too. "Do you have room in Paris for me?" I ask her, because I know once this bombshell drops, I'm probably going to need to hightail it to safety.

"I would love you to come over, but you need to deal with this first. You need to book in with an OBGYN and make sure everything is okay with the baby."

"Do you think something is wrong with it?" I ask, panic seeping through my bones. What happens if I'm sick because something is wrong with the baby. What if I have been eating the wrong things? Drinking? Exercising?

"No, no, I'm sure everything is fine. It's routine," Nell tells me, reassuring me.

"Okay, I can do that."

"I don't mean to pry, but can I ask who the father is? Is he going to support you?"

My sister thinks some frat boy has knocked me up or a struggling artist, which seems to be my usual type. Little does she know I've chosen the perfect baby daddy in Miles. He's older, mature, has a good job, his own place. Hit the jackpot there.

"Babe, it's okay. You don't need to tell me."

She's taken my silent freak out as my answer. I don't want to tell her. And I don't because everything is about to get even more fucked up.

"I don't want you to hate me." Knowing she used to have a crush on Miles, it might upset her to find out I slept with him. "I slept with Miles."

"Miles who?"

"Miles Hartford," I mumble. I'm met with silence as my truth filters through.

"He's so much older than you," she says harshly.

Yes, he's older, but he's not old enough to be my dad. "I wasn't thinking about that when I was sleeping with him, was I. All I thought about was he was hot, and he knew how to kiss, and I thought why not."

"When did it happen?"

"Um, well yeah, okay, this is where it gets weird. I kind of slept with him the night you gave me your ID when you were celebrating going to France. He called me Nell twice, but he was pretty wasted, and I thought he just got us confused because like you were there and then you were gone." Saying it out aloud it sounds way more messed up.

"Please don't tell me you lost my ID at his apartment?" Nell questions me.

"I may have."

"Fuck," Nell curses down the phone.

"What. What did I do? Don't tell me someone stole your identity and like murdered a heap of people and now you're a wanted criminal?" I ask her. Maybe I need to dial down the true crime network binge I've been on.

"No. Worse. I think Remi thinks I slept with Miles and that's the reason he has iced me out."

"Oh. Is that all? I thought it was something bad." Those two fight and hook up more times than I can remember.

"Portia, it is. I love him, and he thinks I slept with his brother. No wonder he hates me!" Nell screams at me.

"Oh shit. Yeah, that's bad."

"You need to tell Miles so we can sort all this out," Nell tells me angrily. "What. No. I can't do that. Everyone is going to hate me!"

"Miles needs to know he's going to be a dad. And you both need to decide together whether or not you are going to keep it."

Nell seriously thinks I would get rid of this baby. My hand instinctively rests on my flat stomach, protecting the tiny bubble inside of me. I get I'm young, but I have the means to look after this baby. I will not be thrown out on the street. Will it complicate my life? One hundred percent. Somehow, this baby got through all my defenses to be here, so it's a determined little thing already. "I'm keeping it. I'm not getting rid of my baby. No way in the world. And if Miles wants me to, he can go get fucked."

"Well then, seeing as you're going to be a mommy soon, you better pull up your big girl pants and break the news to Miles he's going to be a dad." Nell tells me sternly.

"Fuck," I grumble. "You're right. I promise I'll sort it all out," I tell her. I want my sister to be proud of me. "And for the record, I'm sorry I messed everything up with Remi for you." The more I think about it, the more I realize how hurt Remi must be to think Nell had slept with his brother. Now I understand why when I've mentioned Remi around Miles, he's acted awkwardly. Oh no, they have already fought about this. I need to make this right.

"Don't worry about me. I'll be fine. You look after yourself and my niece or nephew."

"Oh shit. That just got real," I say, bursting into tears over Nell's comment. Am I having a boy or a girl? What about names? What surname will they have? Where will I live? I need to build a nursery. Holy shit, this is so much bigger than reading those words on the test.

"I've got to go," I tell my sister.

"I love you, Portia. And I'm here for you anytime you need me okay."

I know she will be.

14

PORTIA

"Honey, we're home," Hannah calls out into the apartment as she walks in with Cora, and as soon as I see my friends, I burst into tears. They both rush toward me and wrap themselves around me, holding me tightly as I breakdown.

"Babe, what's going on?" Hannah asks as she gently strokes my hair.

"You're worrying us," Cora adds.

"I'm pregnant," I say, spluttering through my tears. I hear my friends curse but continue to hold me tightly as I let all my fears and worries out onto their shoulders.

"Your baby daddy is Miles, isn't it?" Hannah asks the serious question once I've finally calmed down. I nod in agreement. She curses.

"Do you think you will keep it?" Cora asks.

"Yes."

"What about Miles? Are you going to tell him?" Hannah questions me.

"He's coming over tonight at nine. Guess I should probably tell him then," I say, looking between my two best friends.

"Do you want us to stay or go?" Cora asks. "You know we will support you no matter what," she adds.

"I know, babe," I say, reaching out and holding her hand. "I think I should tell him by myself. It's time to grow up. I've got a tiny human inside of me. No matter what happens, it's the most important thing in my life now."

"Oh shit, you're going to have to tell your dad." Hannah's eyes widen at the thought.

I love Dad but he can be an overprotective Latin father. He's going to kill Miles when he finds out it's him. What happens if this ruins the two family's relationship? *They don't care about Remi and Nell, why would they care about you and Miles? Because you're knocked up out of wedlock.* Shit, my dad better not try to force Miles to marry me to make an honest woman out of me. This is all so fucked up. Miles is going to hate me after all this. He's going to think I've trapped him. Lying is not a great way to start a relationship with someone. Not that we will have a relationship, I mean, it will be more like co-parenting. Oh, my god, the thought gives me a shiver down my spine. How the hell am I going to keep a tiny human alive? I can hardly keep myself alive most days. What about college? Will I be finished in time, or will I have to defer? Will I be able to work? Does that mean I need a nanny?

"I can see you're freaking out," Cora says, pulling me from my thoughts.

"There's so much to think about."

"You don't need to work it all out tonight though," Hannah tells me.

"I know. It's a lot, you know?" I tell them both. "I feel incredibly stupid I've gotten myself in this situation."

"Hey, it takes two to tango, girl. This is as much his fault as it is yours," Hannah explains.

"I thought you said you used protection?" Cora asks.

"We did. I remember we broke one condom, but I thought I was fine. I am on birth control," I explain to them both.

"Don't forget you were sick around then too from that seafood taco," Hannah reminds me.

And I literally must hold my stomach so as not to gag from thinking about the taco. "What you're saying is it was a series of unfortunate events that have led me to where I am now?" I ask, looking at my friends.

"Bad timing," Hannah adds. She can say that again.

After dinner, the girls say their goodbyes and head out, giving me time with Miles alone to basically change his entire world. My hands feel clammy, my stomach wants to empty itself, a sense of foreboding hits me. The apartment's buzzer makes me jump, pulling me from my internal freak out. I press the buzzer and Miles announces himself and I let him in. I pace around the apartment, nervously waiting for his arrival. There's a knock on my door and I go over and open it.

"Hey, look at you out of bed. You're looking good." Miles greets me warmly, "Here, I got you these," he says, handing me a bouquet of pink peonies. "Thought they might make you feel better," Miles states, giving me smile.

"Thank you so much. These are so beautiful. Come in," I say, holding open the door for him.

I head on over to the kitchen and find a vase for the flowers.

"Are your roommates home?" he asks.

"No. They went out. I wasn't feeling up for it," I tell him as I fill up the glass vase with water and place the bouquet in it. Then I place the vase in the middle of the kitchen counter for the moment. "Did you want a drink or something?" I ask him nervously.

"I'm fine. I won't take up much of your time. I wanted to check on you to see how you're feeling. I can already see you're looking better, you have a nice healthy glow."

I drop the glass I had grabbed in the sink, smashing it. Shit.

"Hey, stop. You'll cut yourself," Miles states as he runs over and cleans up the broken glass. "Are you okay?" He looks down at me, his brows pulled together with concern.

"It slipped," I mumble back to him.

He gives me a frown but continues cleaning up the mess as I awkwardly stand in the kitchen watching him.

"Now that's cleaned up. I might leave you to it," Miles says, wiping his hands on his jeans.

"Stay," I say the word a little louder than I meant to, which makes him give me a strange look. "How's work going?"

"Been pretty busy. That end of summer heatwave had people coming in dehydrated," he explains.

"Glad I've been inside for most of it," I say, giving him a grin.

"Is everything okay, Portia? You seem jittery," he asks.

Oh no. I thought I was hiding my nervousness well enough, but I guess I wasn't, shouldn't be surprised. Seeing as it's his job to watch someone's body language compared to what they are saying.

"We need to talk," I say to him. As soon as those words are out of my mouth, Miles stills as he stares at me. Those green eyes laser focused on trying to work out what the hell I would need to talk to him about. "Maybe we should sit down for this conversation," I tell him as I make my way to the living room and take a seat on the sofa. Miles joins me but takes the armchair across from me, putting significant distance between him and me, which I get.

"Is everything okay?" he asks again.

I think I'm going to throw up. I shake my head at his question and those green eyes narrow on me.

"I do not know where to start," I tell him as my eyes well with tears.

"Hey," he says, noticing I'm visibly upset and moves from the armchair to beside me on the sofa. He wraps his arm around my shoulder and pulls me to his side. "Whatever it is, I'm here to help," he tries to reassure me.

"You're going to hate me," I say, sniffling through my tears.

Miles places a finger under my chin and makes me look up at him. "Hey now. Portia, I could never hate you."

"I think you will." I cry into his hard chest. He holds me against him for what feels like an eternity, not pushing me to explain myself. He continues to hold me tight against him until I can find the strength to tell him the truth. *As hard as this is, Portia, you need to tell him.* If you had told him all those weeks ago, this conversation would be a hell of a lot easier. Now I must drop two massive bombshells in his lap at the same time.

"First, I want to say I'm sorry. I never meant to hurt you or lie to you." Miles frowns at me. I'm not making any sense. I know this. *Just tell him, Portia.* I close my eyes and dig deep to find the strength to get through this conversation. "The night you went home with Nell." I feel Miles stiffen beside me, but I can't look at him, especially not when I'm about to blow his mind in the next five minutes. "It wasn't Nell. You went home with me." Everything goes quiet. The entire universe screeches to a halt at my bombshell.

"What the hell, Portia?" Miles screams, jumping up off the sofa and glaring at me. "What in the fuck did you say?" he glares at me.

"Nell gave me her ID because I forgot mine that night. She met me outside and went home and I came into the club. We were wearing the same dress in different colors. I ran into my ex while I was there and told him I was there with you when he accused me of stalking him. He was with the girl he cheated on me with, and all I could think about in the moment was making him hurt as much as he made me hurt. So, when I saw you waving at me from across the room, I walked up and kissed you."

Miles scrubs his face, not quite believing what I've told him.

"You're a fantastic kisser," I mumble. Miles glares at me, not appreciating the compliment. "I felt sad, and you were making me feel better. I didn't want to stop."

"For fuck's sake, Portia, why the hell did you not tell me?" he asks.

"Because I enjoyed kissing you," I confess. "Would you have kept going if I told you who I was that night?"

Miles scrubs his face again. "Of course not. You're too young."

"Not young enough to spank you or tie you up, was I?" I say back, with a bit of bite to my voice.

"Fuck me," Miles curses, throwing his hands up in the air. "I can't believe I let you do that to me."

"Why?"

Miles glares at me from under his thick black lashes, his chest rising and falling quickly as panic sets in.

"Oh, you hate the fact you liked it so much, don't you?" I ask, teasing him. "You hate the fact I blew your mind that night." I stare up at him. "And you hate the fact you might want to do it again, don't you?"

"What the fuck, Portia?" he yells at me. "No. I do not want to sleep with you again." I raise a brow in his direction. "Fucking hell." He curses again, dragging his fingers through his hair.

"Are you upset you didn't get to sleep with Nell? Is that what the actual issue is?" I ask. Jealousy seeps through my defenses he's upset he slept with me because he truly wanted my sister.

"Hell no. I'm fucking relieved I didn't sleep with Nell. It means I truly never ripped my brother's heart out. I thought I was the biggest asshole in the world for sleeping with the one woman my brother loves more than anything."

Oh.

"That night ripped apart my relationship with Remi. He hates me. He's blocked me everywhere. I haven't spoken to him since because he thinks I slept with Nell."

Explains a lot then.

"How the hell did I not know it was you?" he asks, looking at me.

"My sister and I look similar," I say, shrugging my shoulders.

"I can't believe you and I hooked up," he says as he places a hand over his mouth and stares at me in shock.

"Surprise," I say, waving my hands around awkwardly. Little does he know it's about to get worse.

"Fuck, Portia, I'm too old for you."

"I wasn't looking for anything more than one night, Miles."

"Still, how did I not know?"

"I corrected you twice, but it was in the heat of the moment, so I don't think you were taking it in."

"I'm so sorry, Portia. I…"

"You regret it. I know," I say, filling in his words.

"I regretted that night when I thought it was Nell, but now…I don't know if I can," he tells me honestly. "It can't happen again," he adds quickly.

"Yeah, I know." Because I'm about to blow your mind for a second time tonight and after that, I don't even know if I'm ever going to see you again.

"It was a good night though," he states as he rubs the base of his neck while giving me a heated look. "A great night." Is he flirting with me?

"One of the best," I tell him because it was.

"Never to be repeated."

"Nope."

"Something that is going to stay in our memories."

"Exactly."

He shakes his head as if trying to remove the memories of that night between us. I can tell they are bubbling to the surface.

"And what happened between us is between you and me. No one else knows, right?" he asks.

"About that…"

15

MILES

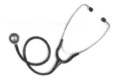

I'm having an out-of-body experience. I cannot believe the person who rocked my world was little Portia Garcia. Don't get me wrong, I am so thankful I never slept with Nell. But the little girl I used to play Barbies with, is the same one that spanked my ass and tied me up while simultaneously rocking my world. I'm floored. Of all the things I thought were going to happen when I came over tonight, finding out it was Portia I slept with wasn't at all on the agenda. Relief is what I am feeling in this moment because I haven't lost my brother for my stupidest mistake. It's going to be tricky trying to get in touch with him, but I have to. I must tell him I never slept with the woman he loves, there was never anything between Nell and I and he needs to get his girl and never let her go again.

What am I going to do about Portia, though? I know I said we shouldn't do this again, but my dick has other ideas as he slowly twitches to life. Thank goodness I don't have to feel bad about all the times I have jerked off to Portia's photos online. I am disappointed, in my mind I still see Nell beneath me that night, and not Portia. Maybe we need to rewrite history and have a round two or something. *No.* That's even worse. You know

now it's little Portia Garcia and taking her to bed now, sober, would be a terrible idea. Technically, I've already slept with her, so doing it again isn't bad, is it? It would explain why I've been drawn to her every single time I've seen her. Why my subconscious won't stop thinking about her. It was trying to tell me it was her you've been thinking about, not her sister. It's why you constantly flirt with her when you see her. Now I know why I was getting déjà vu every single time I've seen her since that night. It all makes sense now.

"It was a good night," I tell her, rubbing the back of my neck, while looking at the beautiful girl sitting before me. Now I know it's her, how did I ever think she was another. "A great night."

"One of the best," she tells me, giving my ego a boost. I'm glad that night affected her the same way it has me.

"Never to be repeated," I tell her, more for me than her.

"Nope."

"Something that is going to stay in our memories," I add. Because most nights it repeats in a loop in my mind while my hand is wrapped around my dick.

"Exactly."

I shake my head because the images of that night are scrolling through my mind and my dick likes what he sees.

"And what happened between us is between you and me. No one else knows, right?" I ask because the last thing I need is her brother Dom catching me in a dark alleyway and busting my balls.

"About that…" she starts.

This doesn't sound good.

"I think you need to sit for the next bit," she says quickly as she nervously plays with her hands.

This doesn't sound good at all.

"I hate dropping these surprises on you like this, but it's all been a bit of a surprise for me too," she says, unable to look at me. "Funny story, turns out I don't have food poisoning," she says with an awkward chuckle. "Guess I should have listened to my doctor because I have morning sickness."

I black out for what feels like a stupidly long time but has only been mere seconds.

"I'm sorry, you're pregnant?" I ask her. She nods. I knew her symptoms would match what I suspected, but she needed to work that out for herself. "Fuck," I curse, standing up. My heart beating uncontrollably out of my chest. "No," I say, shaking my head as the penny drops. "Please tell me you don't think I'm the father," I ask, thumping my chest.

"You were the last person I slept with. We can do a DNA test to be sure, but you've been the only person I've slept with since my ex," she explains to me.

"Oh, fuck," I curse again. I think I'm going to be sick. This cannot be happening. The world can't be this cruel to me. Giving me some of the best sex of my life with someone I shouldn't have even been looking at, but then I've apparently knocked her up, too. No. Oh fuck no. Shit. Fuck. I pace around the room. "Are you sure?"

"I took a test earlier," she explains.

I nod, but I feel like I've sunk to the bottom of the ocean and am slowly drowning. I cannot have knocked up little Portia Garcia. Nope. No way in the world. Shit, Nacho is going to murder me. He's going to feed me to his horses, and I'll never be seen ever again. It can't be mine. I used condoms. I always use condoms.

"We were safe." I stare at her blankly.

"We used condoms. One broke but I'm on birth control so I didn't think it would be a problem, but then I remembered I ate a bad fish taco and was sick so I must have thrown up my pill and it wasn't one hundred percent effective." She explains to me.

Oh fuck!

"Are you keeping it?" The words fall out of my mouth before I soften them.

"Yes." Portia stands up and is almost toe to toe with me as those molten brown eyes glare at me, probably cursing me to hell. "I'm happy to do this alone. I don't need you. I can live off my trust fund for the rest of my days. I'm hardly poor."

"But you're twenty-one," I argue.

"Are you fucking serious?" her voice raises at me. "I wasn't too young for you to fuck, was I?" She pokes me in the chest with her long nail.

My hand comes out quickly and wraps around her wrist, halting her assault. "That's not what I'm saying," I tell her, trying to calm her down, the last thing I want to do is stress out a newly pregnant woman. It can cause all kinds of problems. "You have your life ahead of you. Having a baby is a big responsibility."

Portia shoves me hard in the chest. "Get out!" she screams at me. "Get the hell out." Tears stream down her face.

"Portia?"

She shakes her head. "I know I'm young. I get it. This is not what I had planned for my life. But it's happening. I can't change it; all I can do is embrace it. You may think I'm too young for all this and maybe I am, but I'm going to do the right thing and step up and love my baby. And be the best God damn mom I can be."

"Portia, I'm sorry. I didn't mean to upset you. Tonight has been a lot for me to process. A lot—and I'm not saying the right things to you in this moment because I'm in shock."

Portia's face softens a bit. "I'm sorry I never told you about that night." She lets out a sigh. "I'm sorry this night has changed our lives forever. But I will not make our child feel less than because they weren't planned."

Shit. A baby. Portia and I are having a baby. I thought one day I would have a family but, in all honesty, I thought I would have one later in life, after I got married and settled down. What happens if I'm not good enough?

Portia reaches out and touches my chest. "I think you and I need to talk again tomorrow. You need time to process everything that's happened. You and I have a lot to think about and talk about and I don't think tonight either of us is up for it."

"Portia?"

"Miles, I promise everything is fine. Let's talk in the morning. It's late and I'm exhausted," she says.

I stare down at her face, and I can see how tired she looks.

"Okay, let's talk in the morning," I tell her as I move away and head toward the door.

"Miles," she calls out to me. "I am sorry. I've messed everything up."

"You haven't messed anything up," I tell her as I reach for the door and pull it closed behind me. I press my back against her door and suck in a couple of unsteady breaths before I pull my phone out and text the boys for an emergency meeting at my place.

§

"Okay, we are all here. What the hell is going on?" Smith grumbles at me annoyed I've called him out so late.

"This better be good," Lane says from the screen of my computer. It was too late in the night for him to get a babysitter.

"I bought help," Dylan adds, waving the tequila bottle. He heads on over to my bar and grabs glasses and pours us all a generous shot of tequila. When he hands it to me, I throw it back in one large gulp. The boys are all quiet as they stare at me, wondering what the hell is going on.

"I needed that. My nerves are shot."

"What the fuck is going on, Miles?" Smith breaks the silence.

"There's so much to unpack and I'm still in shock," I say as I explain to them what the hell happened tonight. "The first bombshell is I never slept with Nell."

"What?" Smith says.

"Then who the hell did you sleep with?" Dylan asks.

"Portia," Lane answers for me. "You slept with fucking Portia."

I can hear in my friend's tone he's upset with me. "I didn't know it was Portia, I thought it was Nell the entire time."

"How the hell do you sleep with a chick and not realize it's another?" Dylan questions me.

"They do look like twins," Lane adds. "It is hard to tell them apart, even sober."

"This is good, isn't it? Now you can tell your brother you never slept with his girl," Smith states.

"Yes. But it gets worse," I say, looking at all my friends. "She's pregnant." The room falls deadly silent before it erupts into shouting, cursing, and arguing.

"What the hell?" Smith screams at me, while Dylan is bent over laughing. Lane is giving me a disappointed head shake through the screen. "I don't understand how this happened?" Smith glares at me.

"When a penis loves a vagina, they do a dance and then the stork comes and delivers a baby," Dylan teases Smith, who turns and gives him his best policeman's stare.

"I'm so careful," I tell them. "This time the condom broke. She was on birth control, but it didn't work and now here we are. It has turned my life upside down, so please save any lectures for another day. I'm not up for it." The room goes quiet.

"I'm assuming she's keeping the baby?" Lane asks.

"Yep."

"Her dad is going to kill you," Smith adds.

"Yep."

"How do you feel about it?" Dylan asks.

"I don't know. The fact it was Portia I slept with, not Nell, is enough to blow my mind but this. Fuck," I say, cursing as I drag my fingers through my hair.

"You're going to be in the kid's life, though?" Lane asks.

"Of course," I say, my eyes narrowing on my friend.

"I can't believe you're going to be a dad," Dylan says, shaking his head. "Of all the people you're the last I would ever expect, would have an accidental pregnancy. Don't they teach you that shit in med school?" Dylan teases me.

"You're such an ass," Smith says, punching Dylan in the arm.

"How do you feel about it?" Lane asks.

"It's the last thing I ever expected. I think I'm still in shock."

"You are going to be in so much trouble with your family, you realize?" Dylan adds. No shit.

"Not helping," Smith says, glaring at Dylan with gritted teeth.

"Portia asked to catch up tomorrow to talk. She only found out tonight too, so both of us, I think, are still processing it all."

"Are you going to ask her to marry you?" Dylan asks.

"This isn't the 1950s. He doesn't have to marry her," Smith answers, punching Dylan again.

"I can't even fathom it was Portia I slept with, not Nell, let alone I'm going to be a dad," I explain to them.

"But that's not a no," Dylan says, grinning.

"There's a lot of think about. Both you and Portia are going to have to be on the same page. I think you need to talk to a lawyer regarding co-parenting. What happens if Portia wants to move across the country with your kid? Or overseas? Or meets someone and marries them?" Lane asks me.

Okay, it's a lot of questions I hadn't even thought about yet.

"Where are they going to live? Will you pay child support? What school do you want to send the child to?"

"The baby is only formed and you're already talking about schooling?" Smith asks.

"These things are all important. I know in this moment you are trying to wrap your head about the fact you have knocked someone up but as the only dad in this group, I can tell you there is so much more you need to worry about. Especially with your work schedule," Lane explains to me.

I can already feel a migraine setting in.

"We can worry about that tomorrow, daddy," Dylan tells Lane. "Tonight, let's get our boy fucked up so he can pass out and not worry about anything till tomorrow," Dylan states, raising his glass in the air.

16

PORTIA

That *went okay*, I think as I rub the tears from my eyes. He could have told me to fuck off. He could have slammed the door in my face. He could have even threatened me to get rid of it. I hit him with a one, two punch, and I shouldn't expect him to get back up with no damage. It was a shock to me to find out I was pregnant. For Miles, it must have been mind-blowing, especially since he did not know we had even slept together. I don't think he acted badly, thoughtlessly maybe, but people say stupid shit when they are in shock. I took some of the things Miles was saying to me to heart when he was trying to wrap his mind around everything. I think when we sit down again in the morning, things won't be so heated. We can talk calmly about what we are going to do. This is something that has linked us for life.

"How did it go?" Hannah asks, rushing into my bedroom with Cora hot on her heels.

"She's not crying, so that's good," Cora adds.

"Okay. He's in shock, freaked out, confused."

"But what did he say?" Hannah pushes.

"I told him we need to catch up tomorrow to talk properly as it's an enormous shock for the both of us."

"Understandable," Cora agrees.

"Do you need us here tomorrow?" Hannah asks.

"No. I'll be fine. I promise," I say as a yawn catches me off guard. My lids feel heavy as I lay in bed.

"How are you feeling about it all?" Cora asks, taking a seat beside me on the bed.

"Overwhelmed. I've changed the direction of my life forever," I tell her as my eyes well up again.

"It's going to be okay. You have the two of us and we are going to be the best aunties that little baby will ever have," Hannah tells me as she takes a seat beside me on the other side of the bed.

"Oh my god, you're going to be aunties," I say before breaking down into tears.

My two best friends wrap their arms around me and hold me close to them.

"No matter what, we have you, Portia," Cora tells me.

"Thank you." I sniffle.

"We'll let you get some rest. But if you need us in the morning, we are here for you," Hannah states. I nod slowly in agreement. I know both would stop what they are doing to help me. But I must get used to doing things on my own. I can't call my besties once the baby is here because I can't cope. I need to work shit out myself.

※

Didn't have the best sleep last night. Had dreams of childbirth and Miles delivering the baby, then running away with it. Very bizarre. My girls went off to work and gave me a pep talk before leaving. I've got this. I can do this. The sound of the buzzer makes me jump and I let Miles up. Moments later, there's the knock on the door and I try to stabilize my unsettled stomach. I suck in a deep breath and let it out slowly before opening the door.

"Morning," Miles says, giving me a small smile. He looks good dressed in jeans and a navy shirt with the sleeves rolled up, showing off his tanned, muscular forearms. Every nerve-ending on my body has come alive. I can feel a warmth sweep its way across my body. Strange. Then I notice a basket filled with fruits. My brows pull together in a frown and stare at him.

"This is for you. Thought you might like fruit over flowers." He holds out the basket to me to take, which I do.

"Thanks, you didn't have to get me anything," I tell him. He doesn't answer, but follows me into my apartment. I place the basket on the counter next to the flowers he bought me last night. "Would you like a coffee or something to drink?"

"I'm fine. I'm probably too nervous to drink anything, anyway," he tells me honestly.

"Nervous?" I ask, surprised by his admission.

"You make me nervous." He looks at me with those intense green eyes.

"Me?"

"Yes. I'm worried I might say something and ruin this budding friendship we've started. And I want us to be friends. I don't want our child to grow up with parents who hate each other."

I can see the vulnerability on his face. He is genuinely afraid that our talk this morning could go left, and I will take his child away from him. I couldn't do that; it seems so cruel.

"No matter what, I will never keep you from your child," I tell him, hoping it will settle his nerves. "Let's sit and get all this sorted and put us both at ease."

"You were nervous too?" he asks, genuinely surprised I might be.

"Of course. I had nightmares last night you delivered my

baby and took it away from me because I was too young," I confess to him.

"Portia," he says my name softly.

We take a seat back down on the same sofa as last night, in the same spots putting distance between the two of us. "I guess the first thing we need to sort out is your feelings on knowing it was me you slept with, not Nell."

Miles drags his hand through his hair, nerves still getting the best of him. "I'm happy it wasn't Nell, but..." he pauses.

I can see how he is diplomatically trying to work out how to continue without offending me. *Whatever he says, Portia, it's water off a duck's back. He's entitled to feel that way, take nothing personally.*

He shakes his head. "There's a part of me deep down that's disappointed I don't remember it was you."

Oh. That was not the answer I thought he was going to say.

"When I first saw you in Mom's office, I thought you were beautiful. Little did I know I had spent one of the most amazing nights with you. I'm sorry. Me not remembering must have hurt you. I will say the more I saw you though, the more I had this strange sense of déjà vu."

I had no idea. "Have you been able to talk to Remi?" Miles shakes his head. "I'm sorry I messed things up with your brother. If it makes you feel better, I've messed things up for my sister too by not telling her."

"If the roles were reversed, I'd probably have done the same," he tells me, giving me a smile.

"I'm so sorry about that night."

"I'm not. It was hot," he adds quickly. Typical male.

"It was," I say, biting my bottom lip as my body tingles, thinking about that night.

"I have a question though," he starts, and I nod for him to continue. "The spanking and tying up?" he asks, raising his brows at me.

"Never done that before." I tell him, a blush creeping across my cheeks.

"Really?" His voice raises in surprise. I nod my head. "Wow. Okay." He shifts uncomfortably on the sofa. I can't believe I am talking about this with him. "It was hot. Usually, I'm the one in control," he tells me.

"So does that mean you're going to want to control me through this pregnancy?" I ask him.

"Only in the bedroom." We both still at his reply.

The entire room falls silent and neither one of us moves to say anything, realizing we might have taken this chat a little farther.

"Luckily, that will not happen. Who wants to sleep with a pregnant woman?" I say with an awkward chuckle, feeling my face is on fire with embarrassment.

"Pregnant women can still have sex. Actually, the second trimester women feel in flux of hormones and are extremely horny," Miles explains in his doctor's voice.

"Might need to get a new vibrator then," I joke.

Miles frowns at me for a couple of moments before he shakes his head. "I guess we should talk about the elephant in the room."

"I don't think I've put on that much weight," I say, teasing him.

"I didn't mean…"

"I'm joking, Miles," I tell him. He looks relieved. "Yeah, I think we need to work this out first. Make sure we are both on the same page." He nods in agreement. "Are you okay with me keeping the baby?" I ask him, not like he has a choice because it's my body, but I still should ask.

"Honestly, I still don't know how I feel because this wasn't in my plan."

"Wasn't in my plan either. College is back next week," I tell him.

"Shit, I'm sorry, Portia. I've messed everything up for you," he says, his face crumpled, looking in pain.

"Hey, it takes two," I tell him, reassuring him this isn't all on him.

"You were doing so well. Education is important," he explains to me.

"It is when you're saving lives. I'm decorating rich people's homes. To them it might seem a matter of life and death, but in the scheme of things it's not." He frowns at my comment.

"I can't let you drop out," he adds sternly.

"I'm not. But it's going to be hard being the size of a boulder and trying to get to classes."

"Can you do online?" he asks.

"Maybe. I haven't looked that far into anything. I'm still getting my head around being pregnant," I tell him. "I guess this affects everything." My brain hurts thinking about it all.

"We both have a lot to think about," he adds, both of us falling into silence again, thinking it over. "Are you going to stay here?" he asks.

"For the moment, yes. My girls will support me no matter what, but maybe after one too many sleepless nights they may not be so supportive," I say, shrugging my shoulders.

"What about your family's apartment, the one Nell lives in?" Miles asks.

"Could be an option. Least I would have Rhonda looking after me."

"Her nachos are to die for," he adds.

"How do you know about her nachos?" I question him.

"Had them one day when I went over to check in on Nell when she fell off a table at a club," he explains.

Why does that thought fill me with insane jealousy? That he went and looked after Nell when she was sick. That they hung out. It's irrational, but it's created a pit in my stomach, and I don't like it.

"Or would you go home instead?" he asks.

"Seeing as I haven't told my parents yet, I'm not sure if they will welcome me."

"Please, your parents love you. I can't imagine Nacho and Allison are going to kick you out. Me, on the other hand, I don't think I will ever be invited back. Your father is probably going to kill me. Feed me to his horses or something," Miles states. He's not wrong. My dad is going to lose his mind.

"Have you said anything to your parents?" I ask.

"Not yet. Not until we have worked it all out."

"Maybe we should do it together. Let them know we are a united front. Your mom is going to hate me so much."

"There is no way in the world my mother could hate you. Do you have any idea how long she has been waiting for grand-kids?" Miles gives me a wide smile. "I'm so going to be the favorite for a long time." This has me cracking up. I know how competitive the Hartford boys are.

"I hope we don't strain things between our parents," I add, fearing my father's temper will get the better of him and he's going to say something unforgiveable to Miles's parents and ruin a lifetime of friendship.

"It's probably going to get heated for a bit, but eventually everyone will be okay with the idea. It's not like we can change it," he tries to reassure me.

I let out a heavy sigh because he's right. There is nothing I can do to change the fact Miles and I had a one-night stand which has resulted in this very delicate situation. "Nope, we can't. We are having a baby together." We stare at each other, the realization sinking in, and we both burst out laughing even though this is not a laughing matter. What else can you do because it seriously messed up this situation.

"I know I shouldn't laugh but if don't laugh I'll cry," I tell Miles. He instantly stills, and his face falls as he stares at me.

"I'm sorry," he says again.

"Please, Miles, stop saying sorry. I don't blame you for the situation we are in. It was a series of unfortunate events that has now led to a lifelong entanglement between the two of us."

Miles nods. "When you put it like that." He lets out a heavy sigh at the magnitude of the situation hitting him. "We have a lot to sort out. First things first. We should get you checked out. Make sure everything is good."

"You think something could be wrong?" I ask him. Nell said the same thing. Am I missing something?

"No, not at all. You're a young, healthy woman. I can't imagine anything is wrong at all. But sometimes there are false-positive results, which means you may not be pregnant," he explains. Oh. So, I could be stressing for no reason over my result. "I can make an appointment for you. I know some of the best OBGYNs in the city." It would make sense.

"If you don't mind, that would be great. Put my mind at ease."

"Honestly, Portia. You're young, so there is very little that can go wrong. Of course, there is genetics in play and some people don't know there's a problem until they try for kids," he explains in his doctor tone. What he's saying is everything is out of my control now. "Once we have confirmation everything is fine, then we will need to talk about telling our parents."

"You should probably tell Remi first because he's being weird with Nell," I tell him.

"Shit. You're right." He runs his hand through his hair again. "Remi hates me because he thinks I slept with Nell. He's madly in love with your sister and he thinks I've ruined it. I can't blame him for hating me. What I thought I did was bad."

"How about this? We have the appointment tomorrow. Make sure everything is okay before stressing the family. Once we have the all-clear, we tell your parents and Remi."

"What about your parents?" he asks.

"That's going to be a little harder. Let's see how your parents react to the situation. They are going to be a hell of a lot calmer than mine."

"Sounds fair," he adds. "I'll be here for you, Portia. No matter what, I've got you okay. I know last night I said the wrong things. But know this, I will never let you down, Portia. You can count on me to be beside you throughout this entire journey if you will let me." Aw, that's sweet of him.

"I'd like that. Wasn't looking forward to doing this alone," I confess to him.

"Never. This is my child too. And yes, I never planned on being a dad yet. But the little thing is here now and I'm willing to step up. I think you and I can have a great relationship bringing up our baby together." Tears well in my eyes at his sweet words. Miles gets up and sits beside me and pulls me into his arms and hugs me tightly.

"I'm so scared, Miles," I cry into his chest.

"I get it. Childbirth is hard, but all the fear will disappear when you hold your little bundle in your arms and all the hardship that came before will be gone," he says, reassuring me as he strokes my hair.

"As long as I have you by my side, I don't feel so scared."

"I'm not going anywhere," he tells me.

17

MILES

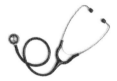

"There's nothing to be nervous about," I tell Portia as we enter the OBGYN office.

"I know, but what happens if something is wrong?" Portia whispers to me.

"Then we will deal with it. But I'm sure everything is going to be okay," I tell her as I grab her hand and lace it with mine, reassuring her. I don't let go, not even when we check in or when we sit down. It's only when the receptionist comes out and asks Portia to fill out some forms that she lets go of my hand. I understand Portia's fears. She's young. She probably has never been around anyone pregnant or even seen anyone give birth. She's been told her entire life having a baby at her age is going to ruin her life. It's been drummed into her for so long I can imagine there is still some uncertainty there. Yes, she is young, but the difference with her situation is she has the financial means to look after herself. She has the support of her two friends; she has my support. We may not be romantically linked, but I still care for her. I still worry about her. I'll do everything in my power to protect her, no matter what. *Even if she is dating someone else?* That thought slivers into my mind. She's pregnant. I can't imagine she will go on dates. *And why not? She's pregnant, not dead.* I frown at my inner thoughts going rogue suddenly. I pull out my phone and try to distract myself.

"She's cute," Portia says, looking at my phone. I take a couple of moments to realize what she is looking at. A girl sent me a message online, and I randomly opened it, not thinking there were photos attached. "Are you dating her?" she asks.

I turn and look down at those molten chocolate eyes that still after everything, draw me in. No. Don't go there, Miles. Stay far, far away from Portia. You've already messed up her life don't mess up her heart too. "I've never met her. She sent me a message."

"Do you get them a lot?" she asks.

"No more than anyone else, I suppose. I'm sure you get loads."

"Most are creepers," she states, shrugging her shoulders. "You know I'll be okay if you date other people. You're not the one who's pregnant," she adds.

Not sure how I feel about that comment yet. "I'm busy at work. Don't have time to date."

"What I mean is, I won't mind you sleeping with other people. One of us should get laid," she says with a chuckle.

Should I thank her for that? I'm not sure how to navigate this conversation because I feel like it will not end well for me. Thankfully, I don't have to say anything because I am saved by the doctor calling us in. We get up and follow the doctor down the hallway and into her white sterile office.

"Hi, I'm Doctor Jennifer Gibbs." She introduces herself to Portia with a bright smile on her face. I went to med school with Jenny. She moved into her field, and I moved into mine. And no, we have never hooked up because she's into girls even though she is stunning. "It's nice to see you again, Miles. How's ER treating you?" she asks.

"Always an adventure," I tell her. She nods and looks over

Portia's paperwork. I can see the tiniest flick of surprise across her face as she reads it.

"So, we are here to confirm if you are pregnant or not?" Jenny looks between the two of us. I can see the questions on her lips about the two of us.

"Yes. Morning sickness seems to have kicked in. I thought it was food poisoning," Portia answers.

"I'm assuming this wasn't planned?" She directs the question at me.

"We both only found out a couple of days ago. Portia's a longtime friend of the family." Not sure why I needed to add that last bit of information. I guess I didn't want Jenny to think I was being stupid with some random girl.

"Right, well, I'm going to need you to lay down on the table in the next room for your ultrasound. If you want Miles to leave for this next bit, let me know?" Jenny asks Portia.

"He's fine," Portia tells her, giving me a small smile.

Jenny pulls the curtain across to give Portia privacy, and we walk back into her office.

"What the fuck, Miles. She's twenty-one?" Jenny whisper curses at me.

"I know. It's a long story," I tell her.

"Of all the people to set foot in my office, you were the last one I would ever suspect." Jenny laughs.

"I know. I was never settling down. Guess life had other ideas."

"Guess it has. So, you've known her for a while then?" she asks.

"All her life. I was at the hospital when she was born," I tell my friend.

Jenny smacks me on the arm. "Oh my god, you're a creep."

"I'm ready," Portia calls out. The look Jenny gives me tells me her questioning isn't over.

"Great," Jenny states before walking into the room where

Portia is, I join her moments later. "Miles, take a seat, please." Jenny says glaring at me.

I do as I am told. Jenny then explains to Portia how this is going to be cold as she squirts jelly onto her stomach and begins moving the wand around. The ultrasound screen comes alive and the tiniest of blips fills the screen. I stare at the black-and-white image, and I feel like someone has punched me in the chest. I've seen this image so many times before but being on the other side —wow. My eyes become glassy. That's my baby.

"This is your baby." Jenny points to the little jellybean on the screen. "This is its heartbeat." She turns on the sound and the loudest thud, thud, thud fills the room. It's so strong. "It's a good heartbeat," she tells Portia, who looks up at me for reassurance. I give her a nod and I can see the relief float across her face as her brows loosen, letting the stress melt away. I look down at her and tears are falling down her cheeks.

"That's our baby," I tell her, grabbing her hand and giving it a squeeze.

"Do we know if it's a boy or a girl yet?" she asks.

"It's a little early. Probably in a couple of month's we should know. Do you want to know the gender?" Jenny asks, looking between the two of us.

"I'm not sure," Portia says.

"If you want it to be a secret, let me know because it's going to be hard for this guy here to not be able to tell." Jenny looks up at me with a smile.

"Of course." Portia chuckles, giving her head a little shake.

"I won't look if you don't want me to," I tell her.

"No. I think it's easier if we find out just in case."

"Will you be having a gender reveal party?" Jenny asks, and I can see the amusement on her face when she looks up at me and I'm giving her a horrified look.

"Hadn't thought about it. Is this what people do? I've never been to one," Portia states.

"There's the gender reveal and baby shower. Then once it's born, you can have a naming day or sip and see," Jenny explains.

"Oh, wow. That's a lot," Portia groans.

"We don't have to do any of that," I reassure her.

"Gives you both something to think about. I'll print you both out some photos of your baby. I'll let you get dressed and we can finish up," Jenny explains to Portia.

I follow Jenny back into her office.

"Are you going to have a DNA test?" she asks.

"I wasn't planning on it. Why?"

"As long as you are sure it's your baby, and she's not, you know," Jenny tries to say diplomatically if Portia trapped me.

"She's way richer than me. I'm poor compared to her trust fund," I whisper to her. Jenny's eyes widen and I can see her shoulders relax a little.

"That's good. Ever since I've known you, you've never thought with the right head. And I've thought one day someone will try to trap you." Jenny glares at me.

Portia enters the room and takes a seat beside me. "Did I interrupt something?" she asks, looking between Jenny and me.

"No," I tell her.

"I was making sure this old guy wasn't taking advantage of you. I've known him for many years. He has a reputation." Jenny gives Portia a wide smile. Is she serious right now? What the hell is she doing?

"Don't you worry. I've known Miles all my life. Those Hartford boys all come with a big fat warning label," Portia adds. This has Jenny cracking up.

"The number of hearts I had to fix during med school I should have become a cardiologist," Jenny teases. "I have to thank him for introducing me to my wife. He broke her heart so badly she swore off men." This is a joke Jenny loves to tell everyone. It's not true though. Yes, I hooked up with Jenny's wife Renee, but I thought it was fun, nothing serious. I told her that morning we couldn't see each other again because I was seeing someone else who happened to be her friend. She was devastated, and Jenny who was my roommate at the time consoled her, and the rest is history. Portia turns and raises a brow in my direction.

"It's not what you think," I try to reassure her.

"No. Miles is a good guy underneath all his ego," Jenny adds. "He's going to be a wonderful dad too." And for a moment, Jenny's compliment catches me off guard and I tear up. Portia reaches out and links her hand with mine.

"I think so too," Portia tells me, and I'm finding it hard to keep my emotions in check.

"Right, well. My work here is done. Portia, your baby, is perfectly healthy. You're in expert hands with Miles. He will walk you through the physical stages of what is going to happen next. All I want to say is, have faith in yourself. I know things are going to get hard because of the unconventional relationship the two of you will have but trust your instincts. People will want to tell you to do this, do that. But in the end, you need to go with your gut. Because Momma knows best," Jenny tells Portia. And I can feel Portia relax at that bit of information.

We thank Jenny and take our photos of our little baby and head on out to the car.

"I can't believe this is our baby," Portia says, staring at the black-and-white image.

"It's kind of surreal," I tell her as I jump in the driver's seat but don't start the car. "You're doing, okay?" I ask her, trying to gauge the level of freak out she might be having.

"I'm fine. I feel great. Excited yet shit scared," she tells me as she looks up at me through her thick lashes. My dick twitches and this is not the time.

"Good, because Mom texted and wanted to meet up for lunch." Portia stills. "I said I would meet her at the office because I needed to talk to her first." Portia's eyes widen. "Could be the right time to tell them."

"I'm not ready to tell my parents."

"We don't have to tell your parents yet. Not until you are ready." I reach out and take her hand in mine again, reassuring her.

"I don't want your parents to hate me."

"They won't. I can promise you that," I tell her.

"Lucky we have these then," she says, shaking the ultrasound images of the baby in her hand.

18

PORTIA

I'm literally shitting my pants as we walk into Miles's family's business. I wave to my co-workers who are happy to see me. I chat with a couple, letting them know I'll be back next week part-time when school starts. Told them I was sick with something and that's why I've been MIA recently.

"It's going to be okay," Miles tells me for the hundredth time. I believe him, but still I'm about to shatter his parents' world.

"Miles, baby." Carrie, his mom, stops in her tracks as she sees me behind her son. "Portia, sweetie, what are you doing here?" she asks, looking between Miles and me. Her heavily Botoxed forehead tries to frown but hardly moves.

"Mom, can we have a chat in your office?" Miles asks seriously. His mom turns and stares at him before turning around and making her way back to her office. "Can you call Dad in here too?" he says.

Carrie picks up her phone and calls her husband, asking him to come to her office urgently. Her green eyes look between the two of us as we take a seat, and I can see she is trying to work out what the hell is happening. Moments later, Leon is walking through the door with a smile on his face until he stops and sees both Miles and I sitting there.

"What the hell is going on, son?" Leon questions Miles.

"Please, Dad take a seat. I need to talk to you about something," Miles says to them both.

"You and Portia are dating?" Carrie says quickly as her eyes look between the two of us again.

"Nacho is going to kill you for dating his baby girl," Leon says, raising his voice at Miles. Maybe this wasn't such a good idea after all.

"Portia and I are not dating," Miles tells them both. His father looks relieved, but his mother looks confused.

"I don't know where to start," Miles says, looking lost in the moment, unsure how to drop the bombshell they are about to be grandparents.

"Here," I say, opening my bag and handing over the ultrasound to them. Carrie takes it from my hand and screams. Leon looks at her and is wondering why the hell his wife is having a freak out and then his eyes land on the scan and he turns his head, his face is pale, his eyes are wide.

"Please don't tell me you're the father?" Leon asks Miles.

"I am."

"Fuck. Fuck. Fuck. Fuck." Miles's father curses while we have reduced his mother to tears.

"That's why you've been sick. You have morning sickness." Carrie looks up at me.

"I'm sorry," I tell her as tears roll down my cheeks.

"It was a surprise. We've only found out. We had the doctor's appointment today to confirm everything was fine. And it is," Miles continues for me as I struggle to find the words.

"What the hell were you thinking?" Leon yells at Miles.

"It was me. All me. I took advantage of Miles when he was drunk. He didn't know it was me. I should have known better." I try to shield Miles from his father's wrath.

"Is it the reason you and Remi aren't talking at the moment?" his mother asks.

"Yeah, because he thinks I slept with Nell, not Portia," I explain.

"Are you fucking serious?" Leon raises his voice again. "Son, I don't understand you. First, you get tangled up with that Tracey girl and almost lose your career and now...you've knocked up the one girl you shouldn't have. Nacho is going to kill you and there is nothing I can do to stop him." Leon throws his hands up in the air. He's known my father for a lifetime. They are best friends. Our families are like family.

"So, it's okay for Remi and Nell to be together, but not Portia and I?" Miles asks his father.

"What did you say?" Leon turns and glares at Miles.

"Don't you bring your brother into this. These are two separate situations," Carrie warns Miles.

"Remi and Nell?" Leon turns to his wife, but she waves him away. "Nacho is really going to kill me now," he mumbles under his breath.

"Ignore him," Carrie says. "Is the baby healthy? How far along are you?"

"Baby is fine and I'm about ten weeks along," I answer her. Carrie looks down at the ultrasound and stares at it for a long time before looking back up at Miles and me with tears in her eyes.

"I'm going to be a grandma?" she asks. Miles and I nod. "Sweetheart, we are going to be grandparents." She waves the ultrasound in her husband's face, and I can see Leon's initial anger subside. "Look, babe. It's a baby." She bursts into tears and comes rushing over to me and pulls me into a hug. "Sorry I'm still in shock," she whispers into my ear and then heads over to Miles.

"Welcome to the family, Portia," Leon says before pulling me into his arms and giving me a big bear hug.

"We're so happy about this little miracle," Carrie says with a wide, tearful smile. "I can't wait to talk with Allison about all the things we are going to do as grandparents."

"About that, Mom." Miles interrupts. "Portia isn't ready to tell them yet." The room falls silent as Carrie and Leon stare at me.

"I only found out a couple of days ago my life's taken a different direction. I know my family. They are going to have so many questions, and I need to sort some things out first before I speak to them. So, if you could keep this a secret for the time being."

"Oh, Portia. Your parents love you so much. And I know your father has a temper, but he loves you. And only wants the best for you," she tries to reassure me.

"I know. I'm still trying to process everything. And I don't feel like I'm strong enough yet to tackle them," I confess to them both.

"Whatever you need, sweetheart, we are here for you," Leon tells me. I appreciate that.

"Things are complicated at the moment as Portia and I navigate through this new life together." His mom's eyes widen in surprise.

"Miles and I are not together," I quickly explain to Carrie.

"I'm not opposed to it," she adds.

"Mom," Miles warns her.

"Not to freak you out, son. But you know Nacho is going to demand you marry his daughter." Leon chuckles.

Miles turns and looks at me. Panic's written across his ashen face.

"He's old school. I'm not ready to tell them yet. He is going to come at us and I'm not in the place to deal with my father's traditional views on marriage and kids," I explain to Miles.

"If you were living together, it might make Nacho feel better about it all," Leon adds.

I can see Miles is becoming more and more freaked out the more his father teases. But Leon's right. These are all the things my father is going to demand of Miles.

"I don't want to live with you," I tell Miles.

"Why not?" he questions me. Which surprises me.

"Because…"

"You two have made me the happiest woman in the world," Carrie says, changing the subject. Were we about to have a fight?

"It's amazing," Leon adds, staring down at the ultrasound again.

"Portia, just know your job here is safe, no matter what happens. You are a talented designer. And I want to keep working with you," Carrie reassures me.

"Thank you," I tell her as tears fall down my cheeks again. Ugh. Hormones suck. I don't think I've ever cried so much.

"Mom, could I borrow your phone for a moment. I need to sort some things out with Remi," I ask her.

"Of course, sweetheart," she says, handing over her phone.

"Honey, all this excitement has built up an appetite. I'm starved," Leon tells his wife. Carrie nods, and they disappear out the door.

"I think it went, okay?" Miles grimaces at me.

"It's a hell of a lot better than how my family is going to react," I tell him.

"I will not let your father push us around, okay?" he reassures me.

"I know. But what my father wants, he usually gets." I sigh, knowing how hot tempered he is. Miles walks up to me and cups my face; the sensation sends tingles all over my body.

"I've got you. You and me against the world. We're a family now. Okay?" he tells me sincerely.

"Okay," I reply, feeling better Miles is on my side. His hands fall from my face and my body instantly morns its loss.

"Right, now I'm going to have to sort out my brother. Fingers crossed he takes my call." Miles crosses his fingers while he dials his brother's number.

"Please don't hang up, Remi," Miles says quickly. "It's important, Remi. Please."

"Thank God." He sighs into the phone. "I found out I'm going to be a dad today." He looks over at me. "Not sure how to say this because I'm confused myself, but I knocked up Portia Garcia." I can hear Remi's voice booming down the phone.

"She's legal. She's twenty-one," he argues with him. "Here's the bit you're going to find funny. Apparently, it wasn't Nell I brought home that night, it was Portia." Miles stares at the phone and frowns. Did Remi hang up on him? "Rem, Remi, are you there. Did you hear what I said?"

"Thanks," he answers awkwardly. "But are you understanding what I'm saying. I never slept with Nell." He tries to reiterate the news. "Remi, I am so sorry I fucked things up between you and Nell. But if you still want her, then you need to tell her how you feel," Miles exclaims.

"What did you do?" he asks Remi.

Oh no, my stomach sinks. I've messed things up between Remi and Nell royally. "Fuck," he curses before hanging up.

"What happened?" I ask him straight away.

"He didn't tell me. But he warned me next time he saw me it might be in a casket." Miles looks pale at the thought.

"That's a bit dramatic," I tell him.

Miles shrugs his shoulders. "Come on. I think we have caused enough chaos today. You're probably exhausted." Now that he mentions it, I could do with a nap and some food. As we walk out of the office, his phone beeps.

"It's Remi," he says, eyes wide in surprise, his brother is messaging him. "He wants Nell's address in Paris."

"What do you think he's going to do?" I ask, worried about my sister.

"I think he's realized he might be in love with her." Miles grins.

19

PORTIA

Miles and I have been communicating with each other most days since we dropped the bombshell on his parents. He checks in every morning to see how I'm feeling, then checks in with me at night and asks how my days are going back at college. It's strange walking back into school again because the last time I was there I was dating Axton and living a carefree life and now I'm hiding a pregnancy to a man eleven years older than me. I've enjoyed Miles's text messages. He's trying, and it's sweet. We have had little time to talk one on one with his crazy work schedule. I guess that's the life of an ER doctor. It's nice; when he has a break, he shoots me a quick text. That I am even on his mind while he is saving lives is nice. He hasn't flirted with me once since finding out I'm pregnant. I don't blame him. Who wants to mess around with a pregnant woman? Not when he has hot nurses at his beck and call every day. Once they find out, he's going to be a DILF, then he's going to have women falling over themselves to be with him.

My stomach sinks a little at the thought. That Miles might date while I'm knocked up with his kid. Because who is going to want to date a pregnant woman? Some creeper with a pregnancy kink, probably. It's so not fair. Miles can still look great with his six-pack abs; women will swoon over him for being a daddy and then there is me. All stretched out looking like shit because I haven't slept in a million years. My boobs are down to my knees and my stomach is no longer taut. Isn't that what they say happens? Fatherhood is going to make Miles look hotter and motherhood is going to make me look like shit. I will say I've noticed my boobs are getting bigger. That's a bonus. Looks like I've had a boob job over the summer. Thankfully, we are coming into the cooler months, and I can hide my ever-changing body.

I haven't told anyone at school about my predicament even though I'm about to hit the twelve-week mark, which is the end of the first trimester, which means things should be okay. There isn't a high chance of me miscarrying or anything. That's been scary the more I've been reading up on pregnancy. If I had read what was going to be happening to me before I got pregnant, then I would keep my legs closed forever. I know millions and millions of women go through this all the time, but holy crap, this is scary. I'm trying to shield my besties from the horror of pregnancy because I want them to have babies too. I mean, I wouldn't wish this upon them now, but in ten years. Oh crap, I'll have a ten-year-old by then. A real-life human and they will only have babies. Wonder what my kid is going to be like? I hope it's a girl because then we can be best friends and go shopping. If it's a boy, I'm going to have no idea what the hell to do with it.

Thankfully, I've been helping Remi plan a romantic apology to my sister. He's hoping he can get her back which has been keeping my mind off my life for the moment and the thought of telling my parents that I've screwed up. Helping Remi is the least I can do for playing a part in tearing them apart. Fingers crossed, Nell accepts Remi's apology, and they can move on with their lives. These two have been dancing around each other enough now and they should finally get together for real. No more games. Honestly, I can't imagine Remi is going to wait long till he proposes as well. He will want his ring on her finger, stat. He's never letting her go now he finally has her. I hope my sister isn't a stubborn ass like she usually is and accepts everything he wants to give her, and they can move on with their lives.

My phone rings, pulling me from my thoughts.

"Hello," I answer, not looking at the screen.

"Thank you. Thank you!" Nell screams down the phone at me. "Remi and I are back together, and we are coming home." She squeals with excitement.

"I'm so happy for you," I tell her. And I am. I feel great I could help make my sister happy again after everything.

"We'll be home in two weeks; have to wrap everything up here."

I'm going to be happy to have her home as I miss her so much and all I want at this moment is for my big sister to give me a cuddle and tell me it's going to be all okay.

"I'm so excited. I miss you so much," I tell her.

"I miss you too. Have you told Mom and Dad yet?" she asks.

"No. You would have heard Dad's yelling from Paris if I had. Miles's parents know and have been so supportive. I've made the twelve-week mark so wanted to make sure everything was okay before telling them."

"Remi and I will be home soon, and we can tell them together. I've got you, babe," she tells me.

"Thank you," I mumble through my tears. "I'm so happy you and Remi are finally together. Now don't mess this up," I joke with her.

"Believe me, I won't This is it. Remi told me I'm stuck with him for life and I'm kind of okay with that. I'm ready for it." I can hear the happiness in her voice.

"Mom and Dad are going to be so happy you are finally together. It's going to take the focus off of me, which I'm thankful for."

"How's things between you and Miles?" she asks.

"As good as they can be," I tell her.

"How do you feel about him?" she asks cautiously.

"It's weird; not going to lie. Usually when people have a baby with someone, it's because they have planned a future together. This is a little complicated, I guess. We are still working things out. It's awkward," I explain to her.

"Well, Remi and I will be home soon and I'm hoping it will make things better or easier."

"Thanks. We'll work it out. We have to. I'm so happy for you, Nell. I'd never forgive myself for messing things up between you and Remi."

"Please, Remi and I did this to ourselves. But never again," she tells me, and I can hear the happiness in her voice.

"I'll let you go. I miss you and I'll see you soon."

"Miss you too, Portia. Can't wait to get home and see you."

And with that, I hang up from our call with a smile on my face.

20

MILES

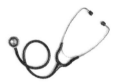

S tirling called me and asked if I wanted to catch up for dinner. We haven't caught up in ages. He's been super busy and so have I. So much so I haven't told him about my news. Guess tonight is going to be the night. I hope he's prepared for what I'm about to drop in his lap.

"Hey," he greets me with a wide smile on his face as I take a seat across from him. He's looking good. Happy, glowing even. What the hell has been going on with him?

"You're looking good," I tell him as I take a seat.

"I feel good," he says with a grin.

The waitress comes over and takes our drinks order.

"What's been going on?" I ask him, curious over his change of disposition.

"Audrey and I are official," he tells me. I'm surprised. Never thought he would fall for his best friend's little sister, even though she's a smoke show. Rhys, her brother, is so protective of her. I remember when Audrey was sixteen, he warned us all away from her threatening to cut our balls off. Please, I was not interested in a sixteen-year-old as a fully grown adult. Except when Audrey was sixteen, Portia was twelve. My stomach turns at the thought.

"I can see it on your face how happy you are," I tell him. "How did things go with Rhys when he found out?"

"Not going to lie. He's still not a hundred percent on board with our relationship, but thankfully his beautiful partner, Ariana, is making him see things differently. It's not such a bad thing we are together. I don't know if Rhys will ever accept the two of us being together."

"Not until you're married," I joke. But Stirling gives me a serious look. "No. You don't plan on popping the question to her?" I stare at my brother in surprise.

"Not yet. It's a little too soon for all that, but it's where I'm headed," he says with a grin.

The waitress brings us our drinks and we order some food as well.

"Congratulations to you and Audrey," I say as I raise my glass up to him and we clink glasses. I'm happy for him. He's always had a crush on Audrey, and I thought it was because she was hot, not because he liked her. Remi feels the same with Nell, but I thought he enjoyed hooking up with her. Not that they were in love. Maybe I'm the one with the problem. Guess people would say commitment issues, but nothing traumatic has happened to me to warrant that thought. I guess what Tracey did to me was bad, but still doesn't make me lose faith in the entire female population. *There's a difference between fucking them and having a relationship with them.*

"Are you not worried about the age gap though?" the question falls from my lips before I have time to soften the delivery.

"At first, of course. That's the reason I've stayed away from Audrey. I'm ten years older than her," he states. There's eleven between Portia and me. The difference is people see someone twenty-five a hell of a lot differently than they see someone who's twenty-one. Those four years at her age are a lifetime. Portia is still in college for fuck's sake. At least Audrey had graduated and wasn't pregnant. "The more I denied my feelings for her, the more I was hurting us both. Believe me, I tried to stay away, especially because of Rhys, but my heart wouldn't let me."

"Did Remi tell you he and Nell are together?" I tell him, changing the subject.

"What?" He chokes on his drink. "No way. Finally. I'm happy for them. Those two hurt each other for no real reason," Stirling says firmly.

"They both needed to grow up I guess," I mumble. "They are on their way back from Paris as we speak."

"No way. I'm happy for them. I would give anything to be a fly on the wall when he tells Nacho, who's basically like his second father, he's fallen in love with his daughter. Nacho is going to freak out." Stirling chuckles as he sips his drink. I don't find it funny. "Maybe Mom and Dad need to be there; at least Nacho can't murder Remi in front of them," Stirling says, laughing again. When the hell did Stirling become a comedian? Thankfully, our food arrives, and I'm spared anymore of Stirling's jokes.

"I bet you must feel relief now Remi and I have found love. Mom can harass us daily for grandchildren," he says with a chuckle. He has no idea how wrong he is on that subject. I've saved him and Remi from daily phone calls from Mom because I'm giving her a grandchild. He should thank me. "So how are things going with your love life?"

"It's gotten a little complicated at the moment."

Stirling arches a curious brow in my direction as he continues to sip his drink. "Let me guess, some nurses found out you were seeing two or three of them at the same time or was it her partner came home early, and you had to jump out the window in your underwear."

I hate him sometimes. "Nothing like that," I tell him. It's much worse. I take a large gulp of my drink, which has Stirling's eyes widening at the movement.

"It's that bad?" he questions me.

I nod. "You're going to be an uncle."

Stirling stills as he takes in my words. "Oh, shit," he mumbles. "I thought you were always safe."

"Of course, I'm safe. This time, a series of events went against me. The odds were certainly not in my favor that night."

"So, it was a one-night stand?" he asks.

"Yes. But it's a little more complicated than some stranger," I explain to him.

"I will not like the answer, will I?" Stirling asks. I shake my head. "Fuck Miles." My brother curses.

"You remember that day we went suit shopping together at Saks. We saw the girls, and we sat around celebrating Nell moving to Paris." Stirling nods. "Well, Nell and I continued partying after."

"Please do not tell me you have knocked up Nell? Because I swear, I'm not above punching you in this restaurant," Stirling tells me.

"No, not Nell. Remi would never have forgiven me for that." Stirling looks relieved. "But I thought I went home with Nell that night."

"What?"

"I was drunk. Remi came over in the morning and found her ID on the floor and all hell broke loose," I explain to him.

"You fucked Nell?" Stirling asks, raising his voice which gets him tuts from the table next to us.

"I thought I did until…" I bite my bottom lip because things are about to hit the fan. "I found out it was Portia who I had actually slept with and now she's the one pregnant with my baby," I say the words quickly.

Stirling's face drops. His mouth moves a couple of times to speak, but no words come out.

"Yeah. I fucked up," I tell him.

"No shit you did. Fuck, Miles. This...I..." he splutters over his words.

"Do Mom and Dad know?" I nod. "And Remi?"

"That's why Nell and he are together. He thought Nell and I had slept with each other and lost his mind over it. Felt like shit after that, let me tell you. Then when Portia eventually confessed it was her I had slept with that night and not Nell. I was relieved because Portia and I had sort of been having a flirtation leading up to the bombshell."

"You're telling me you have been flirting with little Portia Garcia?" Stirling asks.

"She's twenty-one. You of all people shouldn't be righteous about age gaps."

"I remember when Portia was born. I used to babysit her with you."

"Yes. It's weird when you say it like that. But she's grown up now and is stunning."

"So, you were thinking with your dick again," Stirling says, rolling his eyes at me.

"It wasn't like that. She came on to me. Well, I thought Nell was coming on to me. I was drunk and in the moment it felt good," I try to explain to him my point of view.

"So, you want Nell, not Portia?" he asks.

"What? No. I want Portia." As soon as the words fall from my lips, I know I'm in trouble.

"You have feelings for Portia?" he questions me.

"The girl is having my baby, of course I feel something for her," I grumble to my brother.

"But before all this complication you wanted her." Stirling's eyes narrow on me.

"Yes. Okay. Shoot me. I saw little Portia Garcia for the first time as a woman, not as the girl I remember growing up. I thought she was beautiful, and a heap of fun all the times I've run into her," I tell him.

"And what do you feel for her now?"

"I'm going to do my best to help her through these months. I'm going to be the best dad. That's all the capacity I have to think about," I share with my brother.

"I can't believe you're going to be a dad."

"I know. It's scary as shit. Even though medically I know what to do with kids. Parenting wise, I've got no clue," I confess to him.

Stirling's eyes widen. "Have you told her parents yet?" I shake my head. "Oh, shit, you're a dead man walking. Nacho is going to kill you. Remi is going to breeze in, and they are going to think that's the worst thing that could happen, and then you drop this bombshell. And with Portia, who's his baby." Stirling shakes his head at me.

"He's not that bad." I chuckle, but I know he is.

"Rather, you than me."

21

PORTIA

"**O**h my god, I've missed you." Nell squeals when she sees me enter her apartment, with Miles right behind me. She pulls me into her arms and holds me to her.

"I'm so glad you are home," I mumble into her neck.

"Me too." Everything is going to be okay now.

"Nice to see you, man," Remi says to Miles as they bro hug.

"It's good to have you home again," Miles says. "I'm still so sorry about everything."

"It's all good. It all worked out in the end for Nell and me," Remi says, giving Nell a hungry grin. Ugh. These two are going to be intolerable now they are dating in the open. I can smell the pheromones coming off them. Ew.

"How are you feeling about seeing Mom and Dad?" my sister asks.

"Not good at all," I tell her as my stomach does a somersault. *Sorry, baby, I don't mean to stress you out so much.*

"They love you and want the best for you, that's all," Remi adds. He, of all people, should know what my dad is like.

"Thankfully, Mom and Dad will meet us there. Hopefully,

having them there as a buffer will keep things civilized," Miles states. I sure hope so.

"Guess we better get going before traffic gets bad," Remi adds.

"It's going to be okay; I promise," Nell whispers to me as we make our way down to the garage to our cars.

"How are you feeling?" Miles asks as we pull out into the traffic.

"Sick. I'm hoping once we tell my parents everything is going to be okay. But what happens if it's not?" I turn and ask Miles. He reaches out and takes my hand in his and gives it a little squeeze.

"If it's not then you have me." He gives me the biggest, widest smile and it literally liquifies my body. My eyes well with tears. *What? No! Why is that happening? Stupid hormones.*

"Babe?" He turns his face back to me, checking every so often while he drives to see if I'm okay. Oh my god, he called me babe. I'm dead. Panties have incinerated, but I also can't stop crying. This is most confusing. "Did I say something wrong?" His brows pull together, and he looks at me, concerned.

"No." I sniffle. "I'm thrilled you're going to be there for me," I say as I wipe my snotty nose with the back of my hand.

"Of course, I'm going to be there for you. You and me, we are in this together," he reassures me. "I know we probably haven't ironed out everything we need to for the baby. But you can trust me when I say I've got you. You will not go through this alone."

I let out a heavy sigh and curl into the passenger seat. His hand is still linked with mine and I like it. I fall asleep at some point because it's not long till Miles is waking me up and letting me know we aren't far from my parents' house.

"You must have needed that." He turns, giving me a grin.

"We're almost there?" I ask. A sense of doom looms over me.

"Yeah, maybe five minutes. And my parents are probably twenty minutes behind us," he explains.

I nod and stare out the car window at the familiar scenery passing us by. The car then turns into the entrance of the farm. The gate is already open from Remi and Nell as we follow behind them. We make our way along the winding driveway, which is surrounded by white fences filled with polo ponies dotted across the rolling green hills. The trees have lost their leaves and the start of fall has come early at the farm with the sprinkling of orange leaves across the driveway.

"It's going to be okay," Miles reassures me one last time as we pull up out the front of my childhood home. Remi and Nell are already out of the car and my family are there standing on the doorstep. I watch through the window, my parents greeting Remi and Nell happily, all smiles and handshakes. Of course, they are going to love the fact Remi and Nell are together. My dad practically thinks of Remi as his son already. He's now going to have someone to take over his polo team when he retires because my brother Dom isn't interested. He's too busy breeding ponies.

Miles and I step out of the car as we hear my brother greeting Remi and Nell.

"What's going on? You and your sister are freaking out the entire family."

Dom turns as he catches us from the corner of his eyes. He gives me a smile before moving his attention back to Remi and Nell. And that's when I see the realization on his face. The subtle way Remi places his hand on Nell's back to move her toward the house sets my brother off.

"You fucker. You promised." Dom storms out over to Remi and pushes him up against the car, which makes the entire family yell at him.

"I love her!" Remi screams at his best friend. As soon as my mom hears those three words, they have her hyperventilating with delight. "And I'm sick of hiding it from you all," Remi adds.

Mom's face lights up like a Christmas tree. "Oh my god, Nacho. They are in love. I told you it would happen one day. Oh my god, this is a blessing," Mom carries on. "Dom, take your hands off Remi. He's part of the family now," she chastises my brother.

"You break her heart, you're dead," he warns Remi before walking away and up the front stairs into the home to cool down.

"Welcome to the family, son," Dad says, giving Remi a smile.

Wait that's it? Dom is the one that loses his mind, but Dad smiles as if it's no big deal. Who the hell is this man?

Nell takes Remi's hand and gives it a kiss, and my father's face softens and my mom sighs. Mom gives me a wave and mumbles something about coming inside to celebrate as Dad follows her. Remi and Nell stare at each other even more in love, and it's making me sick.

"What the hell happened?" Miles asks me.

"I have no idea. I think someone has body snatched my parents." Miles and I join Remi and Nell as we head to go inside.

"Gee, that went well. Hope Mom and Dad are happy when I tell them they are about to be grandparents."

"I don't think it's going to be as bad as you think it will be," Nell reassures me. But I'm not so sure. Guess I can hope though.

As we step across the threshold, Mom comes running back out letting us know she's asked the chef to prepare canapes for us to celebrate Remi and Nell. She tells us we should all move to the living room; Dad's already in there popping champagne.

"We have much to celebrate and talk about." He grins as Dom hands out the glasses of champagne he has filled to all of us. I hesitate to take the glass, but I do to keep up appearances. Nell glares at me, and I shake my head at her. I'm not stupid, I will not drink it, but now is not the time to drop my bombshell onto the family. "Is this why you wanted to call a family meeting?" my father asks Nell.

"Yes," she answers, taking a sip from her champagne glass.

"Does this mean Remi might be interested in what we've spoken about before?" my father asks, looking over at Remi. What have they spoken about?

"If you are still keen, sir, yes, I would like to come in as your partner on the polo team," Remi adds.

Remi and my father are going to become business partners? When the hell did this happen? What about Dom? I look at my family, and they all seem happy about this recent development.

"Does this mean you might move from the city and stay up here permanently?" Mom asks Nell.

"We haven't discussed anything yet." My sister smiles.

"Remi is here most days. It would make sense if you were here too," my father adds sternly.

"And you can design from anywhere," Mom adds. "You can share my office. I would love to work with you."

What the hell is happening? I've walked into the *Twilight Zone*.

"We don't have to tell them today if you're not ready," Miles whispers to me. I'm so happy he is here, right beside me.

"They seem to be in a good mood. I'm not sure how long this will last," I say, looking up at him. He nods in agreement.

"Nacho, Allison, are you home?" Miles's mom calls out from the hallway.

"Carrie?" Mom turns around, looking surprised her best friend has arrived. She walks over to her and gives her a kiss on the cheek, then greets Leon, their dad, who's right behind them.

"Did you hear the wonderful news?" Mom asks Carrie. Miles's mom turns and looks over at Miles and me to gauge the situation.

"No, sweetie, what news?" she says to my mother.

"Remi and Nell are together. And Remi has become partners in the polo team with Nacho," Mom tells her excitedly.

"Good work, son," Leon congratulates Remi.

"That is wonderful news. Was there anything else?" Carrie asks my mom.

"They will live here full-time," she adds.

"Mom, I didn't agree with that yet. I said we haven't spoken about it yet," Nell tells my mother.

Carrie looks over at Miles and I standing in the corner quietly. She gives us both a little frown. "If you want to borrow our beach house, you're more than welcome," she tells Nell.

"Oh, wow. That is so generous of you, Carrie. Thank you," Nell says.

"We might need to talk to you and Leon about building Nell and Remi a home on the farm, too. I mean, if Remi is going to be working here, it would make sense," Mom explains to Carrie.

"It would have to be on the other side of the farm," Nell adds, chuckling.

"I can't do this," I tell Miles and turn on my heel and exit the living room. I need air as I feel like my throat is closing up and I can't breathe. I don't give Miles time to respond as I place my glass down on the side table and exit.

22

MILES

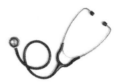

I could feel Portia becoming more agitated as her parents fawned over Remi and Nell revealing they are together and how happy they are over the news knowing full well when we drop our bombshell they will not be as receptive. I watch as her face becomes pale the longer she stands there, and I'm worried. I've been trying to reassure her throughout the day, but it means nothing when you know what the outcome is going to be.

"I can't do this," Portia mumbles to me as she places the full glass of champagne onto the side table and disappears from the room. I follow her because I don't want her to be alone dealing with this. We may not be together romantically, but I hope we are close enough to be at least friends.

"Portia," I call after her. But she's disappeared down the corridor. The slamming of a door catches my attention and I head left to the glass doors that lead outside. As soon as I turn the corner, I see her through the glass doors disappearing around the house, running. I head after her and find her in tears with her face buried against the side of the house. "Portia," I say her name softly as I slow my steps as I reach her. She turns her head to the side; her eyes are red from crying. Her make-up has run, but still somehow in that moment she's never looked more beautiful. Her broken image pulls inside of me, opening a door deep below that has been shut for years. Next thing I know, she is wrapping her arms around and hugging me tightly as she sobs. "I've got you," I tell her, while stroking her hair. I hold her to me while she lets it all out. I know she's been trying to be strong, but I also know she must be so scared, she's young, none of her friends are at this stage in their life yet and as much as they are there for her, they don't understand fully how life changing this is going to be. I mean, me, a thirty plus doctor with experience with babies, can't comprehend how much my life is going to change. All I know is I'm going to have to be there for Portia. She needs me and I can't let her down.

"I'm sorry," she mumbles against my chest.

"You don't need to apologize for anything," I tell her.

"I think I had a panic attack."

"I think so," I say, running my hands down her back, hoping it will take away the anxiety she is suffering.

"Everyone thinks Remi and Nell being together is the best day of their lives. Like the missing piece my dad has been searching for. My mom is already planning the wedding and then counting down to kids." She sniffles.

"Your mom is going to be happy once she finds out our news," I try to reassure her.

"I don't think they are," Portia mumbles, tightening her arms around me.

"If they aren't, my parents are. They may have been in shock at the beginning, but now they can't wait. You know Mom's already started plans on a nursery in their home," I tell her.

Portia pulls back and looks up at me. "Really?"

I nod. "Yes really. Know you aren't alone in the excitement of this baby." I reach out and caress her face with my hand. Smoothing the frown lines across her forehead, wiping the mascara filled tears from her cheeks, she's probably going to need to freshen up before going back in there, otherwise her parents are going to know something is up.

"Do you mean it when you say you'll be there for me?" she asks quietly.

"One hundred percent," I tell her honestly as I stare down at her, those chocolate brown eyes all innocent and wide as they stare back at me. I hate the tingle that's moving across my body as I'm not supposed to feel anything like that toward her. I promised myself we were just friends having a baby together. Nothing romantic can happen between us purely because it will complicate things. I can't keep being the bad guy with women. Portia and I hold a look between us for way too long until she surprises the hell out of me and wraps her hand behind my neck and pulls me to her lips. No. This wasn't supposed to happen. My mouth opens for her on instinct and that night between us floods my bloodstream with endorphins, my dick twitches with need and for the briefest of moments, I push her up against the house and kiss her back.

"Shit," I curse as I jump away from Portia. "I...I shouldn't have done that," I tell her, running my hand through my hair.

"That was all me. I'm sorry. I think my hormones took over at that moment. And I don't know what came over me to kiss you like that."

"It's fine." I wave her apology away; she never has to apologize for putting her lips on me.

"I keep messing up," she mumbles.

"Hey, no," I tell her. "It was nice. I wasn't saying no now. But I think us doing anything will complicate what we have," I explain to her.

"I agree with you," she says, giving me a friendly smile. "You have nice lips and sometimes it's hard not to remember the way they felt on me."

Shit. A groan falls from my lips, surprising us both. "Portia," I warn her.

"Of course, you don't remember it the way I do," she says, shaking her head. "I'm going to go upstairs and freshen up and then we are going to tell everyone our news," she says confidently. I nod in agreement. "Okay, I'll see you back downstairs in five." And with that, she's gone.

I turn the corner and nearly walk right into my mom.

"Everything all right, sweetheart? I came to check on you both," Mom asks, surprising me.

"She needed a moment. It was a little much for her in there," I tell her.

"Yes. It was not at all how I thought Nacho would be over the situation, but he treated Remi as if he was a son. They have spent so much time together over the years."

"And you think because Nacho doesn't know me, he will not be as welcoming?" I ask her, putting my hands in my pockets.

"I think if Remi had told Nacho Nell is pregnant today it would have gone a hell of a lot different." Mom gives me a small smirk. Right, dating is fine, pregnancy not so fine. "Nacho is a traditional guy, so having a baby out of wedlock will be a lot for him to compute."

"I will not let him say anything to hurt Portia," I warn her.

"I wouldn't expect anything less of you, my sweetheart." She takes a step toward me and kisses my cheek. "I'm so very proud of the man you have become. This may not have been in the plan for either of you, but the world works in mysterious ways."

"Thanks, Mom." No matter how old you are, sometimes you still need your mom.

"Now, come on. Let's get back inside and prepare for the inevitable fireworks." She chuckles.

It's another twenty minutes before Portia rejoins the group looking like nothing has happened. She gives me a small smile as she heads toward her parents. My heartbeat increases with nerves as I realize it's go-time. I put my empty glass down and make my way over to where Portia is, hovering in the background, unsure of my place. Portia gives me a nod and a head flick to show she wants me by her side. Her parents are talking with my own, fingers crossed they might buffer the news.

"Mom, Dad, sorry to interrupt but I need to tell you something," Portia says confidently. Her parents frown at her intrusion into the conversation but she has their full attention now. "Look, you will not be happy about what I'm going to tell you both," Portia warns them, "but it is what it is," she says with a heavy sigh. Nacho and Allison look at each other and you can see they are trying to work out what Portia is on about. "It wasn't planned, but it's happening." My mom tries to give Portia a silent *"You've got this"* with her eyes. "I'm pregnant."

The entire room stills, you could hear a pin drop. Portia stares at her parents, who are looking at her like she's lost her mind.

"What did you say, sweetheart?" her mom asks.

"I'm three months pregnant," Portia tells her.

"What the fuck did you say?" Dominic curses from behind, glaring at Portia. I can see Remi is ready to restrain his best friend if needs be.

"And I'm the father," I say, linking my hand with Portia.

That's when things went south quickly. A hand comes out and punches me in the jaw, which puts me on my ass. It startles me so much I'm hearing everything as if I'm underwater. The screaming and shouting are muffled. It was Nacho. Portia is screaming, her mom, my mom. My dad is holding Nacho back. Dominic is screaming at me and is ready to rip my head off.

"Dad, stop it!" Nell is screaming at her father.

He's cursing me out to my father, who is pulling him away from me, trying to get him to settle down.

"I'm so sorry." Portia holds her hand out for me and helps me up off the floor. "I honestly didn't think he would hit you."

"It's fine," I tell her.

"It's not. Come on, let's get you away from all this and find you some ice." She pulls me from the living room and back into the hallway and we head down to the kitchen. "You didn't deserve that."

"Kind of did. I knocked up his little girl." I give her a shrug of my shoulders. She shakes her head and pushes through the double doors which lead into the kitchen. "Chef, can we get an ice pack?"

He looks up from his station at me and yells at someone to get me an ice pack. A young chef runs into a large commercial fridge and comes out with an ice pack and hands it to me. I position it onto the bruise I can feel is coming up. The kitchen staff are trying not to look at the drama happening before them but are failing. Portia takes me back outside and there is still arguing, echoing down the hallway.

"Let's give them all a moment before we go back," Portia warns me. So, we stand there in silence while I keep the ice pack on.

"Leon, your kid is a piece of shit!" Nacho screams. "He took advantage of her. He's eleven years older than her. He's ruined her life."

"It takes two to make a baby, Nacho," my father yells back at him.

"I can't let my dad take the heat," I turn and tell Portia. She nods in understanding, and we head back into the living room.

"You piece of shit!" Nacho screams as he tries to go at me again.

"Fuck you, Nacho. That is my kid. I will not have you disrespecting him like that!" my dad yells as he stands in between Nacho and me.

"It was all me, daddy. I tricked him," Portia explains

to her father. He turns and looks at his daughter and frowns. "I pretended to be someone else."

I don't think Portia telling him she pretended to be her sister to sleep with me is what he needs to hear right now.

"Why, sweetheart? Why would you do that?" her mom asks.

"Because Axton broke my heart. That night he was there with the girl he was cheating on me with rubbing it in my face. I saw Miles and used him to hurt Axton as much as he hurt me. Little did I know how much I would end up liking him," Portia tells them as she looks over at me. I'm going to have to find out about this asshole later. "We spent the night together. He had no idea we had until I dropped the bombshell on him weeks ago."

"You found out weeks ago and never told us?" her mom asks, looking hurt her daughter didn't confide in her.

"Why would I when I knew Dad was going to act like this," she says, looking over at her father.

"Baby, it's because I love you. That's why," Nacho says as his face softens toward his daughter. "This man is so much older than you. He is no good."

"Dad, he's a doctor. If he wasn't who he was and was my age, you both would be excited I was dating a doctor," Portia tells them.

"Are you dating?" Nacho questions her.

"No. We aren't. We never were. It was an accident," Portia tells them.

"But what about college, sweetheart? You're so close to finishing?" Her father frowns at her.

"And I will," she tells them confidently. "I've already spoken to my teachers and asked if I could take the exams earlier due to me giving birth around finals and they said yes. I will graduate after I've had the baby."

I did not know Portia had organized this already.

"I have promised Portia a job whenever she wants," my mom adds.

"You knew about this?" Portia's mom questions my mom.

"I told them after I found out. I was too scared to tell you both for this very reason," Portia tells them both as she looks over at me with the ice pack on my face. Nacho's face falls as he listens to his daughter's words about being too scared to tell him her secret.

"I never want you to feel you could never tell me anything, Portia," her mom says as tears fall down her cheeks. Portia's face falls a little before she rushes into her mom's arms and hugs her tightly as she dissolves into tears. Nacho moves over and hugs them all tightly too.

23

PORTIA

Tempers simmer down after the shock of our announcement, but there is still a large underlying tension between both families. I know Mom's hurt over me telling Carrie first about my pregnancy. I did what was best for me in the moment. My parents burst out crying again as I showed them the ultrasound. They both couldn't believe it as they stared at their grandbaby. My brother is still being a jerk to Miles, and I don't think there is any love lost there.

"Will you be marrying my daughter?" my father asks Miles as we sit down to eat.

"Dad!" I warn. "Miles and I are not in a relationship."

"Yes, you are, you're having a baby together," he states angrily.

"We are friends," I explain to him.

"Is my daughter not good enough to marry?" my father turns and asks Miles, who looks like a deer caught in headlights.

"Dad, you don't have to get married to have a baby," Nell tells him.

"It's the right thing to do," he tells her.

"But they aren't in love," she tries to explain it to them.

"Then why did they sleep with each other?" he asks her.

Nell's eyes widen at my father's question, and she shakes her head.

"I know you've had plenty of nights like that before Allison," Leon teases my father. Carrie chokes on her champagne, as does my mom, and the room goes quiet.

"Never irresponsible enough to knock any of them up though," my father bites back. This is getting awkward. "Don't you think it's going to be hard on the baby then if you're not living together? How are you going to split time between the two of you? Can't imagine Miles is going to have time after work to hang out with the baby. Don't you work twelve hours a day?" My father turns and glares at Miles.

"I have days off," Miles answers him.

"Right, so you're going to be a part-time dad. Leave it to Portia to do the heavy lifting," he says.

"That's not fair, Dad. We haven't worked all of that out yet. We are both still processing the news," I try to calm him down.

"Don't you think this should have been sorted out by now? Have you spoken to lawyers to put a co-parenting agreement in place?" he asks.

"Not yet. I wanted to make sure I didn't lose the baby before organizing any of this. Wouldn't be any point if I lost it now, would it?" I yell at my father, losing my patience as I get upset with him.

"Sweetheart." My mom tries to calm me down. "Fighting like this isn't good for the baby." She aims her comment at my father.

"I'm asking reasonable questions," my father argues back.

"You are asking very valid questions, sir. Portia wanted to wait till she was over her first trimester before saying anything. She didn't want to jinx anything by making plans," Miles explains to my father. I didn't want to plan anything in case something happened. My father has valid points about the living situation. Miles is going to miss out on so much time with the baby because we will live apart from each other. I've been thinking about maybe moving back to Bridgehampton to be with my family for support because I can't have a crying newborn in the apartment waking Hannah and Cora up all night. That's not fair.

"Did something happen?" Dad asks, concerned.

"No. The baby is healthy. I didn't want to get my hopes up if mother nature had other plans," I explain to them.

"Do you know if it's a boy or a girl?" my brother asks, his rage simmering for the moment.

"Maybe next month we will know," I tell them.

"Does that mean we can have a gender reveal party?" Nell asks excitedly.

I look over at Miles and shrug my shoulders because we hadn't thought about it.

"That's what people do, don't they?" Miles adds.

"Can I organize it, please?" Nell asks.

"I want to help," Mom adds.

"And me too," Carrie says, waving her hand in the air.

"This sounds expensive." Dad chuckles for the first time since finding out I'm pregnant.

"Expensive for me," Miles adds.

My father's eyes widen, and then he bursts out laughing. "There's a silver lining in this situation. All baby parties are to be paid for by the baby's father."

What the hell is happening? Is my father drunk?

"Seems fair," Miles adds.

"There's also the baby shower," Nell tells Miles.

"Is that not the same as the gender reveal?" Miles questions her.

Nell shakes her head. "Oh no, that's a party to celebrate if you're having a boy or a girl. The baby shower is where everyone brings gifts for the baby."

"And you have to be there," Remi adds, his eyes narrow on his brother.

Miles and I are getting ready to go as we head back to the city.

"I'm so sorry you didn't think you could come to me with your news," Mom says, pulling me to the side.

"Dad punched Miles, that's the reason," I tell her.

"I could have told your father gently."

"We shouldn't have to walk on eggshells around Dad," I tell her. My father is a good man, and I love him with all my heart, but he is hotheaded. He reacts first before thinking about it.

"I understand, sweetheart, but he loves you, that's all."

"Then he needed to have faith in me."

"He still sees you as his little baby girl. You'll understand once you have your own baby," Mom tells me. "But we both love you with all our hearts, Portia. And daddy may not show it today, but we are very proud of you. This is going to be a hard journey on your own, but I have faith in you.".

"I'm not on my own, I have Miles," I tell her with a frown on my face.

"He's going to be there for you for the big stuff but for the everyday things you're going to be alone for them. And that's hard," she explains. I know my mom means well, but I don't want to hear it now.

"Please, let me work it out for myself. Okay?" I ask her.

"Okay, my sweetheart. I love you. I'm here for you," she tells me as she gives me a kiss and a hug.

Miles and I say our goodbyes and jump into his car to head back into the city. We sit in silence for a long time, mentally processing what happened.

"Today could have been worse," Miles says as he turns to me, and we both burst out laughing.

"How's your jaw?" I ask, reaching out and touching the bruise that's there. Miles winces at my touch.

"I'll heal." He gives me a sad smile.

I let out a heavy sigh. "I know I shouldn't have been surprised at how today went, but I am."

"They are your parents. Of course, you wanted them to accept the news happily. But they're human."

Miles is right. But a girl can hope can't she?

"Your dad had a point that hit home with me," Miles says.

I look over at him and frown. What on earth could my father have said that could resonate with Miles? There wasn't anything nice said between my father and him.

"When he was talking about separate homes. How I wouldn't be able to see my baby all the time, especially not after work."

"I would never keep your baby from you," I add quickly, hoping he doesn't think I would be like that.

"I know you wouldn't. It's not that. It's just...the more I thought about it today, the more I realized all the milestones I would miss during your pregnancy and after," Miles says, keeping his eyes on the road, not looking at me. Is he worried about what he's confessing to me? "I don't want to be a part-time dad. When I thought about having kids, I thought I would be there through it all. Enjoying feeling the baby kick for the first time or changing the baby's diaper."

Oh. I've never thought about those things because the baby is stuck to me. I don't have to worry about missing all those milestones because I must be there.

"Sorry, that's...never mind," he adds quickly as the car fills with silence.

"No," I say, reaching out and placing a hand on his thick thigh. "Please, tell me what you're thinking because I don't know what I'm doing. This is all new and scary for me too."

Miles turns his head and gives me a smile, as his hand lies on top of mine, which is still on his thigh. "What are your thoughts on the living situation, then? I don't want you to miss out on anything unless I buy an apartment next door to yours. Is there one for sale?" I say with a chuckle.

"Not at the moment. Guess I could keep an eye out or you could move in with me until we worked it out," he says the last bit of the statement quickly.

"Move in with you?" My voice raises.

"I knew it was a terrible idea," he replies, then silence falls between us. "Actually, no it's not," Miles says sternly. "I think it's a great idea. You have your own personal doctor on standby. I get to be a part of your pregnancy. Our child will be born into a home with two parents living together. The more I think about it the more I know it's a good idea."

"I don't," I say quickly, which makes Miles pull his hand from mine. His knuckles have turned white while he clenches the steering wheel. "We hardly know each other," I add, hoping to soften the blow. "You could have an annoying habit like, I don't know, eating sardines before bed."

Miles bursts out laughing. "Sardines before bed?" He shakes his head.

"I have pregnancy brain and it was all I could come up with."

"I can assure you I don't eat sardines, so it won't be a problem," he explains to me.

"What about if you have a date and want to bring her home. Then I come out waddling like a duck and she's like you didn't tell me about a baby momma. My rounded belly would be a huge cock block," I argue with him.

"Thank you for worrying about my cock, but I can assure you it will be fine," he adds smugly.

"Of course it would be. You're not the one that's going to end up the size of a house. Your life is going to go on as if nothing has happened. Whereas I'm going to be stuck with nothing but my hand to help me." I moan, crossing my arms over my chest. The car falls silent again. Did I push him too far? I thought we were joking. My eyes flick to the side and I see his knuckles white as he clenches the steering wheel again. "I will not be shamed about masturbation, Miles." I huff beside him. "It's healthy," I grumble. "You should be happy I'm fucking my hand and not another man's dick."

"What the fuck, Portia." He raises his voice. I'm not sure what I said wrong.

"It's not my fault your generation isn't open and communicative about sex," I add with a bratty pout. Miles just shakes his head and mumbles incoherently to himself until we make it back to my apartment.

"This conversation isn't over," he warns me.

Did I miss something because I could have sworn for the past hour we had been driving in silence?

"What conversation?"

"The one about you moving in," he states, those green eyes narrowing on me.

"Oh, I thought we had agreed it was a bad idea," I say, grabbing my bag.

"No, we didn't," he argues back.

"Um, yeah, we did. You said something about sardines and cock blocking, and I agreed," I say, waving my hands in the air. As I undo my seat belt and jump out before he says any more.

"Portia!" Miles yells my name. "This isn't over," he warns me before jumping back into his car. Ignoring him, I head on into my apartment. I'm ready for bed.

"Hey, girl, how did it go?" Hannah asks as I walk into the apartment exhausted. I make my way over to the living room where my roommates are sitting watching TV and flop down beside them on the armchair.

"That good, huh?" Cora adds.

I tell them everything that happened and the strange car ride home with Miles.

"That's sweet," Cora says.

"Sounds controlling," Hannah adds.

"No, it's not. It must be hard for the dads. They experience nothing during pregnancy, unlike the moms. He's worried if you're apart he might not feel connected to the baby. Like aren't you supposed to talk to it, so it knows your voice when it comes out," Cora explains.

I have no idea, maybe I need to read up on it. "Don't you think that's weird though, moving in with him?"

"No weirder than you getting knocked up by a man who thought he slept with your sister," Hannah adds with a smirk. I roll my eyes at my friend. "You could get a new home together."

Maybe that's not such a bad idea. His apartment, though luxurious, is small. It was very much a bachelor pad from memory.

"If you bought it, then if anything went sour you wouldn't have to be the one to leave." Hannah has a good point. "And as much as we love you. This apartment isn't set up for a baby either. Where would you put the crib, in your walk-in closet?"

"Who knew Hannah could be so wise," Cora says, bursting into laughter.

"It's something to think about, that's all. We love you and we're not trying to kick you out in the least. Cora and I can't wait to be aunties to your little nugget but living here is a short-term situation. Babies come with a lot of stuff." This is true. Now everything works here, but Hannah's right. Where would I put the crib in my bedroom? The baby can't sleep with me in the bed. Don't they like have to be older for that? Maybe I should have a place for me and baby we can call our own.

"I may have forgotten to mention I kissed Miles today as well," I confess to my girls. Who start peppering me with a million and one questions. "I was having an emotional breakdown. He was kind, and his lips were there, and I went for it. He kissed me back for a couple of moments, then pulled himself back and realized it was a bad idea."

"You two are going to bang if you live together." Hannah chuckles.

"Least she can't get pregnant twice," Cora jokes.

24

MILES

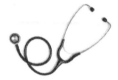

W e've all headed over to Lane's house for guys' night because his sitter is sick and he can't get one last minute, which is fine. I make my way into his apartment, where the rest of the guys are hanging out.

"Miles." Jaxon, Lane's son, sees me and comes running toward me. He wraps his little arms around my waist and gives me a big hug.

"Hey, little fella. How are you doing?" I ask him.

"Good. Dad won't let me stay up and hang out with you all." He pouts.

"It's a school night," Lane tells him. Jaxon's little shoulders slump but he nods in understanding.

"Promise we will have another guys' night on the weekend, and you can join in," I tell him. His little face lights up and he gives me another hug before hightailing it back to his room for bed.

"I'm going to say goodnight and I'll be back," Lane says, walking down the corridor to Jaxon's room.

"Look at you being all good with kids," Dylan teases me as

Smith hands me a beer and I take a seat on the couch in the living room.

"I did a rotation in pediatrics. Got all my skills there," I tell Dylan.

"Or maybe you're giving off daddy vibes," Dylan says back.

"Do I need to arrest you for saying that?" Smith arches a brow in Dylan's direction.

"Look, I'm down for handcuffs," Dylan says back, giving Smith a wink, making the detective shake his head as he drinks his beer.

"Anything good happen at work today?" I ask them both.

They both shake their heads. Seriously?

"I'm sure the detective caught a couple of bad guys, but he's being humble," Dylan says, teasing.

"Nothing I can talk about," Smith adds.

"What about you? Did you save any lives today?" Dylan asks.

"A couple. It was crazy busy today from the full moon last night. The ER gets chaotic," I tell him.

"See, if I didn't have such a big dick, you two might intimidate me." Dylan chuckles.

"That was not the right time to walk back into the conversation," Lane says as Smith hands him a beer. "What's happened?"

"Nothing worth mentioning. But we are all waiting patiently to find out how the baby daddy reveal went with the grandparents. Judging by the bruise on his cheek, not so well," Dylan says with a grin.

Smith and Lane turn and look at me. Both of their eyes narrow on to my jaw.

"Yeah, Daddy Garcia was not happy about me knocking up his little princess," I tell them as I take a sip of my beer.

"Sorry," Lane says sincerely.

"Thanks, man. I knew it was going to be a shit show, but seeing it was another thing. Portia got upset because everyone was so excited about Remi and Nell announcing their relationship and she knew it wouldn't be the same for her," I explain to them. "Thankfully, my parents were there, but it nearly turned into a brawl. It was insane."

"Sorry, man, that's fucked up," Dylan tells me.

"Least they know now," Lane adds.

"How's Portia?" Smith asks.

"She was pretty upset on the day but seems to be okay now. Her mom is trying, and her dad is grumbling through it still. Her sister is talking about organizing a gender reveal party or something."

My friends all laugh. Assholes.

"How's things between you and Portia then?" Lane asks.

"Good. We talk most days."

My friends all stare at me like I've lost my mind.

"But something her dad said to me in the heat of an argument resonated with me. He was talking about how much I'm going to miss with us being apart during the pregnancy and after the birth. I told Portia I don't want to be apart from my kid."

"What does that mean?" Dylan asks.

"I told Portia she needs to move in with me," I explain to them.

"You told her?" Lane asks, his voice raising.

"Yeah. I told her I didn't want to be apart from our kid."

"But she has a choice?" Lane pushes.

"Yeah, I guess she does, but I don't want to miss out on a second of my baby's life." What do they not understand?

"Let me guess that conversation didn't go down too well?" Lane asks.

"We argued about it, yes."

The boys all raise their brows high while looking at each other. What am I missing?

"How can you be so clueless?" Lane states. "You can't tell a hormonal pregnant woman what to do. The only loser in that scenario will be you. Women are stubborn on the best of days, but when they have a million and one hormones running through their body while they literally are growing a human, they don't want to be told what they can and can't do," Lane explains to me.

"But what about me?" I ask them.

"Honestly, Miles, this isn't about you," Lane says seriously. "This is all to do with what is best for mother and baby. If that means she is living in a small apartment with her girlfriends, then that is what she is doing. If she wants to move back home with her family than that is what she is doing."

"Don't I get a say?" I ask him.

"If you were a couple, then yeah, but you're not."

"That doesn't seem fair," Dylan adds.

"It's not. But mother and baby's health are what's important, especially when she is still early on. Keep her stress levels down," Lane explains to us.

"So, me demanding we move in together probably wasn't good for her stress," I say. Lane nods in agreement. "You can't tell me you would have wanted to miss any moment with Jaxon."

"No way in the world. But I was married, and things are different when you're a couple. I'm not going to lie, things are going to be hard for you co-parenting but talk with her about your wants, your fear of missing out, and come to an under-standing you are both happy with," Lane tells me, giving me sage advice.

"I never want to double wrap my dick more," Dylan adds. We all shake our heads at him.

"Is there a chance you and Portia might want to have a rela-tionship?" Smith asks.

"A romantic one?"

"Yeah. Seems like what Lane is saying is if you and Portia

were dating, it would make things easier," Smith states, shrugging his shoulders.

"You know Miles hates commitment," Dylan answers for me.

"He's already got an enormous commitment having a baby with someone," Smith argues back.

"Not by choice," Dylan adds.

"I don't want to lead her on," I explain to them both.

"Do you like her?" Lane asks.

"Of course, I do. She's great."

"But she wasn't in your plan," Smith says.

"No, she wasn't. I mean, I didn't even know I had slept with her. I still can't put the two together in my mind."

"Maybe you need to sleep with her again," Dylan says.

"No," both Lane and Smith shout at Dylan.

"Do not listen to him for advice. It's terrible," Lane says, glaring at our friend.

"Aren't pregnant woman horny all the time?" Dylan states.

"This is not porn," Smith adds.

"Some women get horny while pregnant, especially in the second trimester. It's the extra hormones and blood flow," I explain to Dylan.

"See, doc says so," he adds with a grin.

"If you two stumble into bed together, don't break her heart because it's not like some woman who can block you on the socials. She can block you from your child," Lane warns me. He's right.

"Lucky I will not sleep with her then," I tell him.

The room erupts in laughter. I glare at my asshole friends. I'm glad I never told them we kissed the other day because I would get more of a lecture.

"Fuck you all," I curse them out.

Later in the night, my phone rings, waking me up.

"Hello." I answer it without checking who it is.

"Miles?" I hear Portia's distressed voice down the phone and I'm sitting up wide awake.

"Is everything okay?" I ask as panic moves around my body. I jump out of my bed and head to my closest to get changed.

"I went to the toilet and found blood." Portia breaks down crying. "I'm so scared."

"It's going to be okay; I promise. I'm on my way. I'll be there in ten," I tell her.

"Thank you."

I grab my gray sweatpants, a white T-shirt, and a black hoodie. Then I grab my joggers that are at the front door from my run earlier and put them on. Grab my wallet, phone, and keys and head out the door. My mind has turned into doctor mode as I try to go through all the different scenarios for why she might be bleeding. I don't know how much it is. Could be a lot or it could be a little. I jump into my car and thankfully at this early hour the traffic is light and doesn't take long for me to arrive. There's a park out the front, and I jump out and rush toward the main entrance.

"Mr. Hartford, Miss Garcia called down and said to let you up straight away," her doorman states as he lets me through the glass doors and into the elevator. He's already hit the button to her apartment for me and next thing I know I am stepping out into her hallway. My hand reaches for the knob and it's open. I rush inside her darkened apartment and toward her room. I find her crumpled in bed, crying.

"Hey, there, I'm here now," I tell her. The relief on her face when she sees me cracks open my chest. I pull her into my arms and hold her tightly while she cries. "I've got you, babe," I reassure her.

"I'm so scared, Miles. Did I do something wrong?" she asks.

Her face is pale, her eyes a little sunken, she looks exhausted. I haven't seen her in a week, and she's changed so much.

"Was there a lot of blood?" I ask her.

"I don't know what a lot of blood for pregnancy is?" she states.

"Is it spotting like when you wipe or is it gushing?" I ask her.

"When I wipe," she explains to me.

"Do you have any cramping or anything like that?" I ask her, she shakes her head indicating no. "You noticed it when you wiped?" Those round chocolate eyes stare up at me all innocently as she nods, letting me know she only noticed it wiping. "I think everything is going to be okay," I tell her. "Sometimes women experience spotting when it's around the time of their period or sometimes it happens. But I'd feel better if we get you to the hospital, to be sure. You're looking a little pale," I tell her.

"Okay," she says quietly.

25

PORTIA

I'm a little disorientated as I wake up, the bright fluorescent lights making it hard to work out where the hell I am. A strange beeping sound pulls my attention and I realize I'm in hospital. What in the hell? Then last night comes flashing back to me. Seeing the blood. Calling Miles and having him come to get me. As soon as he wrapped his arms around me, I knew I was safe. I remember him mentioning going to the hospital to get checked out. He thought it wasn't anything to worry about, but he wanted to be sure.

"You're awake," Nell says, greeting me.

That's when I look around the room and see my two best friends, my mom and Carrie, all sitting in the hospital room with me. What the hell is going on? Am I dying? Is there bad news? Is that why there are so many people here.

"Sweetheart, you look so much better," Mom says, planting a kiss on my cheek.

"What's going on?" I ask her.

"Miles called us after they admitted you. You had some spotting, which turned out to be nothing. Thank goodness. But when they ran some tests, they said your iron levels were down and you were dehydrated probably from your morning sickness. Cora and Hannah said it's been pretty bad," Mom explains.

"Isn't morning sickness supposed to be bad?" I say, mumbling through my dry mouth.

"It can be. Seems like you got your terrible morning sickness from me. I ended up in the hospital with all of you because I couldn't stop throwing up," she tells me. Oh. I thought this was normal. I didn't realize it wasn't. I feel silly now.

"They have given you a blood transfusion which is working because you have some color in your cheeks," Mom explains.

"I feel better. Like I have more energy," I tell her as I sit up in bed.

"Miles has been worried about you. He said he would be back in an hour. He had to go to his shift in the ER. There was a large car accident, and they needed everyone. That's why he called us to make sure when you woke up you wouldn't be alone," Carrie told me. That's sweet of him. I'm a little over-whelmed by everyone being in my room.

"Is the baby okay?" I ask.

"Yes, sweetie. The baby is fine. They are running some tests, but your OBGYN was here and told us she sees nothing wrong," Mom explains. Relief fills me. I know having a baby wasn't in my plans, but now that I am, I don't want to lose it. I want this baby so much. Tears fall down my cheeks at the thought of losing my baby.

"Oh, sweetie, it's okay. It's going to be okay," Mom says, giving me a cuddle. "I was talking to Daddy, and we both think it's a good idea if you come back home to the farm. We can look after you. I can make sure you're eating well. Chef will make sure you are eating all the best food. Your sister and brother are back too. The whole family is there," she tells me excitedly.

"What about school?" I ask her.

"Do you need to go? You're going to be a mom; you will not have time to work," Mom says. Is she serious right now?

"I'm going to go grab us some coffees," Carrie says, standing up from her chair as she ushers Cora and Hannah out with her, leaving Mom and I alone. Carrie could sense I was about to lose my mind at any moment.

"You want me to give up on school?" I ask her.

"I'm sure you don't need a degree to decorate houses," she says. Mom's dismissal of my career feels like a dagger to the heart.

"I guess the same could be said about fashion design too," I bite back, knowing it will hurt my mom.

"Fair point," she says through gritted teeth, agreeing with me. "But going to school and being pregnant is putting extra stress on you when all you need to be doing is looking after yourself so baby is healthy. You've already ended up in hospital."

"But you worked while you were pregnant."

"And I ended up in hospital each time," she says, letting out a sigh. "I was stubborn. My mom told me the same thing I'm telling you. I get it now in this moment why my mom was so worried about me. You never want to see your child hurt or sick. My instincts have kicked in and all I want to do is protect you, Portia."

"By smothering me and telling me to give up on my dreams."

"Is that what I'm doing?" she questions me.

"Feels like it," I tell her. I can see her face drop as she takes in my words.

"I keep messing everything up," she says as tears well in her eyes. "I love you, sweetie, so much and I'm trying to protect you but I'm making things worse."

"Mom. I know you're trying to protect me, and I appreciate it, I do. But I'm trying to work this all out too. I'm an adult now. I need to work things out for myself," I explain to her.

"Duly noted," she says, wiping her tears away.

"I still love you and Dad. And maybe I can come up on the

weekends and you can look after me then," I say. Mom's face lights up at the thought. My mom isn't trying to be mean; she wants to look after me during this time. Maybe I need to give a little as do they.

"Hey, you're awake," Miles says, standing in the doorway. My breath hitches seeing him dressed in his scrubs. Oh, wow. That's hot. The stupid machine beside me beeps constantly and sort of makes a funny sound which pulls Miles's attention.

Mom looks at me with a wide smile. "I'm going to give you two a moment," she says happily before leaving the room.

"Are you feeling okay? The machine went a little wild there," Miles asks, staring down at me.

"Um, yeah," I reply, embarrassed my body betrayed me so much at that moment. Miles frowns as he looks between the machine and me. "I'm fine. I saw you in scrubs for the first time and thought you looked hot, that's all. There's nothing wrong with me, maybe mentally," I say quickly.

Miles stills for a moment before bursting out laughing. "I'm flattered I caused such a reaction from you." Jerk. He's smiling down at me as if his ego didn't need to be stroked. "But in all seriousness, how are you feeling?" he asks as he takes a seat beside me on the bed.

"Better, thanks to you," I tell him.

"When you called me last night, I was so worried. I would never have forgiven myself if I wasn't able to get there in time," he confesses to me, and I can see the worry etched on his crinkled forehead.

I reach out and grab his hand and give it a squeeze. "But you were."

Miles nods, but I can see he is a little shaken over the incident. "I heard your mom mention you moving back to the farm to monitor you. Maybe it's a good idea at least someone is around in case something happens." He looks up at me with those bright green eyes and there's a storm of regret flashing behind them.

"I thought you wanted me to move in with you?" I ask, a little hurt over his change of mind.

"I did. I do. But I understand now it was too much to ask of you. We hardly know each other. If the best thing for you is living with your family, then you have my support, Portia," he whispers.

"I don't want to live with them. They will drive me crazy," I tell him. "I also don't want you to miss out on time with the baby. I want the baby to hear its father's voice." Miles gives me a small smile. "I also don't want to move into your bachelor pad," I add. "Haunted by girlfriends past." This makes him smile wider. "My girls suggested I buy my own place and you could move in with me," I tell him as I bite my lower lip nervously.

"Move in with you?" he asks.

"Yeah. There is no space at all in my current apartment and everyone keeps telling me babies come with a lot of stuff. So, I've been thinking about moving anyway," I explain.

"And you wouldn't mind living with me?" he asks cautiously.

"I'm sure we could find something big enough so we would each have our own personal space. All that matters is baby gets to know its dad," I tell him as I look up into his face.

"You want me to help you find something?" he asks.

"Sure, if you have time. I've been looking online this week. I've found some places, but I think something with a yard would be nice," I tell him.

"But do you want to be in the city? We could look further out and I'm happy to commute," he asks. I hadn't thought about not being in the city.

"I'm not sure," I tell him.

"How about this? I have the weekend off. Why don't we

go for a drive out into the suburbs and see if there is anything nice out there? We can then look at places during the week in the city and see what works." I'm not opposed to that suggestion, I guess.

"And if you still have your apartment, you could crash there when needs be." Like when he wants to hook up with girls. Miles nods in agreement. "Let's not tell our folks yet until we've found something. You know they are going to read into it all and I don't need that stress."

"I'm fine with that. I know my parents will have whatever we look at guttered and remolded." He chuckles.

"I have a condition, though. This will be my home and I will decorate it the way I like," I say, pointing my finger at him.

"As long as it doesn't turn into a Barbie house, I think I can live with whatever you pick."

"Shoot, I was hoping to recreate my Barbie dream house. Don't you remember how much I loved playing with mine?" I tease him, which makes him groan.

26

MILES

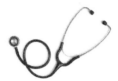

Portia didn't want me to speak to my parents about the idea of the two of us moving in together and I get it; knowing each of our parents they will think we will get together and where we both are now, it just isn't a possibility. Have I ruled out anything happening between Portia and me? Never say never. Do I want to sleep with her again? Yes, I'm only human. But I'm also old enough to know it would mess everything up.

I spoke to my boys about Portia's idea of us moving in together, and they thought it was a better idea. That it was her place I was moving into, which gave her security and stability for the baby. We then got onto the topic of homes and where to live with the family until Dylan came up with the craziest of all plans and said to commute between The Hamptons and the city. It's anywhere between a thirty-five to forty minute helicopter flight. It gave me a moment to think if I could do that. Then later in the week I heard some doctors talking about a surgeon that commutes from his home in The Hamptons via helicopter and how he loves he can get out of the city and be on the golf course in twenty minutes after landing. Not sure if that's me, but why not?

Our first call this weekend is homes in The Hamptons.

"Why are we heading to my parents' place?" she asks as she notices the direction we are heading.

"Hear me out," I say before she yells at me to turn around. "You would be close to your family up here. I can commute to work via helicopter and be in the city quickly. Our kid would have the beach, family nearby as my parents have a holiday home close to your parents. We could get a dog, maybe some chickens. I could build a vegetable garden," I explain to Portia. I'm met with silence, so I turn to her, and she is staring at me wide-eyed.

"Who the hell are you?"

"Was this not a good idea?" I ask Portia, worried I'm totally off base with my thoughts.

"You've caught me off guard, that's all," she states. "This wasn't at all what I was expecting. You would be okay with commuting like that?"

"Well, the other area I was looking at was Greenwich, Connecticut, and that's over an hour's drive or more by train. Some of Stirling's friends live out there and commute into the city," I explain to her.

"What about bad weather? Can't imagine the helicopter would work then."

This was a good question and one I hadn't even thought about. "Maybe I could transfer to a hospital closer," I add.

"I thought you loved working at your hospital," she asks.

"I do. I did. I kind of messed up and I'm thinking now I've possibly messed up my chances of ever getting anywhere there anyway," I confess to her.

"What do you mean, you messed up?" she asks.

"It's a long story." I tell her.

"Lucky, we have a long drive." She says turning her head and giving me a bright smile.

Damn, she's breathtaking.

I never wanted to tell Portia about my stupidity over falling for Tracey and finding out she was sleeping with my boss to get the promotion we were both going for. Relationships were against the rules between staff, and I got into trouble from my superiors, granted I did not use my position of power to get laid, unlike my boss who demanded Tracey keep sleeping with him even when she got the promotion. I was lucky to keep my job. I fucked up big time with Tracey, and I know now my career is suffering because of it. Getting the crap shifts, overlooked for promotions and extra training. Before I found out about Portia, I had applied for a couple of positions around the country at other hospitals, but I've not heard from them. I'm assuming I never made it to the short list. Which I'm fine about because now my life has taken a different direction.

"That's not fair." She says when I finish my story. "Yes, you broke the rules but what she did was so much worse,"

"They were both fired, and their reputations ruined," I add.

"You're a brilliant doctor, they would be stupid to lose you," She states sincerely.

I turn my head and look over at her, her face is serious with a tiny frown press against her forehead. She would go into bat for me if I needed her too. In that moment I know Portia would have my back if I needed her to and a strange calm settles over me.

It doesn't take us long until we are at the first house.

"Oh, my goodness. It's beautiful." She gasps as we drive up the driveway to a traditional Hamptons-style shingled house. The realtor walks out and greets us, and he starts his spiel about the home. All the stuff I couldn't care less about because it's up to Portia in the end. I follow her around to the back of the home and stop. Wow. In the back garden is the pool and beyond is the bay, which stretches out to the ocean. As far as the eye can see is nothing but blue water. I can imagine what this must look like in summer with all the boats on the bay, BBQs in the yard, kids splashing in the pools. It's a chilly day but at least the sun is out even if there isn't much warmth in it.

"Wow, this is nice," Portia says, joining me. "I could see the little one running around the backyard kicking a ball."

I grin. "We could get a boat to moor at the dock and then on the weekends we could go sailing."

"Do you know how to sail?" she asks me.

"Kind of. But I'm sure I could learn."

The next house is as equally impressive as the first one and the one after and so on until they all blur into a one. I will say it was nice to get out of the city for the weekend, even if the weather is freezing. We've stopped for lunch, and Portia has chosen a little Italian restaurant for us tucked away in the village. I'm starved. We take a seat and quickly order. I watch Portia devour the fresh bread they brought to the table while we wait for lunch.

"So, what are your thoughts?" I ask her, dipping my bread in some olive oil.

"Loved them all. I think I would be happy with any of them. There wasn't too much wrong with them."

"We have a couple more to look at a little further up the coast," I tell her.

"Do we have time to go for a walk along the beach? I'm dying to dip my toes in the sand."

"Of course, we have plenty of time before we head back to the city," I tell her as we both settle into a comfortable conversation over lunch.

We head on down to the beach. After seeing our last home, we take off our shoes, roll up our jeans, and head out onto the cold sand. The beach is empty as the blue sky has turned gray as a storm is threatening to roll in. The dark clouds are far off on the horizon, so there's plenty of time before it hits.

"This is what I have needed. To get out of the city and recharge my batteries," she tells me as we stroll along the beach.

"You're a beach girl then?" I ask.

"I guess. I love the city and the country too," she explains to me as I watch a couple of crabs scurry away into their holes in the sand. "I've never thought about what I want in my future before. It seemed like such a long way away. But little one," she says, rubbing her stomach, "had other plans."

"I know you were working with my mom. Is that what you wanted to be, an interior designer?" I ask, curious of what her dreams might have been before I came along and messed them up.

"Yeah. I've loved design. I guess I get it from Mom, but instead of designing clothes, I enjoy creating homes. Nell is more into the clothing side. I like fashion, but I'm not driven by it like my sister. I'm more laid back."

"You're not interested in becoming an influencer like your sister?" I ask.

"Not really. I know people would kill to have the following I have and make the extra money I do from it, but it's not what drives me. Maybe one day I can be an interior design influencer; that would be pretty nice," she explains to me and we fall into a peaceful silence with each other as we casually walk along the beach, neither one of us in any sort of hurry, enjoying each other's company.

"Have you always wanted to be a doctor?" she asks me.

"Yeah. Ever since our dad's accident. I remember visiting him in the hospital and watching in awe at the doctors helping him walk again. That's when I knew I wanted to do that."

"Wonder if our kid will follow in your footsteps," she ponders.

"Or they might follow in yours." I chuckle. "I can't even fathom that we will have a tiny human this time next year. With its own little personality and everything. It's mind blowing." I shake my head. "My friend Lane, he's a single dad. He's already on me about looking at schools and things."

"Oh my god, is that a thing? We need to have our kid on a list while it's still in the womb? I only thought that was in the movies?" she asks, horrified.

"I don't know. But he seems to think it's important and I guess he would know." I shrug, looking as confused as her.

"Guess we are going to have to pick a home sooner rather than later."

Suddenly, an all-mighty crash of thunder startles us from our conversation and the first heavy drops of rain fall on us.

"We should head back to the car before we get drenched," I say as we hasten our steps, but it's too late. The clouds open. By the time we get back to the car, both of us are soaked. I open the car and we both jump in.

"Shit. I'm going to ruin your car." As we sit down, the wet feeling seeps through every inch of our bodies.

"It's fine. I'll get it looked at when we get to the city. I don't know about you, but I don't have a spare set of clothes and I don't feel comfortable taking you back to the city sitting in damp clothes. That won't be good for you or the baby."

We stare out of the windscreen, which is being pelted with thick rain drops. It looks crazy out there.

"We could go to your parents' place and warm up," I suggest.

"No," she answers before I finished the words out of my mouth.

"Our family's holiday house is up the road. We could

go there and dry off," I explain to her; she might feel more comfortable there.

"That sounds perfect," she says through chattering teeth.

27

PORTIA

We get to Miles's parents' beach house and make a mad dash inside. We kick off our shoes and toe off our socks, then lose our jumpers as soon as we enter the house.

"I'll grab us some towels," Miles says as he runs down the corridor. Moments later, he is handing me a couple of towels. I wrap my hair up first before wrapping the other towel around my body, hoping to stave off the bitter cold that's seeped through to my bones.

"What are you doing?" Miles asks. His green eyes are staring at me wildly as I take off my jeans.

"I was going to get undressed here so I don't run through the house wet," I tell him. Carrie would kill us if she knew.

"Oh," he says as his eyes land on my bare legs. Goosebumps prickle across my skin and I'm not sure if it's from his intense stare or the cold. My T-shirt is the next item of clothing I wiggle off. It gets stuck on the towel drying my hair and I'm seconds away from flashing Miles as I try to maneuver it over the towel. "Let me," he says, taking the towel off my hair and then removing my T-shirt from its wet clutches. The shirt hits the floor with a thud and the sound reverberates through the home. I look up at Miles and his green eyes are shimmering with heat, which lights a fire in my veins. Because the next thing I know, I'm launching myself at Miles and capture his mouth with my own. I wrap my arms around his neck, which means my towels fall to the floor, exposing me in my underwear. His wet jeans and shirt feel like ice against my exposed skin, and I shiver as he presses himself against me. But I don't care because Miles Hartford is kissing me back. He moves me the couple of steps until he presses me against the wall. A shiver falls down my back as I feel his erection through his wet jeans.

"Shit, Portia," Miles curses as he steps back away from me. He scrubs his face, and he looks horrified that he's kissed me. I'm standing in front of him in nothing but my see-through underwear, utterly exposed. His green eyes scan over my body and my nipples feel like steel pressing against the fabric as a frown forms across his face. Humiliation creeps up my body like a vine and all I want to do is get away from him. And so I do. I bolt up the main staircase and run into the first room I find and slam the door shut; tears streaming down my face. The room is dark and moody with its navy walls and dark wooded furniture. I don't have time to marvel at the stunning aesthetics Carrie has applied to this home as I bolt toward the bathroom. I slam the door shut there as well and sink to the floor. My butt hits the cold tiled floor, but I don't care as I dissolve into a million pieces.

There's a heavy knock on the door behind me. "Portia!" Miles calls out my name. "I didn't mean to upset you," he says. But he did. "Babe, please open the door so I can see if you're okay." His tender words warm my chest and I hate that my hand twitches to open the door for him.

"Leave me alone, Miles," I say with a sniffle.

"I can't. I need to know you are okay." His fingers tap lightly on the door. "Please, let me see you're okay and then I'll leave you alone." I pull myself up off the cold tiles and open the door to the bathroom. I stick my head out and see his handsome face staring back at me with a storm raging across his tense face. "I'm so sorry I kissed you, Portia. I…I shouldn't have done it." Huh. He thinks he made the first move. I'm pretty sure it was me. "We had a great day and then I had to ruin it." He scrubs his face again, agitated.

"You don't have to apologize, Miles," I tell him.

"I don't want you to think if we move in together I'm going to push you up against a wall and kiss you like I did." Please, will he? I can't imagine saying no to that in the slightest.

"Miles, I kissed you," I confess to him. I don't want him to beat himself up over something he didn't start.

"Why?" His question catches me off guard.

"Because in that moment I wanted to know what it was like to be with you and not have you think it was my sister." And with that confession, I slam the bathroom door shut and lock it.

After a long hot shower, I get changed into the clothes I find on the bed laid out for me, a gray fluffy robe. It feels like a bear hug as I wrap myself with it. I suck in a couple of unsteady breaths as I make my way downstairs to face Miles. I can hear him walking around downstairs and I steel myself to see him. He's in the kitchen and looks like he's plating up some food.

"Great, you're here. I ordered in food. I thought you must be starving. I've thrown our clothes into the dryer. If you have anything else you want to dry let me know and I can pop it in there," he says, giving me a warm smile. Right, we are going to pretend that kiss didn't happen. That's fine by me.

"I'll go grab my underwear. It's still upstairs in the bathroom," I tell him.

"No, you eat. I'll go grab them and take them to the laundry room," he says, giving me a nod and heading upstairs to deal with my wet underwear.

I stare down at the plates of food. He's ordered Chinese, Italian, and Mexican. Doesn't bother me; I could eat it all. This baby has an enormous appetite. Once I've piled food onto my plate, I head on over to the living room and take a seat beside the fire he has started; the heat warms my toes. The TV is on talking about the wild weather pummeling the coast.

"Your clothes should be ready in an hour," Miles tells me, making me jump as I'm absorbed in what I was watching. He takes a seat on the large sofa in front of the TV. I took the armchair so I could be close to the fire. We eat in relative silence as we watch the TV and weather. "I don't think we will make it back to the city tonight." The rattling of the windows and the howling of the wind were a dead giveaway.

"That's okay. I don't think it would be safe driving in this, anyway," I mumble, shoving some noodles into my mouth. "I'll text my friends to let them know I'll be back tomorrow. Don't want them to worry." I go to grab my phone which is normally glued to my hip. Miles jumps up and heads over to the front door and grabs my bag and brings it back to me. "Thank you," I say, grabbing the bag from his hand. Our fingers touch for the briefest of moments, and a sizzle of electricity shoots up my arm. Miles must feel it too as he gives me a small smile and sits back down in his chair and stares back at the TV. I fish into my damp bag and pull out my phone. I send the girls a quick text letting them know I'm fine, but I'm caught in bad weather and staying the night in The Hamptons.

Hannah: You're in The Hamptons?

Portia: We got caught in a crazy storm. I nearly froze to death. Miles thought it was better to get warmed up here while our clothes dry.

Cora: Sounds romantic.

Hannah: I thought you'd look at Brooklyn or something.

Portia: He was talking about commuting via helicopter to the hospital or something.

Cora: Mom does it during the summer.

Hannah: It's so far from us.

Portia: It's just an idea.

Cora: Portia is having a baby. She can't raise it in the city.

Hannah: We were raised in the city.

Cora: When we were teenagers.

Hannah: Hang on. Are you naked with him?

Portia: No. I'm in a robe having dinner watching the news.

Cora: You sound like an old married couple already. It's cute.

Hannah: Has anything happened?

How the hell am I supposed to answer this? I must take too long because Hannah fills in the blanks.

Hannah: You did. Oh my god, Portia!

Portia: It's not like that. We had a moment, and I kissed him.

I confess to my friends.

Portia: He freaked out and now I feel stupid.

Cora: Hey, you're not stupid.

Cora: Was it a good kiss?

Portia: Yes.

Hannah: I told you the two of you would bang.

Portia: I will not have sex with him. It was a moment.

Cora: It's okay if you do.

I hate my friends sometimes.

Portia: Look, I'm not in control of my hormones now. They are making me do stupid stuff.

Hannah: Exactly. You are going to combust if you don't get laid.

Portia: I think I can control myself.

Hannah: Doesn't sound like it.

Seriously? Who has friends like these?

Cora: If you hold it in while pregnant, you might explode.

These girls are not helping.

Portia: Are you wanting me to sleep with him?

Hannah: YES!

Cora: YES!

What? My friends have lost their minds.

Portia: You two are bad influences. I will not sleep with him.

Hannah: BJ?

Portia: Fuck you both. Good night.

I text them back as I put my phone down and shovel some more food into my mouth.

"Everything all good?" Miles asks.

"Yeah. My friends are being annoying, that's all," I tell him, feeling the heat on my cheeks from their conversation. Now my mind is filled with images of Miles naked in my bed.

This is not good.

28

MILES

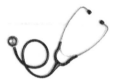

"**I**'m heading to bed. I'll, um, see you in the morning," Portia says.

"Okay, see you in the morning," I tell her. I let out a sigh of relief because things between us are a little awkward after that kiss from earlier. Did the kiss blow my mind? Yes. Was it wrong? Yes. Will it happen again? Probably. Is it right? No. There's a shimmering sexual tension between us and if she was any other woman, I would have taken her against the wall without a second thought. But I'm finding myself second guessing things between us. I can't let my dick mess things up. I have too much to lose. Shit. I curse, raking my hands through my hair. Maybe tomorrow will bring some clarity, but what I know is the more time I hang out with Portia, the more I like her and wish we might have met under different circumstances. That I didn't sleep with her, thinking she was her sister. That I didn't knock her up. If all those things hadn't happened maybe something good could have happened between Portia and I. *Lies.* The voice inside my head screams at me. *If you hadn't done all those things, there is no way in hell you would have given little Portia Garcia a chance.* This was probably true. But

I appreciated how much she had grown up. *You would have tried to sleep with her.* No, I wouldn't have because my mom would have cut my balls off if I had. *Lies again.* That voice screams at me. Yeah, my subconscious is right. I probably would have been a dick and slept with her and then been on my merry way and not given her a second thought. I would never have changed my ways. Not that I thought I was that bad or anything. *You were.* Okay. I was bad. But I haven't slept with anyone since Portia and that night. Which has been months. Must be a record. Maybe the two of us are sexually frustrated. And that's manifesting into something between us. I don't know. This is all so new to me. I sit back and start flipping the channel until I can find something that will take my mind off the half-naked woman upstairs that tastes like sweetness and sunshine.

There's a constant buzzing somewhere around me and I can't work out where the hell it is. It's driving me crazy. It starts up again and I jump up from the sofa and go hunting for the sound. Eventually I find it on the armchair Portia left earlier. When I look down, I see her phone has slipped down the side of the chair. I reach down and see a heap of missed calls from Nell and texts from her friends. Something serious must be going on, so I head on up to the room she is staying in to give her, her phone back. The door is slightly ajar, so I stick my head in to see if she's fallen asleep because I don't want to wake her up if she is. What I wasn't expecting to see when I stuck my head through the doorway was Portia's hands between her thighs and small moans falling from her lips. I'm frozen as I watch her hands slide between her creamy thighs as it moves furiously inside of her, in my room, on my bed. My dick is standing to attention, and I know I shouldn't be watching because it's wrong and it's a complete invasion of her privacy and yet I still don't look away. Then I hear her say my name across her lips as she comes, and I swear I'm moments away from coming myself. She was thinking about me as she touched herself. I'm not sure what to do with this information.

I step back from the door and press my back against the wall, swallowing deep breaths in trying to get my dick under control. Then her phone buzzes in my hand, which surprises me, and I drop it. Shit. The phone drops with a loud thud. Double shit.

"Miles?" Portia calls out.

"Yeah, it's me," I say, trying to mask the heat lacing my voice as I step into the doorway of her room. "You left your phone downstairs, and it's been buzzing all night," I tell her, shaking the phone in the air. Her cheeks are still pink from her orgasm and those chocolate brown eyes are wide as she tries to assess if I caught her or not. "I think your sister is looking for you." I walk over and hand her the phone. My eyes land on her fingers which were inside of her, and I wonder if I could smell orgasm still on her fingers? I lick my lips at the memory of her sweetness on my lips.

"Thanks," she answers warily. "I'll call her, let her know I'm safe."

"Great. Well, I'll leave you to it." And I turn on my heel and back to my room where I pull my dick out and moments later, I am coming over the images of her fingers inside of her.

⸎

"Morning," I greet Portia as she comes down from the bedroom all dressed.

"Thanks for my clean clothes."

"Not a problem. I went out to the bakery and got us some treats," I tell her, waving my hand over the buffet of pastries I bought.

"They look amazing," she says, her eyes lighting up as she grabs a croissant and takes a large bite into the flaky pastry. "Oh my god," she mumbles around her bite as a groan falls from her lips. Similar to the one she released last night, and my dick instantly twitches to life, remembering the sound.

"I've organized some showings today down in Brooklyn, then we have some uptown," I explain to her.

"Fantastic. I'm excited to see what there is. I loved all the homes from yesterday. I worry it's too far from work for you and maybe too close to my parents." She chuckles.

"If you decide to stay in the city, then I might buy us a beach house. We could have the best of both worlds," I explain to her.

"It could work, but only if it is something you would be interested in."

"After looking at all those properties yesterday, I could see us running around with the little one. Maybe eventually filling the backyard up with cousins if Remi and Stirling decide to have kids," I tell her before biting into a Danish. Her eyes land on my lips as I bite into the pastry. Interest flares behind those chocolate eyes. Is she thinking about my mouth being somewhere else? Is she committing it to memory, so the next time her fingers slide between her folds, she is thinking of me?

"Do you think they will have kids soon?" she asks

"One day maybe in a couple more years."

"Seeing as our parents are already planning Remi and Nell's wedding and they're not even engaged," she says, rolling her eyes. "Once they're married, I think Mom and Carrie will expect grandbabies."

"Guess you and I have given our siblings a bit of grace before being hounded." I chuckle.

"We're so thoughtful, aren't we?" she says with a giggle.

We're heading back toward the city and it's a beautiful fall day, last night's storm is a distant memory as the sun is out and blue sky sits on the horizon.

"I have a question. What do your friends think about our situation?" she asks me.

"They're happy for me but also think I'm an idiot for letting it happen," I tell her honestly.

"It was an accident. We were unlucky," she says, turning to me with a frown on her face.

"No, they think I was stupid for sleeping with you in the first place." As soon as the words are out of my mouth, I realize how bad it sounded.

"Oh."

"Shit, that came out wrong. They think I was a dick for even going there with you when I thought you were Nell. I broke bro code." I turn and explain to her.

"And now they know it wasn't my sister you were with."

"They think that's even worse," I tell her. "Look, I've made stupid decisions in the past led completely by my dick. My ego knowing no bounds because in that moment all I cared about was getting the girl home and having my way with her," I tell her, swallowing over my confession. "That's what happened with you. Even though it wasn't Nell I took home, in my mind it was still her and I knew she had a past with Remi, and I didn't care because I was feeling it. I pushed Remi and his feelings to the back of my mind because I told myself he didn't care about her. That she was a booty call." With every word I'm saying, I feel the disgust dripping down my insides. "I haven't been a good guy in the past, Portia. I'm a fuck boy and I realize that now."

"Were you honest with all the girls you were with?" she asks me. I nod, showing yes. "Then what more can you do? You told them you were there to have fun, to scratch an itch, so to speak. I mean, the reason I hooked up with you was out of revenge as I had run into my ex that night," she says casually, but her words hit me in the chest, and I don't know if I like it. "We were both honest with each other that night, even when we were drunk. We both agreed to it being one night and one night only. If the women you are with don't respect the boundaries you have put in place for the night, then that's on them. If the roles were reversed, the men would be in trouble for not respecting the woman's wishes. So, the same should apply for you too," Portia tells me honestly. I turn and look over at her. I'm surprised by her comments, and they've thrown me for a loop.

"Have you spoken to your ex since then?" My hands grip the steering wheel tightly. What happens if she wants him back? If he wants her back? They have history together. I don't want another man bringing up my child. Would he move in with us? Oh, hell no. My child is only going to be calling me daddy.

"Hell no. He's a piece of shit. We were together for two years. And he dumped me literally on the footsteps of the plane on our way to Mexico to celebrate his graduation. He walked back onto the plane and into the arms of one of my friends. Screw him. She's the biggest gold-digging whore, she's probably screwing all his friends. I mean she did at college, so you know," she says with a shoulder shrug. "Once he got his NFL contract, he turned into the biggest dick. The entire two years we were together, he had slept with all my supposed friends and their friends too. How do you look your friend in the eye knowing you fucked their boyfriend? I'll never understand it," she says, shaking her head. Wow. I had no idea it was that bad. "So, I'm sorry I used you for revenge, but boy did it feel good," she says with a chuckle as she looks over at me.

"Seeing as I'm a recovering fuck boy, use me any time you want," I tell her. Portia stills at my words. It sounded less flirtatious in my head, but now I've said it out loud. Yeah, sounded like a come on

"Have you been seeing anyone?" Portia asks quietly.

"I haven't been with anyone since you," I tell her honestly.

"Work's been crazy, then I found out about the baby, and I've been processing this new life."

"Wow, I'm surprised."

"Like I said, I'm a recovering fuck boy." I turn and give her a smile. "What about you?" *Please say no.*

"Seeing as I have spent a month hurling my guts up, the last thing I wanted to see was a dick." She gives me a smile.

"And now?" I ask, my voice dipping huskily, which wasn't my intention.

"Now it's all I can think about," she explains, biting her bottom lip.

Shit. My hands white knuckle against the steering wheel.

"But I'm not looking to date anyone," she adds.

"So just sex then?"

"Yeah. But I don't want to dress up and do the whole wine and dine thing. I want to get to the action. Maybe I need to buy a better vibrator or hire a gigolo," she says, bursting out laughing. "I can't believe I confessed all that to you. Forget what I said. Stupid hormones."

Silence falls between us as my dick feels like it's about to punch a hole through my jeans. "What about me then?"

"What about you?" She turns to look over at me, a small frown across her face.

"Use me for sex."

Portia chokes on my words and looks flustered by my comment. "Excuse me, what the hell did you say?" she questions me.

"We are about to live together, so my dick is on tap. You don't have to get dressed up. Neither one of us needs to impress the other. You can't get pregnant again. I mean, we're stuck with each other for life, so you know I will not stalk you."

"Won't sex complicate all this?" she asks, patting her flat stomach.

"Not if we communicate with each other. Look, at the

moment, I'm not interested in dating. My focus is on work and this baby. You've said you're not looking to date anyone because your focus is on college and the baby. I mean, we had a pretty good night the first time, from what I remember," I say to her as I look over. Portia's cheeks have a pink hue to them.

"Yes, we sure did," she says, rolling her eyes at me.

"Well, I'm cheaper than a gigolo because I'm free," I joke with her.

"This seems…I…" Portia's lost for words, and I don't blame her because I kind of can't believe what I'm suggesting.

"You said I'm honest with the women I'm with. I tell them exactly what I want, as do you. I'm sure you and I can be honest with each other and say this would be a friends with benefits situation. It works for where we both are in our lives. We are focused on our baby. I know I sure as hell am not interested in someone else getting to spend time with you and baby when I can't.

"How long does this arrangement go for?" she asks.

"I know the second trimester is going to be your horniest. By the third, things will get harder, so I guess while you feel the need. I'm here," I explain to her.

"What about feelings?" she asks.

"Are you looking for a relationship?" I ask her. She shakes her head, indicating no. "Neither am I. And once the baby is here, neither one of us is going to have time for anything else except for it. We will want sleep over sex." I laugh.

"What will people think?" she asks.

"We don't tell them. I mean, we will already be living together, so whatever happens under our roof is our business," I explain to her.

"And you would be okay with hooking up with a pregnant chick?" she asks. The fact she's even contemplating my crazy suggestion has me ready to leap across this car and consummate it here and now.

"You're a beautiful woman, Portia," I tell her, which makes her blush.

"Fine. I can't believe I'm agreeing to this. But only once we have found a place to live," she tells me. "It would be weird before then." If that's the way she feels, then I'm ready to buy now so I can have her in my bed again.

"That's fair. I agree."

"Should we shake on it?" she asks.

With one hand on the wheel, I reach out the other and hand it to her. We shake on it and as soon as our skin touches, electricity runs between us. Portia gasps and pulls her hand away. Oh, we are going to have so much fun.

29

PORTIA

After spending the weekend with Miles looking for homes, we've continued the search during the week. Every night we have met after his shift and looked at houses in the city. We would then go to dinner before he would drop me home like a gentleman with a kiss on the cheek and a list of homes to see the next day. But I still can't stop thinking about his proposal of being friends with benefits or baby daddy with benefits it should be. And boy, how do I want his benefits. Every night I come home from searching for houses and think about his smell, and the way he links our arms together as we walk along the sidewalk so no one bumps into me. The way his green eyes sparkle when he talks about work and who he saved that day. It's been nice. I notice I'm looking forward to our nightly house hunting. Is that sad? Hannah and Cora tell me we're dating, but we're not. We are looking for a family home to raise our child together in. When I say it like that, it's weird. My friends don't get it, they don't understand why I'm doing this even though they suggested it at the beginning. Maybe they thought I wouldn't do it. The thought of playing Suzy home-maker used to make me gag, but now I'm getting excited if the home is in the right school district and if I can entertain in the kitchen. I don't cook. It's confusing but I'm going with it. All the pregnancy books say I'm probably nesting, which seems a little early, but apparently, it's a thing. Some women go crazy with it. I think as an interior design student I'm on the normal level of house loving.

"Are you going out with Miles again?" Hannah asks, glaring at me over her magazine.

"If you must know, I'm going out to dinner with Nell and Remi," I tell her.

"Is Miles going to be there?" she questions me.

"Yes. He will be, but so will Stirling. It's a family dinner," I explain to her.

"Sounds like a couple's dinner to me," she says, giving me a grin.

"Would you stop it? It's not like that and you know it."

Hannah smirks. "The flowers on the counter say differently."

Fine, she got me there, but who doesn't enjoy getting flowers? It was thoughtful of him to give them to me when I told him about a horrible bout of morning sickness that had wiped me out for a couple of hours.

"Be careful. The lines between the two of you are becoming blurred. And I'm here for it as long as he doesn't break your heart," my best friend warns me.

"I'm not giving him my heart," I tell her.

Hannah smiles and shakes her head at me. "Have fun," she sings out to me as I hear the knock on the door. Miles is picking me up to take us to the restaurant.

"Hey, you look gorgeous." Miles smiles, greeting me with a kiss on the cheek. My chest flutters at his compliment and my skin tingles where his lips have touched. I'm wearing a black minidress with black knee-high boots and a sparkly long cardigan. I thank him for his compliment as he ushers me into the elevator. "So, have you narrowed down your choices?" he asks as we descend to the basement where he's parked his car.

"I did like that house in Carroll Gardens, in Brooklyn. It has a two-car garage, the bottom courtyard, and the rooftop terrace with views over the city. I could imagine entertaining up there, watching the New Year's Eve fireworks. It's still commutable to the city. Heaps of families and playgrounds. It gives us the space but for half the price of the city," I explain to him.

"Yeah, I did like that one. But then I compared it to what we could get in The Hamptons for the same price and it's like, ugh." He's not wrong there. I love The Hamptons, but maybe it might be something to think about when it's time for school. I think while the baby is young, I'd like to stay in the city close to my friends. Will my friends still want to hang out, though?

"I did like the historic townhouse in Tribeca. It had a gorgeous courtyard. Close to the river, and there's a heap of parks to walk around. But close enough to everything. And uptown is only a subway ride away," I explain to him.

"Then there was the duplex on the Upper Westside walking distance to Central Park and close to your girls on the Upper East," Miles adds. I did like that one as it was in a magnificent spot and close to the girls, but the rooms were a little smaller, so do I sacrifice for location? This house hunting business is hard, so many things to think about.

"I have a lot to think about," I tell him with a smile.

Miles opens the car door for me and closes it, then jumps into the driver's seat. We head out into Friday night traffic, talking about his day and what funny things happened in the ER. I told him about college, filled him in on the gossip of who was dating who, and what drama was currently happening and before we knew it, we were at the restaurant. The valet helped me out of the car, and I waited for Miles to join me, and we walked into the restaurant together. I'm a little nervous because this is the first time we have all been together since our baby announcement. I know Remi is fine with me, but I do not know if Stirling will be. Plus, this isn't a date, so the other two couples are going to be all lovely dovey and Miles and I are going to be us.

"Portia." Nell squeals my name from halfway across the room before running up and pulling me into a tight hug. "You look practically glowing." She giggles. "Show me your belly. I want to see it," Nell questions me.

"I don't have a belly yet."

"Bitch, of course you don't." She chuckles, running her hand over my stomach. "But your boobs look amazing," she says, giving them a squeeze.

"Babe," Remi says, clearing his throat.

"Oh sorry, forgot where I was." My sister grins up at him before he pulls her face to his and places a kiss on her lips. She lets out a sigh of contentment and a pang of jealousy hits me. Will I ever get that? Will I ever have someone worship me the way Remi does Nell?

"Portia, oh my god, it's been too long," Audrey says, pulling me into a hug. "Congratulations on the baby. We're going to be family." She smiles widely.

"Miles and I aren't together," I answer her nervously.

"Well, you're having a baby together. That's pretty together," she says. I guess, on a technicality.

"Portia, congratulations." Stirling holds out his hand for me. I take it and give his hand a shake. "Thank you for giving Remi and I breathing room on the grandkid front." He chuckles.

"Happy to be of service," I tell him.

"Come, let's sit and order. I'm sure Portia's starved," Miles says, pulling out a chair for me. Everyone's eyes watch Miles's movements around me. I take my seat beside Miles, and he pours me a glass of water before I have even asked him. He then places his bread roll on my plate without stopping his conversation with his brother.

"You two seem familiar with each other?" Nell questions me.

"We've hung out all week looking at homes," I tell her.

"Who for?" she asks. I realize I may have forgotten to inform Nell of my hairbrained idea to move in with Miles.

"Me and the baby."

Nell's eyes narrow on me. "And that's all that's happened?"

"Yes," I answer her under my breath, horrified if Miles heard her.

"That's nice of Miles to help you. Why would he be doing that?" Nell questions me, and I can see it already. She smells something fishy. Reaching out, I squeeze Miles's leg under the table, and he excuses himself from his current conversation.

"Nell, it's good to see you again. I hope my brother is treating you well?" he asks.

"Very. Portia told me you've been helping her house hunt. That's very kind of you to help my little sister, especially when you are so busy," she says, tilting her head as if to peer into his mind to see what the real reason is. Miles's face doesn't react, but he soon catches on I have told no one about our plans.

"Excuse me, sorry to interrupt," Miles says, clearing his throat. "But Portia and I wanted to let you all know we have been looking for a house together and once we have found the perfect home, we will move in together." The table falls silent.

"What the hell, Miles?" Stirling is the first to crack.

"I want to be a hands-on father and I can't be if we live apart. Portia is going to need help with a newborn, so it's only natural we move in together. Into something family friendly," he explains.

The table is still in shock over his revelation.

"Are you and Portia together?" Remi asks.

"No," I answer for us. "I will buy the home and Miles will move in with me." Relief falls across my sister's face, while the others end up nodding in understanding.

"Well, congratulations then," Remi says, holding up his whiskey glass into the air. Everyone else follows, giving us both their well wishes. Miles links his hand with mind under the table and gives it a little squeeze.

"Are you sure about this?" Nell whispers.

"Yes. No matter what happens between Miles and I, I will never lose my home."

"This is your life. I'm happy if you're happy," she says, wrapping her arm around my shoulders and pulling me into her side.

"I'm scared, Nell. And having a doctor on call will not make it so scary."

"Is that the only reason?" she asks.

"Baby comes first. Miles and I agree on that." My hand falls to my stomach and strokes it. Nell wishes me well, but I know she is going to have more questions but isn't going to push the subject right now. But it's coming.

The night ended up being a heap of fun. Nell even filled us in on her plans for our gender reveal. I didn't care what the theme was. All I want to know is it a boy or a girl.

"We need to catch up soon," my sister tells me. I agree and give her a hug before Remi gives me a hug and tells me to look after his niece or nephew. Stirling does the same. Both of Miles's brothers seem excited over the prospect of being a cool uncle. Somehow, it's turned into a competition between the two of them. We say our goodbyes and head back to my apartment.

"That went well," Miles says.

"Thankfully. Was a little awkward after announcing us moving in together."

"You know our moms will be on the phone to both of us tomorrow questioning the news of the two of us living under one roof," he says with a smile.

"I'm sure Mom will have a million reasons why it's a bad idea," I tell him, rolling my eyes.

"I've got you, so it will be okay," Miles turns his head and tells me.

A little while later, we are pulling into my basement and parking.

"Thanks for tonight. I had fun," I tell him as we park.

"I had fun too." He parks the car and turns in his seat, giving me his full attention. "I've had fun this week hanging out with you."

"You say that as if it's a surprise."

Miles chuckles. "That's not what I was getting at. It's been nice house hunting and doing dinner together."

"I'm up for dinner. Baby is always hungry," I tell him with a giggle, rubbing my belly. Miles smiles, but those green eyes narrow on me, and something flashes across his face.

"Can I ask you something?" he asks. I nod, still captivated by his eyes. "Can I kiss you?"

Wow, was not at all what I was expecting him to say, and he's caught me off guard. But he takes that as my answer, and I can see that my hesitation has ruined the moment as he moves away from me.

"Sorry, Portia, I shouldn't have asked that. You looked so gorgeous tonight and I...I don't know what I was thinking." While Miles is rambling on, I've taken off my seat belt, dropped my bag, and am launching myself into his lap. Which surprises the hell out of him.

30

MILES

I knew I shouldn't have asked to kiss Portia. What the hell was I thinking? *You were thinking how beautiful she looked and you had an overwhelming desire to kiss her.* Well, she looked good. She's glowing. I've heard people say pregnant women glow but never seen it until that moment. As soon as the question slipped out of my mouth, and I saw the confusion on her face, and I knew it was a bad idea. Next thing I know, Portia is launching herself into my lap, her ass is beeping the horn and she's giggling.

"Yes, you can kiss me," she says.

I pull the lever for my seat, so it slides back, giving her room. The last thing we need is security coming down and checking on us. I pick her up by the hips and position her better in my lap. My hand winds its way up her back until it's gripping her neck and I'm pulling her to me. She comes willingly and the moment our lips touch is like an ignition spark, and we detonate against each other. Weeks of being around each other, getting to know the other one outside of who we knew during childhood, the flirtation. It's all been simmering underneath the surface between the two of us and now finally we have given each other permission to give into it.

"I need more," Portia mumbles against my lips as her hands undo my pants.

"We're in a parking lot?" I tell her. Any moment someone could walk past and see her in my lap. I hope the security cameras are not facing this direction, otherwise the guys will get a free show. Then I remembered the tinted windows so no one can see in, but we can see out. Thank fuck I took the optional upgrade.

"I don't care, Miles," she hisses at me as her hand furiously tries to pull me from my jeans. I should give the woman what she wants. So, I do. I help her by unbuttoning my jeans and pushing them as far down as I could get them, which releases my dick from its confines. "Fuck, I forgot how huge this thing is," Portia states, staring at my dick.

"Guess I should remind you then?" I grin, cocking a brow at her.

"Oh, hell yeah," she pants. Portia wiggles herself over my dick and I'm thankful she's wearing a dress.

"What about a condom?" I ask.

"I'm already pregnant and we both haven't slept with anyone since."

She's right. Damn, my dick thickens at the thought of taking her bare. Something I never do because I've never wanted to end up in the situation I am in now. I grip my dick and I run the head of it through her folds. Damn, she is soaking.

"Please, Miles," she pants as I tease her.

"This time I'm going to take my time and enjoy it. Commit your moans to memory," I tell her.

"I don't want you to take your time. Hurry and fuck me," she says through frustrated teeth and before I tell her I promise to make it worth her while, she impales herself onto me.

"Shit," I hiss, feeling her warm walls around my dick. My entire body stills as my nerves feel every twitch, every sensation as she moves. Portia slides herself over me, taking control again, and I don't care one bit. She can take whatever she wants from my dick. She rides me like a damn rodeo queen, taking her pleasure when she wants it and how deep she wants it. My hand slips between her thighs, pushing her G-string to the side. My fingers find her wet cunt, so I press a thumb against her clit as she rides me, giving her the friction she needs to be pushed over the edge.

"Yes!" Portia screams, throwing her head back as she continues to ride me. "Fuck me, Miles. Please, harder. Give it to me."

I do as I'm told and give her exactly what she wants as my hips thrust into her, fucking her deeply.

"More, Miles," Portia moans as my thumb puts pressure on her clit. My balls tingle, but I try to stave off my orgasm until Portia has hers. The windows of my car are fogging up and the groaning of the car is moving to our frantic beat. If anyone walked past right now, they would know exactly what we are doing, but I don't care. I'm so far gone. "Oh my god!" Portia screams as she convulses around me, which sends a chain reaction to my dick as he furiously continues to move between her thighs. Then I throw my head back and release a guttural groan as I come inside of her. We both take a couple of moments to come back down, each of us panting. Portia leans down and kisses me slowly and languidly.

"That was so good." She grins, pressing her forehead to mine as she slowly rocks against my still hard dick.

"It was a great way to end the night," I tell her as I nuzzle my face into her throat. "Next time I would like to be somewhere there is a little more room."

Portia chuckles. "Yeah, I have to agree. Lucky, I do enough yoga to move in this small space."

I look up at her and push her sweaty hair from her

face. She looks so gorgeous, all flushed and sated. "I needed that."

"Me too," she says, agreeing with a sigh. "I better get going upstairs," she tells me.

"Hold on." I tell her as I reach behind her and open the glove box and pull out some tissues. "You're going to need these." Her eyes widen in understanding. I gently pick her up and deposit her back onto the seat. She quickly wipes herself, throwing the tissues into her bag.

"Well, thanks for that," she says awkwardly, now the fog of our orgasm has disappeared.

"When will I see you again?" I ask her. Portia stills with her hand on the door handle.

"To do it again or something else?" she asks.

"Both," I reply.

"Um, well…" she mumbles.

"I was going to check out a house tomorrow if you wanted to come. It's around the corner," she tells me.

"I'd like that."

"Okay, well then, I guess I'll see you back here tomorrow about ten," she says.

"Sounds good. We could go grab some lunch afterwards. Maybe do some baby shopping."

Portia's eyes widen. "You want to go baby shopping? I thought guys hated that."

"I think it might be fun." She nods and gives me a smile before she reaches for the door again. "Oh, and, Portia." She turns and looks at me. I reach out and pull her to me again and kiss her one last time. "See you tomorrow." She smiles and gets out of the car on shaky legs and if that doesn't make me feel like the king of the world.

"Morning," I greet Portia with a kiss on her cheek and a ginger tea as I know she's still not feeling the best in the mornings. "Did you sleep well?" I ask her.

"I did actually," she says, taking the cup of tea from me. She smells it and lets out a contented sigh which hits my dick directly. I like I made her happy with the tea. I enjoy making her happy. It gives me this warm feeling inside, which is alien. I thought it was heartburn at first. Now I realize it's me enjoying seeing her smile. "One of the best night's sleeps I've had in a while," she says, taking a sip of the tea. I had a fantastic sleep. Also, my balls weren't hurting as much, but my dick was. He wouldn't stop thinking about her moans and groans, the way she begged for me to fuck her harder. I had to settle him down again once I got home.

"Where are we off to?" I ask her, changing the subject before I pull her into the hallway and fuck her again. She rattles off the address as we head back down to the foyer as it's within walking distance of her current apartment. Once we step out of the warm foyer of the building, the icy wind hits us. I'm glad I bought her tea to keep her warm. We meander our way through the busy streets until we arrive at the building. Oh wow, it's a townhouse within walking distance to Central Park. And for the price she said it was, it seems like a steal, so it must need a ton of work. It's in a great location. I'm close to work. Portia isn't far on the subway to college, a great school district. It's in the heart of everything. The realtor meets us at the front door with a wide smile. He directs all his spiel and questions to me. Dick. I tell him Portia is the one buying it; it has nothing to do with me. He looks a little flustered by my comment and finally starts directing everything to her. It's five stories, with bedrooms on the four upper levels. There is a courtyard out the back of the kitchen and a massive terrace off the bedroom on the higher level. Amazing wooden floors, fireplaces, recently painted, all updated; it's move in ready. The realtor leaves us to it for a couple of moments to chat.

"I love it," she says, her chocolate brown eyes flickering with excitement.

"Me too," I tell her.

"I think I should get it. Don't you?" she asks me.

"Yes. It's perfect. There's enough room we can all have our space. There's room for the baby to grow into its spaces," I explain to her.

"What do I do now? I don't know how to negotiate," she whispers to me.

"I can take care of it. If you trust me."

"Yes. I know I should be like yay I'm an independent woman, but I'm so out of my depth. The realtor is going to see me coming and I will not get a deal."

I can see how worried she is, and I want to help her. "I've got you," I tell her, pulling her into me and placing a kiss on her temple. "Let's make an offer. Then we can go shopping and start planning the nursery." Portia's eyes light up. She's like my mom. Whenever Mom gets sad or stressed, if you offered to take her shopping for the house, it would perk her up.

31

PORTIA

iles and I are on our way to our gender reveal party at my parents' place up in The Hamptons. I'm excited to find out what we will be having. Our OBGYN was very careful with our last checkup she gave nothing away because Miles would have known straight away. It's been an exciting time, finding out if we are having a little boy or girl and finding out I got the townhouse. I get the keys next week and I'm itching to get in and decorate as soon as I can. My mind for the past month has been swirling with design ideas. How I want my room, the baby's room, even talking to Miles about his bedroom. Speaking of Miles, we've been hanging out more and more, even after getting the house. We speak every day; go out to dinner at least three times a week under the guise of talking about the baby, but Hannah and Cora think we're falling for each other. *We're not.* Cora, I would expect this romantic bullshit rose-colored glasses from, but not Hannah. Look, I enjoy hanging out with Miles. We're having a kid together, so shouldn't I like my baby daddy, especially if we are going to co-parent together? If I'm honest, I'm looking forward to us living together. I'll get to hang out with him more without having to sneak out behind my roommates' backs. There's no way in the world I would tell my girls we are sleeping together. They already think something more is going on. I do not want a lecture.

Since that night in the parking lot where I practically jumped Miles in the front seat of his car, every time we catch up, we can't seem to keep our hands off each other and end up back at his apartment or a hotel, whichever is closer to get it on.

For example, the other night when he sent me a message that read.

Miles: *Meet me at the hotel in an hour.*

This is all the text said; straight to the point. I remember the tingles rushed over my body in anticipation. The same ones I get every time I'm around him. Every pore in my body feeling flushed, every nerve on high alert. I can feel how wet I am already between my legs thinking about him.

My mind wanders back to the other night.

I jump in the shower, get all my bits cleaned, and get dressed. I grab my red fuzzy sweater dress, black knee-high boots, and my new underwear I bought the other day for Miles. A gorgeous black lace set. My stomach is fuller and now I look like I've eaten way too much food, but it's cute. I've rubbed it more; I can feel the tiniest bit of stretch as the baby grows. And my boobs, wow, they have gone up an entire size and I don't know when they will stop growing. Not that I'm complaining because now I have the boobs I've wanted. Even if it's for a little while until the baby destroys them, I'll enjoy them. I put a little light makeup on because let's be serious, we both know why we are going there. I don't have to impress Miles.

"Where are you going looking like a whore?" Hannah asks, catching me as I creep out. Shit.

"Hey, I'm dressed casually, thank you very much," I tell her, running my hands down my dress.

"It's eight on a Tuesday." Hannah smirks.

"I'm catching up with Miles. We are going over some ideas for the house," I tell her.

"Does it matter what he thinks? It's your house," Hannah adds.

"He still has to live there. We're talking about the baby too," I explain to her.

"Convenient." She chuckles.

"What does that mean?" I ask her, a little annoyed at her questions.

"Why are you hiding the fact you are going off to hook up with Miles," Hannah questions me.

"I'm not."

"You may fool Cora because that girl is innocent, but you can't fool me, sweetheart. I wouldn't judge you," Hannah states.

"Sounds like you are."

"I want you to be careful, that's all. Am I happy you are getting laid? Yes. More power to you. And Miles Hartford is fine. I'm worried about your heart, that's all," Hannah says softly.

I let out a sigh and walk over to where she was on the couch and sit down beside her. "Fine. I'm meeting up with Miles at a hotel."

"I knew it." Hannah grins.

"I like him. I like what's going on between us. I don't want to lose this because I want a good relationship with him for our baby's sake. But I'm not falling for him," I explain my feelings to Hannah.

"Okay, fair. And what about him? What are his feelings?" she asks.

"I don't know. He's happy he's getting laid," I say with a shrug.

"So, it's exclusive?" she questions.

"We're not sleeping with other people; we agreed on that but not because we only want each other. It's more convenience as we are both so busy."

"*Friends with benefits who are exclusive and moving into together while having a baby. Sounds like a relationship to me,*" Hannah says.

"*It's not though. We are friends who, yes, sleep together. And are having a baby and are about to live together. Friends can do that with it not meaning anything,*" I exclaim to her.

"*Okay, okay, I get it. You're just friends. I'm saying be careful. Your hormones are all out of whack so old Portia may think like that, but new hormonal Portia might think differently,*" Hannah explains. I understand her concern and will make a note of it. "*I'm just looking out for you, boo. And no matter what happens, I'm here for you,*" Hannah says, placing a reassuring hand on my leg.

"*I know you are and I appreciate it,*" I tell her.

"*Okay, go get laid. I will sit here watching sport. And shoving popcorn in my mouth.*" Hannah smiles. I lean over and give her a hug and rush out the door.

A little while later, I arrive at the hotel, collect my key from the receptionist downstairs, and head on up to the room. I give the hotel door a knock to warn him I'm here before swiping the key across the lock and unlocking the door. The green light flashes and I enter the room as excitement rushes across my skin. The door clicks shut as I walk down the corridor, which brings me out to the bedroom where Miles is standing, looking out the window at the city below. He's dressed in jeans, a blue dress shirt with the sleeves rolled up, and he's bare foot. He looks so handsome. Of all the people to be accidentally knocked up by, I hit the jackpot with him. Miles looks over his shoulder at me. Those green eyes flare with heat as he takes in my outfit. He then turns fully and grins.

"*Take it off,*" he commands.

I do as I am told and pull the red dress up over my head and let it fall to the floor. Miles's eyes widen as he takes in my new underwear.

"This is new?" he asks. I nod as my teeth sink into my bottom lip. "Did you buy this for me?" I nod again, as heat rushes across my cheeks. Miles strides across the room, those green eyes laser focused on me. His hand reaches out and runs along the edge of my lace bra grazing my nipple, which pulls a moan from my lips. "Your nipples have become so sensitive." He grins as his voice deepens. "I bet I could make you come by playing with them." He wouldn't be wrong. The tiniest of grazes sends sparks across my body. His finger runs along the other side and goosebumps lace my skin. "I've missed you," he confesses, catching me off guard. It's been a week since we've seen each other due to him being busy and doing a couple of double shifts, as they were short staffed. He still checked in on me via text, though. "We've been spending so much time together I didn't realize how much till you weren't there." His hands pulls the straps of my bra down my shoulders, exposing my breasts to him. His fingers lazily run along my skin and over my hardened nipple, teasing me. "When something happens to me, you're the first person I want to tell." A small frown forms across his fore-head, as if he's not sure how he got himself into this situation. "I like it," he says, the frown turning into a smirk as he drives me crazy, playing with my nipples. He's torturing me and I love it.

"Me too," I say, agreeing with him. His smile widens at my comment.

"Glad we are on the same page then," he says as he takes a closer step toward me. His hand grabs my chin and tilts it up, so I am looking at him. "I want you, Portia." Miles's voice deepens with desire.

"How do you want me?" I ask, quirking a brow at him. This makes him smile and his eyes flare with need.

"Let's start with you on your knees with my dick in your mouth," he growls, taking a step back. I sway a little as desire rushes over my skin and I fall to my knees. I'm still wearing my knee-high boots, but Miles loves me in them with nothing else on.

I unhook my bra and throw it away from me as Miles undoes his jeans and pulls himself out. He is already so hard for me.

A man like Miles Hartford, a known playboy, getting hard over a girl like me, blows my mind. Yes, it is via forced proximity, but he could have found out about the baby and said thanks and never got involved until after it was born, or he could have never gotten involved at all. He also could have continued his playboy life, and some other girl could be on her knees right now for him. But it's me. I look up at him and he gives me a heated grin as he runs his dick across my lips, teasing me. I let my mouth fall open for him and he hisses as my tongue slides across the tip, licking the bead of pre-cum from his dick. "You've never looked more beautiful than in this moment on your fucking knees worshipping my dick." Miles smirks. I move my head forward and envelop him inside of my mouth and suck him down. He's not so cocky now I have him where I want him. "Yes," he hisses as his fingers dig into my hair. "God, I love fucking your mouth." He curses as he thrusts further down my throat. We must be careful with the gag reflexes now because one night he got a little enthusiastic and made me gag and I threw up all over his feet. That was bad. We both have PTSD from it. Miles is careful not to hit the back of my throat as he thrusts into my mouth while he whispers dirty things to me. My underwear is saturated, and my body is on fire. I could probably come just by sucking his dick. These pregnancy hormones are no joke. "If you keep going like that, I'm going to come down your throat and I want to be nestled inside your delicious pussy instead," Miles growls. Yes. Yes. Yes.

Next thing I know, Miles is pulling his dick from my mouth and his hands are underneath my arms and lifting me up off the floor.

"I bet you are soaking?" Miles smirks as he lays me against the bed.

"Come and find out," I say, wiggling my brows suggestively at him.

Oh boy, does he ever, diving between my thighs he rips off my underwear and throws it over his shoulder and his mouth is diving between my legs seconds later. Groans of appreciation vibrate from his lips as he feasts on me. He's gone crazy between my legs like a starving man, licking, sucking, moaning while my body liquifies into a puddle of blissful goo. My fingers drag through his hair as I hold on for dear life. Then he presses a thick finger inside of me and I'm done for. It's like he has the key to the hidden areas of pleasure inside of me and with one flick of his finger, he is opening it all up and my body is ready to float away over the edge into oblivion.

"Fuck, yes," I curse as he inserts another finger filling me up as his skilled tongue continues lapping me up as if I'm the finest wine until he twists his hand and his fingers hit the magic button inside of me and send my back arching against the bed and his face as I scream my release probably waking up the entire floor, but I don't care. Miles chuckles against my pussy at the response he has pulled from me. Cocky bastard. Especially when I finally come down from my orgasmic high and look down at him, still between my thighs, those green eyes staring up at me as if I'm the most beautiful woman in the world. Something cracks inside of me, and Miles seeps through, and I don't want him to.

"I love watching you come." He grins as he wipes the back of his hand across his mouth, but I can still see myself all over his face. He then positions himself on his knees as he grabs my legs and widens them for him. He then pulls me down against his dick and we both moan at the connection. My heart is beating uncontrollably outside of my chest, and I don't like. "I'll never get sick of sinking inside of you, Portia." I never will either, the thought strangles me, and I gasp. Now is not the time to be dealing with whatever this is. So I push it back deep down in my chest, locking the box and concentrate on Miles fucking me into oblivion.

32

MILES

Wﾠe are driving up to The Hamptons for the gender reveal and Portia has fallen asleep, but the tiny moan that falls from her lips has my dick's attention. Is she having a sex dream? This is not at all what I need before we see the family again. I'm nervous enough as it is because last time I was driving up here it didn't go so well. I'm hoping Nacho and Allison are a little more welcoming this time. They have to be, don't they? It's their grandkid's gender reveal. I've invited my friends up as well to celebrate. It will be the first time they will meet Portia and I hope they don't say anything to upset her. I haven't told them about my deal with Portia being friends with benefits, they wouldn't understand. Lane would give me a lecture about leading the girl on, Dylan would curse me out for sleeping with one woman for so long, and Smith would grunt and tell me I'm an idiot for thinking with my dick.

"Hmm, Miles," Portia murmurs beside me. What in the hell? I nearly hit the brake and cause an accident at hearing her breathlessly say my name. What the hell is going on in her head? I see a farm up ahead with a long dirt road and nothing around it except for pumpkin patches. I turn off the road and drive up the dirt track. My dick is begging to come, especially as Portia keeps mumbling my name under her breath.

"Portia." I touch her lightly.

"What?" She sits up with a start, shaking her head, looking confused why we are in a pumpkin patch.

"What the hell have you been dreaming about?" My voice is hard with tension.

"Huh?" She stares at me, still a little groggy from waking until her eyes widen and she covers her mouth in surprise.

"You were over here moaning and groaning my name. I nearly had a damn accident over it. My dick is fucking steel," I tell her as I grip myself.

"Oh. I'm so sorry. I was ...you know, thinking about the other night," she explains to me as her cheeks flush.

"Get into the back of the damn car, Portia," I tell her. She scrambles out of the door and into the back. "Lay the fuck down and take your underwear off," I growl as I get out of the car and rearrange my dick. I look around the empty rows to make sure we are truly alone, I don't want a police officer breaking up our fun and hauling us off to jail for indecent exposure. By the time I've come around the car and opened the back door, Portia is there in the back with her underwear off and her legs wide open. Good girl. I place a knee on the back seat and lean forward. I swipe my fingers through her folds and find her soaked. Fuck, she is perfection. I then suck her off my finger and grin. I quickly unzip myself and give my dick a couple of tugs before I slip into her. Both of us moan as I sink into her inch by glorious inch.

"We're going to have to be quick, otherwise we will be late," she tells me.

"It's your fault we are going to be late with your little fucking moans beside me. How the hell am I supposed to drive while you're there practically getting off without me," I growl at her.

Portia's eyes widen until a mischievous smirk falls across her face. "Good to know you can't handle me getting off without you."

"I'm the only one allowed to give you pleasure," I tell her, accentuating my point with my dick, which has her eyes rolling back in her head. "Do you understand me?"

"Yes," she screams as I hit her deeply. Her hand falls between her thighs as she furiously touches herself, her cunt tightening with each of my thrusts, practically strangling me. It doesn't take me long till we are both coming. "Happy now?" she asks.

"Always when I'm inside of you," I tell her, placing a kiss on her cheek. "Here, better clean yourself up, we don't want anyone knowing our dirty little secret."

"What, you love the fact that I'll be walking around the party with you still inside of me?" she questions me.

"Fuck yeah. The hottest thing in the world knowing you're still wet from me," I tell her.

"Who knew you had a breeding kink, Miles." She chuckles as she cleans herself off.

"Is that what it's called coating your pussy with my seed and leaving it there. If it is, I'm all for it," I joke with her. She throws the sex towel at me, making me jump out of its way. "Hey, you nearly got jizz on my shirt. Would not be a good impression for your father."

"Come on, let's get going before Dad kills you for being late."

A little while later, Portia and I walk into the seventh circle of hell. Oh shit, it looks like a blue and pink confetti machine has vomited everywhere. Why are there so many balloons? And babies made from balloons?

"Finally, you made it." Nell rushes up and greets us.

"Sorry, I keep forgetting I have to stop a million times to pee," Portia tells her sister who thankfully smiles and takes

Portia's word for it. Nell ushers Portia away and I head into the party to see if my family and friends are here.

"This is insane," Smith says, greeting me with a stern look on his face.

"I'm in love with these," Dylan states devouring a pink and blue deviled egg.

"We have a bet going we think it's going to be a girl. Karma for all the girlfriends past," Lane jokes. Dick.

"I'm not that bad. He's worse," I say, hitting Dylan in the chest.

"Hey, I'm not the one with a baby momma," he groans.

"So where is she? Are you scared to introduce her to us?" Smith asks.

"To be fair, one look at me and she'll forget all about this dickhead," Dylan teases. I turn and glare at him, which makes him laugh even harder, almost choking on his deviled egg.

"Has something happened between you and Portia? You seem awfully protective?" Smith raises a brow at me. Stupid detective gene.

"This is my kid's gender reveal," I answer him, but he doesn't seem convinced. "There she is," I say, pointing to the crowd. As if she could sense me, Portia turns around and gives me a wide smile.

"Can see why you've kept her away from us," Dylan adds. I thump him in the chest again, which makes him chuckle.

I wave Portia over and she excuses herself from who she was talking to and walks over to where I'm standing. I place a comforting hand on the base of her back, needing to be connected to her. She gives my friends a bright smile before turning to me, waiting for me to introduce them.

"Portia, let me introduce my friends. This is Lane. He has the little blond boy, Jaxon, running around. This is Smith, and this is Dylan, he's Australian so ignore him," I tell her.

My friends all greet her warmly and it doesn't take long

before she is laughing and joking with them as if she's part of the crew. A thought flashes through my mind of us grilling in the summer in the back courtyard, a sleeping baby in her arms, while the boys come over and watch the game. Would it be like that? What happens if she meets someone? What happens if she realizes all she ever wants from me is friends with benefits? Do I want something with her? It's the significance of the day has me being all weird. I like Portia, of course. She's great. Do I want something more? Could I even give her something more? Does she even want me? I know she wants my dick, but would she want to date me? I'm too old for her.

"Portia, Miles, it's time!" Nell calls out from the stage area. We both look at each other and I can feel the anticipation building inside of me. I'm moments away from finding out what the little bump is. Boy or girl, I don't care as long as it is healthy. That is all that matters. Portia and I stand in front of a huge archway made of pink and blue flowers, our family standing in front of us and then our friends, all waiting patiently for the moment. I can see how excited the moms are at this moment. They are both clinging to the other in anticipation. "Okay, here you both go." Nell hands Portia and me a silver tube. "When I say go, you will twist the bottom of the tube and whatever color comes out is what you will be having," Nell explains excitedly.

"You ready?" I ask Portia. She nods but looks a little freaked out.

"Okay, Portia and Miles, are you ready to find out what you are having?" Nell says to the crowd. "In Five.Four.Three.Two.One…" *Pop!*

Portia and I both twist the bottom of the tube, and an enormous bang happens, followed by bright blue smoke. Shit, does that mean? Oh my god, I'm having a boy. A son. I'm going to be a dad. I drop the tube and before I even process what I'm doing; I turn toward Portia and grab her face and kiss her in front of everyone.

"I love you, Portia," I tell her before pulling away from her, and her mom is pulling her away from me. Portia's chocolate brown eyes are wide with confusion over hearing those three little words I've said to her.

It felt right in the moment, and I meant it.

"Congratulations, sweetheart, a boy," Mom says, pulling me into a tight hug. My father does the same.

"What the hell were you thinking?" Stirling says, pulling me in for a congratulatory hug. Huh? "You kissed Portia in front of everyone as if you were a genuine couple."

"It felt right in the moment," I tell him. He shakes his head at me before Remi comes over.

"I knew it. You better not fuck her over," Remi says under his breath. "She's family and I will fuck up your shit."

"We're not together."

"You basically came out to everyone with that kiss." Remi glares at me. Did I? I know I was happy over finding out we were having a boy and yeah, I may have confessed to Portia I loved her, but people will not think we are together, will they?

33

PORTIA

I'm in shock.

Not only did I find out I'm having a boy. Miles kissed me in front of our entire party and then whispered he loved me. He didn't mean it. There is no way in hell he meant to say those three little words to me. He was swept up in the moment. He didn't mean them. Thankfully, my family pulled me away, congratulating me before I could react. What would I have said? Do I love Miles? I don't know. It seems a little soon, doesn't it? I thought we were only friends.

There's a knock on the door of my childhood bedroom and I walk over and let them in.

"Oh, hey," I say, surprised to see Miles standing there. I hold open the door for him to come in before closing it again.

"Are you hiding from me?" he asks, a frown forming on his face.

"No," I answer quickly.

Miles turns and narrows his eyes on me.

"Maybe," I say, changing my answer.

"I fucked up. I'm sorry. I shouldn't have kissed you like that in front of everyone. I bet you've had the Spanish inquisition from your family. I know I have." Miles chuckles.

"They had a million and one questions about it. I told them nothing was going on; you were excited we were having a boy. Then Nell told them we were moving in together and then all hell broke loose and now I'm here. Hiding away from them," I explain to him.

"It wasn't because I may have told you I loved you?" he says confidently.

"I know you didn't mean it," I say, waving him off.

"How do you know that?" he asks. I'm stumped. Miles walks over to me and cups my face. "I love you, Portia. You and I are family. You don't have to say anything back to me because I know you're not there yet. But know I'll be here waiting for you when you do," he says firmly before kissing my lips. I'm in shock. "I'll see you downstairs," he says before leaving me alone in my room. What in the fuck? Miles loves me. No. There is no way in this world he means that. I pull my phone out and text my girls.

"What is it?" Hannah says, bounding into my room with Cora on her heels. I look up at them and burst out crying.

"Oh no, did you want a little girl?" Cora asks.

I shake my head. "No, it's Miles," I say with a sniffle.

"I'll fucking kill him," Hannah sneers.

"He told me he loved me," I tell them. The room falls silent, so I look up to see what they think of that bombshell.

"This is so exciting. I knew it. The way he kissed you when he found out he was having a boy. He was too comfortable around you. That was a genuine moment. You two have been hooking up," Cora says.

"How do you feel?" Hannah asks.

"I don't know. He said he will wait for me," I explain to them.

"What does that mean?" Hannah asks.

"It means he is going to love Portia until she is ready to share her true feelings. He is going to wait however long it takes to fall in love with him too," Cora states confidently. Hannah and I both stare at her. "What? Well, do you love him?"

"I don't know. I feel like he's said it because he's wrapped up in the day's emotion," I explain to my friends.

"Do you want a relationship with Miles?" Cora asks.

"I don't know."

"You've been having a relationship since the moment he found out about the baby. You've been dating for months," Hannah states.

"How would he know whether he loves me or not?" I ask them both.

"Miles is older. Older men know what they want," Cora adds.

We both turn and look at our friend.

"Are you talking from experience there, Cora?" Hannah asks.

Cora's cheeks flush at Hannah's comment. Busted.

"Spill the tea," I tell her.

"There's nothing to spill. I've dated older men before. They aren't like guys our age; they know what they want and go after it. They are experienced," Cora explains.

"Experienced in the bedroom," Hannah jokes.

"Of course, they are. And they are much more giving than college guys," Cora says, rolling her eyes.

"I need to know more, but we will circle around to that later. We need to sort out Portia's life first," Hannah says.

"There's nothing to sort out. I'm going to bury my head in the sand and forget Miles ever said anything." Both my friends shake their heads in shame at me. It's the easiest way to protect my heart because it's not my heart he will break, it will be our baby boy's, too.

It was a quiet drive home after the reveal party. Thankfully, I didn't have to pretend to be tired as I fell asleep as soon as I sat down in the passenger seat of Miles's car. It's not until he wakes me up, I realize we aren't at my apartment, he's brought me to his own.

"What are we doing here?" I ask him as he helps me from the car.

"I wanted you to spend the night with me," he says, shutting the car door behind me.

"Miles, I'm not in the mood for sex. I'm tired," I say crankily.

"Lucky I'm not in the mood either and all I want to do is curl up on the sofa with you," he says with a grin as he takes my hand and escorts me into the elevator. He pushes the button to his floor, and we ascend to his level. He doesn't let go of my hand until we get into his apartment. "Did you want a drink or something to eat?" he asks, heading toward the kitchen.

What is going on? I'm so confused. "Miles, I think we need to talk," I say, unable to cope with his weird mood. He stops what he's doing and gives me his full attention. Suddenly, I feel something weird in my stomach and clutch it. Miles's face pales as he rushes over to check on me.

"Portia, what is it. Are you okay?" he asks, looking me over, trying to work out what's happening.

"The baby. I felt the baby." I tell him as tears well in my eyes. "A brief flutter in my stomach. I thought it might have been gas, but it's the baby."

"Our little man is moving. Do you think I could feel it?" he asks.

"Not sure. Try."

Miles put his hand on my stomach but shakes his head. "I think it might be a little early yet for me to feel it," he says, sounding disappointed.

"It won't be long till our little one is kicking a soccer ball around in my stomach," I tell him with a chuckle.

"Can you believe we're having a boy?" he says in awe.

"I was happy either way. But now we know what we are having. I have so many ideas for the nursery," I say, grinning up at him.

"What about names?" he asks.

"I haven't thought of any," I confess.

"Will he have my surname or yours? Or will we do a double-barreled surname like Garcia-Hartford or Hartford-Garcia?" Miles asks.

"I don't like the sound of that. I'm okay with him having your name. Maybe Garcia could be his middle name," I suggest.

"I like that," Miles grins.

We then spend the next couple of hours arguing over boy names. Who knew it would be this hard? I must fall asleep as I feel Miles picking me up and carrying me into his bedroom. He's slipping off my boots and taking off my dress, then my bra before placing a T-shirt over my head. I'm too tired to care, as I lay down in his bed. I roll over and slowly crack an eye and watch him get changed.

"Stop looking at me like that, Portia, unless you want me to do something about it?" Miles says with a grin.

I bite my lip as I contemplate how tired I am. And if I want him to do something about it. The thought has my body running hot.

"Portia, I'm warning you." Miles narrows his eyes on me, and I take him all in from where I am lying down. His broad chest, the tiny smattering of hair across it. Then my eyes travel down along his taunt stomach over his abs before they dip to the waistband of his pajama pants. His dick is standing tall and proud, straining against the waistband. I love the fact I can make a man like Miles hard. The look of complete and utter desire is glowing from beneath those green eyes and are directed straight at me, has me squirming in my spot. I move around under the covers a little and produce my underwear. Miles's eyes widen as he stares at the red fabric. I then throw it at his chest. He captures them and grin, he then brings them up to his nose and smells them.

"I can smell how fucking turned on you are, Portia," he says, running his nose all over the fabric. That's hot. It shouldn't be, but it is. He then throws them on the ground and places a knee on the bed before pulling the covers off me. I let him. My legs fall open for him and a moan falls from his lips. His hands grab my ankles and haul me across the bed. He runs his fingers through my slit and places them directly into his mouth. "Perfection." Miles groans as he closes his eyes and saviors me as if I'm a fine wine. He slides his pajama pants down and the tip of his dick glistens with pre-cum as he leans over me and slides himself right into me, no need for foreplay. I'm turned on. I love the feeling of him sliding into me, filling, stretching me. It has my eyes rolling back in my head. He leans over me on his elbows as his lips run along my throat.

"I will never get sick of sinking into you. It's the best feeling in the world," he whispers into my ear as he moves. Sliding out of me almost fully before thrusting hard back into me with a grunt as he moves me up the bed. I wrap my legs around his hips and pull him deeper into me, making him touch those parts of me only he seems to touch. Miles fucks me slowly, taking his time, prolonging my need. His hands are fisted in my hair as his teeth nip the sensitive curve of my neck. Something is different tonight in the way he is fucking me. Usually, we are frantic and can't seem to get our clothes off in time and most of the time we can't so we fuck around them, but this slow and languished rhythm is making my skin itch with anxiety as if he might make love to me. Not sure if it is what I want, especially not after his confession earlier today. No. I don't want this, not yet, not now. My chest constricts. So, I do what I need to do and flip him over and take the control back. Arching my back, I slip back onto his dick and begin riding him like the good girl that I am. How dare he try to make love to me. It's sneaky and underhanded. So, I punish him for it. I don't let him take control. I concentrate on taking my pleasure from him. This is what I want from him. This is all I can handle at the moment. Anything more I'm not ready for.

"Yes, yes, yes!" I scream as I spasm around his dick and moments later he is coming too. I fall against his chest exhausted from everything; my eyes close as his heartbeat lulls me to sleep.

"Portia," Miles calls my name and I mumble something incoherently. "Did you fall asleep on me?" he questions me and again I mumble something. I feel his chest rumble with laughter, then he picks me up and rolls me to my side and I snuggle into the pillow. My eyes are heavy and I'm unable to stay conscious anymore. I feel something cold between my legs as the bed dips. I let him do whatever he needs to do as I fall asleep into the dark abyss.

34

MILES

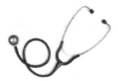

"Yes, Miles, yes. Harder!" Portia screams as she rides my dick. Damn, this dream feels real as if she is actually fucking me. Then I feel the pinch of my nipple and my eyes shoot open and I've woken up to Portia riding on my dick. How? What? When did this happen? Not that I'm complaining. My hands come out and grip her hips as she takes what she wants. Now I'm awake, I move my hips and push into her deeper, which has her sighing. She rolls her hips and rubs her clit against my stomach, and it sets her off and I'm not far behind her. She rolls off me and gives me a contented sigh. I'm still in a daze. I had no idea Portia was fucking me. Thank God my dick was ready to play.

"You can wake me up like that anytime you want," I tell her as I roll over and pull her back to my chest and nuzzle her neck, which makes her giggle.

"You were asleep?" She squeals, turning around in my arms to stare at me. I nod. "Oh, my gosh, I'm so sorry. I took advantage of you, and you did not know." Portia gives me a pained expression as her forehead crinkles.

"Babe, I'm not upset at all. My dick is yours to do with what you want. Anytime of the day or night," I say with a chuckle.

"You reached out to me, and your hand slipped between my legs and um, I thought you knew what you were doing," she says with a frown.

"Guess I was having a pleasurable dream about you then." I give her a smile. She still doesn't look convinced. "Come on, let's have a shower and get dressed. I'm taking you out shopping. Now we know it's a little boy, I thought you'd be dying to get everything you need for the nursery."

"Yes," she says, her eyes lighting up. "But I have no clothes."

"Lucky I got your friends to pack some for you. Your bag is at the end of the bed," I tell her.

"You had this planned."

I nod at her because I had it planned. I wanted to spend the night with her after we found out about our baby. Then, knowing her like I do, I knew she would want to go shopping instantly.

"Our moms will meet us there as well," I tell her, biting my lip at that bit of information. Her eyes widen with surprise.

"You organized for them to come too?" she asks.

"Yep. Nell will be there too as well as your roommates," I explain to her.

"Everyone is coming?" she questions me.

I nod. "Then we are going out for lunch." Those chocolate brown eyes blink at me, trying to work out if I'm joking or not. "Get ready and let's go," I tell her.

"Hey, honey," Allison greets her daughter. Then the rest of her friends and family do as we step into the baby shop. Portia looks a little overwhelmed by the attention.

"Hey, sweetheart, how are you doing?" Mom greets me. "I'm so excited." Mom smiles at me. I can see it on her face as she takes in the shop filled with all number of baby paraphernalia. Are we going to need all this?

"The shop does a baby registry. All you have to do is pick the things you want, and people will buy it for you for your baby shower," Nell explains to Portia, who is staring down at a sheet of paper. Sounds like an awesome idea.

"How are things going between you and Portia? The two of you seem to get along well," Mom questions me as we stand back and watch everyone tell Portia what she needs to tick for the register.

"Yeah, we are getting along great. I think I'm lucky to have knocked her up," I joke with Mom, who gives me a swift slap in the chest which makes me chuckle.

"I saw the way you kissed her at the party yesterday. Everyone saw the way you kissed her. Is something going on between the two of you? Nacho almost had a heart attack, you know." She gives me a knowing grin.

I let out a heavy sigh. Maybe I should talk to Mom about the feelings I'm developing for Portia. "I like her, Mom. Really like her, but I don't think she's there yet," I turn and tell her.

Mom's eyes widen at my confession, but she nods and smiles. "It's probably all a big change for her. So many life-changing moments are happening. She's trying to finish college before the baby comes. She's bought her first ever house. Her body is transforming. She probably isn't interested in doing things other twenty-one-year-olds are into at the moment because of the pregnancy. She's had to deal with the fallout of telling her parents her news. As much as I love my friends, they can be overly critical of things. Not maliciously, but because they love their kids and want what's best. But they forget to listen to what their kids want sometimes." Mom nudges my shoulder. "And Portia might fear falling for you. She could be protecting her heart, protecting her baby's too."

"I would never abandon my child."

"I know you wouldn't, sweetheart. It's not the child I think Portia worries about you abandoning." She spells it out for me. "She might think the feelings you have for her are about the baby. If you want something with Portia, long term, you want to create a family home, then tread lightly. You need to make sure you are all in, sweetheart," Mom warns me. "Is that what you want?"

"I feel like it is. But I'm scared too. What happens if Portia doesn't have feelings for me? I'll be looking from the sidelines at my child and whoever Portia decides to have a future with," I confess.

"If it happens, then you will deal with it. You can't control other people's feelings, sweetie. No matter how much you might want things to be different. The fact she will move in with you is a big step to building something strong together."

"You think?" I turn and ask her.

"I do. You're building a life together and that bond will get stronger the longer the two of you are together. Remi says the two of you have been spending a lot of time together."

Thanks Rem. "We have been as we were looking for a house."

"And after that?" she pushes.

"We continued seeing each other," I tell her. She smiles and nods as if my answer explains it all. Portia looks over and smiles at me before she's pulled in another direction by her sister.

"I think her feelings are there toward you, my sweetheart, but she's scared. Give her time, reassurance, and if this is what the two of you want to be together, raise your little one as a family, then you have my full support. You know how much I love Portia. She's a talented and beautiful girl. I would love to one day call her my daughter-in-law," Mom says with a wink.

Wait, hang on now. I think this conversation has taken a severe turn left. The look on my face must say it all, as my mom bursts out laughing at me.

"Don't look so scared. A baby is more of a commitment than a ring," she tells me before joining the rest of the women.

35

PORTIA

I t's moving day. I'm so excited. I'm moving into my very first home. Look at me adulting like a champ. All the deliveries are arriving at the townhouse today. Miles and his brothers are on standby to help. This morning they are moving Miles's furniture from his apartment to the townhouse. I had little to take over, mainly my wardrobe as most of the furniture was joint purchases. My brother Dom is helping me move all those boxes. I'm leaving my bed here as a guest room for the girls, in case I want to stay over some time. I wanted all new furniture in my new home. Downstairs we have the main living areas but up on my bedroom level I have my bedroom en-suite and walk in closet but on the other side of the floor I have two bedrooms with a shared bathroom. One will be the baby's nursery and the other will be my office or lady cave. The painters have already been through, thanks to Carrie for organizing some last-minute trades for me. The carpets have been steam cleaned and everything should be sparkling.

"I can't believe this is your house, Portia." Cora stares up at the five-story townhouse. "You're such an adult," she says, giving me a grin.

"You did good," Hannah says, nudging my shoulder as we watch everyone come and go.

"I think I'm going to be happy here. Baby and I," I muse, looking up at the beautiful building.

"And Miles," Cora adds, giving me a smirk.

"Of course, with him, but he's not staying with me forever," I tell her.

"You sure about that?" Hannah says, raising her brows at me. I'm not getting in this with my friends, now is not the time.

The day speeds by quickly. By the time the sun is setting, they set the house up. My bed has been built, and I made it earlier. It was the least I could do, seeing I could lift nothing. Miles's room was complete. I made his bed too. My walk-in closet has most of my clothes hanging up, my shoes are in some sort of order. My handbags are placed on the top neatly. It's not perfect, but it will do for the moment, as my energy levels are fading quickly. I put all my toiletries away and pull out my new towels too. My mom hung my curtains while Dad put together a beautiful outdoor set for the terrace off my main bedroom. It will be too cold to use it at the moment, but by summer it will be perfect. The nursery I will leave till last since I want to spend my time putting it together, plus we have the baby shower in a couple of months, and everyone made me put a lot of things on the register so it might all be coming then, who knows?

I ordered a heap of pizzas, salads, and drinks from the local pizza place and everyone is downstairs hanging out in the kitchen and living room. Everyone's freshly showered after working all day, helping me get this place up to a livable standard.

"I want to raise a toast to you all," I say to the group as tears well in my eyes. "I know these last few months have been a major change for you all. But I can't thank you enough for showing up today and helping me with the next phase of my life," I explain to them as tears run down my cheeks. "I've never felt more loved than I do right now," I tell them, holding up my soda into the air and saying a cheers to them all. Everyone gives me a round of hoots and hollers.

"We are so proud of you too, sweetheart, for everything," Mom calls out, raising her glass of champagne to me, tears running down her cheeks too. It means the world to me she said that, acknowledging how much I have matured these past months since finding out about the baby.

"And congrats to my brother too. For being the best role model for his child," Remi says, holding his beer up to acknowledge his brother.

Shit. I didn't mean to make this day all about me because this is Miles's home too.

"I couldn't have done it without you, Miles," I say, walking over and wrapping my arms around him. He hugs me back tightly and I can feel everyone's eyes on the back of me, but I don't care; he deserves this moment.

"Thanks, babe," he says, kissing my temple.

It takes a while for everyone to eventually leave, but they finally do and both Miles and I sit down on the sofa exhausted. I close my eyes for the briefest of moments, and then I feel a kick. Ouch. "Oh my god, quick," I say, my eyes flying open as I grab Miles's hand and place it on my stomach. "Little man is kicking. Can you feel it?" I ask him. When I look up at Miles, I see those green eyes shimmering with awe and wonder as tears fall down his cheeks.

"I can feel him. Faintly, but I can feel him," Miles states.

"He might be a football player with a kick like that," I tell him with a chuckle.

"You can be whatever you want, little man. Mommy and Daddy will support you as long as you are happy and healthy," Miles says to my stomach. His words are like an arrow to my heart, and tears well in my eyes as the magnitude of his words hit me. Mommy and Daddy. That is going to be us. Me and him.

Miles Hartford and Portia Garcia forever linked because of this little human inside of me. Wow. It's all becoming real now. "You've made me the happiest man, Portia," Miles says, the awe still thick in his words. "I don't know how I'm ever going to repay you for giving me the gift of our son."

Damn him. That was the sweetest thing I've ever heard. I lean forward and kiss him as emotions take over. Miles kisses me back and neither one of us pushes to take it further. We are caught up in the magic that is having a baby.

"Morning." Miles greets me in my bedroom with a tray filled with pastries, fruit, and a decaf coffee. He's pulled the curtains in my bedroom, letting in the tiniest slivers of fall sun into my room. The days are getting darker and the air crisper. There will probably be snow coming sometime soon after the weather has taken a turn. At some point this morning, while I've been asleep, he's come into my room and started a fire for me. The crackling of the logs filters through the room. He takes a seat beside me on the bed and steals a couple of strawberries from the plate.

"Fantastic," I tell him. "I'm sorry I passed out on the sofa but yesterday was exhausting."

"What do you think of your new home?" he asks me.

"I love it. I love it so much it makes me deliriously happy. I can't believe this is mine, all mine," I tell him, popping a blueberry into my mouth. "What about you? Did you sleep well?"

"I did, actually. The room is perfectly dark, so as soon as my head hit the pillow last night, I was out like a light." He grins, taking a sip of his coffee.

"Thank you so much for yesterday. I couldn't have done it without you. I hope you know how much I appreciate it. Appreciate you," I tell him honestly; I want him to know that.

"I know you are, Portia. But if you want to show me how

much you appreciate me, there are other ways to thank me," he states with a flirtatious wink. I shake my head as I bite into my croissant. We sit there together eating breakfast and enjoying each other's company. "Do you have any plans for today?" he asks.

"Other than moving things from where my mom put them, no," I tell him, which makes him smile.

"I'm going to go for a run in Central Park. I love being this close to it. Then I'll have to go to work as they have called me in tonight." I try to hide my disappointment, but I don't do a good enough job. "Don't worry, I'll be back by six in the morning and I'm happy to wake you up with my tongue if needs be."

"Promises, promises," I joke with him.

"Challenge accepted," he says, stealing another strawberry before kissing me on the cheek. I watch him leaving my bedroom, feeling hot and flustered. Not sure if he was joking or not. Guess I'll find out in the morning.

I spend my day puttering around the house, rearranging things. Before Miles left, he warned me not to move anything heavy, he would do it when he comes home. I told him I'm pregnant, not an invalid, but he didn't care. He got all growly and angry at me, which was all kinds of hot. But now I'm lying here in this big old home alone for the first time and I've creeped myself out. I probably shouldn't have watched true crime before going to bed because every creak, squeak, and groan has me jumping thinking I'm about to be murdered by a serial killer. Maybe I should have gone for a home with a bellman, at least then I would know the chances of me dying were next to none.

You've got this, Portia. You've stayed at home by yourself when your parents have gone away. This is true, but they have a staff of ten on site, so no matter what, there were still people there.

You can do this.

36

MILES

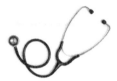

I counted down the minutes of my shift so I could get home to Portia. I bet she is all sleepy and soft curled up in her bed. I told her I was going to wake her up with my tongue between her legs. My dick has been throbbing all shift, thinking about sinking into her again. It feels weird coming home to this new house instead of my apartment this morning, but seeing how happy Portia is about her new home makes it all worthwhile. I don't care where I lay my head at night as long as it is near her— that is all that matters. We are going to have a talk at some stage about the two of us, but she has enough on her plate at the moment I'll wait till things settle down, maybe at Thanksgiving we can talk about what's happening between the two of us.

Mom and Dad are working on a project in the Caribbean for a client and she's asked Portia to assist her for extra credit toward her degree. Once Portia's parents found out she was going and wouldn't be with them for Thanksgiving, they invited themselves onto the work trip, as did Remi and Nell. Stirling isn't coming because he fucked up with Audrey and wants to win her back, so he's having Thanksgiving with her family. That fool is head over heels in love with Audrey.

Now we are having Thanksgiving in a tropical location, Remi has confessed to me he is going to pop the question to Nell on this trip. I think he is fucking crazy. They have only been together for three months but he's like

"I've been in love with her all my life." Which I get, but still. He of course likes to remind me I'm the one having a baby with Portia, so I don't have a leg to stand on with my judgy comments. And he's right. In the same time Remi and Nell have been back together, I've fallen in love with Portia, so who the hell am I to say they are moving fast.

After a quick shower, I head on down to Portia's level and push open her bedroom door. I quietly sneak toward her bed and still.

What the fucking hell?

She's not there. Panic grips my heart as I look around her bedroom. Maybe she's gotten up to pee, she's been doing that a lot. I walk into her en-suite and it's empty. Where is she? Maybe she went downstairs while I was having a shower. I rush out of her bedroom and down the stairs to the living area and she's not there.

"Portia?" I call her name out into the townhouse. She must be here. "Portia, are you home?"

Silence.

Did she go for an early morning walk? Why would she? She's never done it before. Why start now? *Because of Central Park.* Maybe. I head toward the front foyer and grab my phone out of the bowl where I dropped my keys. There are no missed calls, no messages letting me know she won't be home when I get back from work. Don't panic, I'm sure she's fine. I quickly pull up her social media to see what she tagged last. It's a photo of her in bed saying she's watching TV in her new home. Then where the hell is she? I pull up her number on my phone and wait for her to pick up. Shit. What the hell do I do? What happens if someone's taken her? It can happen. Stirling told me it happened to Rhys's girlfriend's best friend and Smith worked the case. So, it happens.

Smith! I need to call him. He will know what to do. I pull his name up and dial him.

"Hey, man, I'm at work. What are you doing calling so early? You working a late one too?" he answers.

"I've got back from work and Portia is missing!" I yell at him down the phone.

"Has anything been taken? Were the doors locked when you arrived home? Did you notice anything suspicious?" Smith goes into detective mode instantly.

"No. Everything was fine. You checked the alarm system yourself. She posted at 9:35 p.m. last night she was in bed watching TV. And I've gotten home, and she's not here. Where the hell is she?" I ask my friend as I rake my fingers through my hair.

"She's at the Waldorf Astoria," he says down the phone. "The last known ping of her phone is near there. I'm assuming she's checked into the hotel for the night. Why would she do that? Did you two have a fight?" he questions me.

"No. Nothing like that at all. I don't know why she would be there."

"Maybe she got scared of being home alone and stayed at the hotel?" Smith suggests.

"You think?"

"I don't know unless she had a date with someone."

My stomach sinks at the thought. There is no way in the world she's hooking up with someone at a hotel. I wasn't home. She could have done it in her own bed if she wanted to. No. Portia wouldn't do that to me. No way in the world.

"Now you know where she is, find out. Good luck, man," Smith tells me before I hang up. The Waldorf is only a couple of blocks away, it won't take me long to jog it. The entire way, I keep calling her phone, but it just rings. Fucking hell, Portia, I'm going to kill you when I find you. Eventually I make it to the hotel and stride in, hoping I don't look too much like a sweaty mess.

"Hi, I'm here to see Miss Portia Garcia," I tell the receptionist who gives me a once over.

"And your name, sir?" she asks.

"Miles Hartford," I tell her.

The receptionist types into her computer and scans the screen. "I'm sorry, sir, Miss Garcia has put a do not disturb sign on her room. We can't call her to let her know you have arrived," she explains to me.

"Can you give me her room number then?" I ask.

"No, sir, I can't."

Fuck. I curse internally. "Guess I'll wait for her then," I tell the receptionist. She gives me a nod and turns back to her computer. I walk over to some chairs and take a seat. If I must wait all day for her to walk past me, then so be it. I fall asleep at some point because it's Portia's voice that wakes me up.

"Miles?" she calls out to me.

I jump up off my chair and stride over to her. I'm so happy to see her safe and sound I grab her face in my hands and kiss her passionately. Relief floods every inch of my body.

"Don't you ever do that to me ever again, you hear me," I tell her sternly as I cup her face. "I thought I'd lost you. I thought something had happened. I was going out of my mind, Portia."

Those chocolate brown eyes widen at my distress. "I'm so sorry, Miles, I didn't think. I was watching true crime documentaries last night, and I scared myself to death. So, I checked into a hotel because I couldn't sleep by myself," she explains to me.

"I've been calling your phone all morning," I tell her.

"I didn't take my charger and my phone died. I'm sorry, Miles," she says, her brows knitting together.

"You're safe now. That's all that matters," I reassure her.

Portia wraps her arms around me and pulls me into a tight

hug. "I am so sorry to have worried you. I didn't think about how you would feel coming home and I wasn't there."

"I was so worried for you," I say, stroking her hair.

"I know. I can see it on your face. I promise I won't do anything like that again. Next time I'll leave a note and make sure my phone is charged," she says, giving me a grin.

"Next time don't watch true crime when I'm on night shift," I tell her with a chuckle.

"Deal," she says with a smile.

"I love you, Portia. Do you understand that? When you weren't there, I thought someone had ripped my heart out of my chest. I had gone insane."

Portia stands there wide-eyed, taking in my words. "You love me?" she asks.

"Of course, I do. I told you the day of our gender reveal how I felt. I've been too worried to tell you again because you seemed skittish over the idea, and I didn't want to pressure you. But when I thought I'd lost you, Portia. The thought of you never being in my life again was incomprehensible," I tell her.

"I thought you said it because of the baby," she says.

"The baby may have brought us closer, but it's not the reason I love you. I love that you are carrying our son, of course. But I cannot imagine spending a single moment without you in my life, Portia. Those couple of hours this morning when I thought I'd lost you made me see it clearly. I want you, Portia. I want you and I to be a family. I know it's a tremendous leap of faith, but I'm all in. Everything," I confess to her. Tears are running down her cheeks and my thumbs swipe them away. "You think you could handle dating an old guy like me," I ask her with a grin.

"Yes," she squeaks through her tears. Wait, did I hear her correctly?

"Yes?" I ask, wondering what the yes is for.

"I want to try, Miles. You and me as a couple, dating. I want to be a family," she explains to me.

"You do?" I question her again, not quite believing my ears.

"You're an easy guy to fall for, Miles Hartford," she says with a bright smile across her lips. I can't believe it. She's fallen for me too.

"Can we go home now and consummate this?" I ask.

Portia bursts out laughing and wraps her arms around my neck tightly. "Take me home and fuck me, Miles."

She does not need to ask me twice as I grab her hand and haul her out of the fancy hotel, grabbing the first cab we see, and hightailing it back to our apartment.

37

PORTIA

iles and I have been going great. We both seem to fit into each other's lives seamlessly. We have our routines. He goes to work, I go to college, and Mom sends Rhonda over to cook and clean for us seeing as Nell lives the majority of her time up in The Hamptons with Remi on the farm and not down in the city apartment like she used to. Rhonda is a lifesaver. Before Rhonda arrived, Miles and I were eating out most nights or getting takeout, both of us too exhausted to cook, but now that we have Rhonda and her home-cooked meals, I'm in heaven.

Miles has invited his boys over to watch football most Sundays. Lane brings Jaxon over and I get to test out my mothering skills on him. It's hard. Thankfully, Cora has been dropping over on football Sundays, seeing as Hannah works that day on her brother's telecasts. It's been good having time with her, and she loves hanging out with Jaxon. She's a natural at this kid business.

Now Stirling and Audrey are back together, we have been doing a heap of double dates with them both, since they still live in the city and their apartment isn't far from the townhouse.

Audrey is so sweet; I knew her growing up, but only as my sister's best friend, not as a friend herself. We've somehow fallen into bliss. Who knew relationships could be like this? I sure as hell didn't. Miles is an attentive lover as well as a thoughtful boyfriend. He brings me flowers when he finds out I'm having a bad day. He rubs my feet while we watch true crime together. He doesn't get upset when I fall asleep before him after promising to blow his mind with a BJ. He doesn't get frustrated over missing out. Is this what it's like dating a man, not a boy? Why have I not dated older before?

We are having our checkup before we get on a plane for Grand Cayman. My family, of course, highjacked my work trip because we would be away for Thanksgiving and Mom didn't want to miss it with her grandchild even though it's inside of my stomach so you can't do much with it. She's excited about the baby, so I didn't fight it too much. I'm so looking forward to relaxing by the pool, having the sun on my skin, and the sand between my toes. The weather in Manhattan has been horrible lately with a cold snap hitting the city. It's freezing cold.

"I can't remember the last time I took a vacation," Miles mumbles, sipping on his beer, looking awfully relaxed.

"This is our first vacation together with little one," I say, rubbing my stomach.

"The start of many more." Miles leans over and kisses my cheek while rubbing my stomach. Little man gives his daddy a kick in agreement which has us laughing.

It's not long till Miles is waking me up and pointing out the window at the turquoise sea below us. As soon as the doors open on the plane, the warm weather hits me and it feels amazing. There is a fleet of cars waiting for us on the tarmac to take us to the vacation rental our parents organized for the holiday week-end. It's only a ten-minute drive from the airport to the villa and as soon as we drive up to the home, nothing but the turquoise

ocean and the purest white sand greets us. This is exactly what I
needed.

Our room is facing the ocean and is only a couple of steps to
the beach, and the pool is on our right for easy access. It's all
white to offset the bright blue ocean. There's an oversized king
size bed in the middle of the room facing the ocean and behind it
is the en-suite and walk in closet.

"I'm never leaving this room," I tell Miles as I flop down on
the bed, which feels like I'm floating on a cloud. "Actually, I'm
never leaving this bed. It's divine."

"I'm okay with us never leaving our bed," Miles says as he
leans over and kisses me. A moan falls from my lips as I pull
him toward me on the bed. He comes willingly, wrapping his
enormous arms around my body. His hand slides down my body,
but I'm wearing jeans and he doesn't have easy access, instead,
his hand gives my ass a hard squeeze. There's a knock at the
door and I groan in disappointment at whoever decided it would
be a good idea to interrupt our snuggle time.

"Sorry to interrupt," Carrie calls out from the door. "Portia, if
you're up for it, I'm popping over to the client's house to do a
walkthrough if you want to come." I still at Carrie's words.

"Go on." Miles grins as he sees how excited I am. I jump off
the bed and head over to the door and open it for Carrie.

"Yes. I would love to," I tell her.

"Great. Go have a shower to freshen up and we'll leave in
twenty, okay?"

"Okay," I tell her as I close the door. I do a little excited
dance as I head toward the bathroom.

"I'm a great multitasker," Miles states as I pass him laid out
in the bed.

"You have ten minutes. Come join me in the shower," I call
out to him over my shoulder. Miles has never moved so fast.
Next thing I know, the shower is turned on and he is naked, stepping in underneath the water with his hand gripping his already

hard dick. I take a little longer to wiggle out of my jeans thanks to my stomach, but I eventually get in and as soon as my toes hit the tiles Miles is on me. Pulling me to him and kissing me passionately as the water cascades around us. Then he spins me around and my hands hit the tiles. I fall to my elbows and my belly almost touches the wall. Miles runs his fingers through my folds, making sure I'm ready for him before he pushes in. Both of us hiss as he enters me from behind. One hand comes around and covers my mouth while the other plays with my breasts. I'm a screamer and will be hella embarrassing if my family hears me screaming the bathroom down.

"Be quiet, Portia," he growls into my ear as he pushes into me. Yes. I will never get sick of Miles fucking me. I don't think anyone would ever be able to fuck me as good as him. He continues to fuck me slowly, but consistently. I know he's getting close when the hand on my breast moves to between my thighs as he strums my clit. It doesn't take long till I'm shattering into a million pieces, and he is not far behind me.

Miles spins me around and moves me under the water as his hand cups my pussy and cleans himself from between my thighs.

"I will never tire of fucking you," he murmurs to me as he brushes the water from my face before leaning down and kissing me. "I never thought I could ever be this happy," he confesses to me. Oh. Wow. I wasn't expecting that. "Anyway, you better jump out, don't want to be late," he tells me with a hard slap on my ass as I move out of the shower. I look over my shoulder and he gives me a heated smirk which shoots me in the clit, and I'm seconds away from walking back into the shower and fucking him again. "Go," he says to me, knowing exactly what I'm thinking. He shakes his head while soaping himself up.

It was so exciting sitting in on the client meeting with Carrie and Leon. My job was to take notes of what the client wanted, liked, anything he said in the conversation about what he wanted to do in each of the spaces. By the time we get back to the villa, it's dinner time and my mind is swimming with a million and one ideas. Ideas Carrie asked for me to share with her on the way home in the car. She explained how some ideas may or may not work in certain areas and I swear I learned so much more from that lesson than I have this entire semester at school. I miss going into the office and shadowing Carrie, but she told me to concentrate on school and once I graduated and had enough time off, she would have me back in the office again, but only if I wanted to. She told me she would design a nursery at her office so if she needed to be on grandma duty she could be, or if I wanted to work, I could bring the baby with me. I couldn't ask for better grandparents for my surprise baby than them. I did well getting accidentally knocked up by the one person who had the best family.

38

MILES

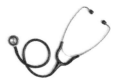

"Stop freaking out, she is going to say yes." I try to calm my brother down, who looks like he's moments away from hurling his guts up. It's Thanksgiving, and he is going to propose to Nell tonight at dinner. I've taken him for a walk along the beach to relax him. He's already thrown back two tequilas in quick succession. If he keeps going, he will not remember proposing. And after the shit he and Nell have been through, she deserves a magical proposal.

"I'm going to remember this conversation when you propose to Portia," he grumbles at me.

"I don't know if it will happen." I chuckle.

Remi stops walking, and I take a couple of steps and realize he's not beside me anymore. His face looks like thunder, as his green eyes narrow on me, and he looks like he is moments away from punching my lights out. What's his problem?

"Are you telling me after everything you will not marry Portia?" he questions me with a frown.

"Dude, come on, we have only been together for a little while. I think it's a little premature to be talking about marriage," I tell him, shaking my head.

"You're having a kid together."

"We don't need to be married for that," I tell him.

"I know. Do you love her at least? Because if you string that girl along because she's convenient or feel compelled to because she is having your baby, I will gut you," my brother warns me.

"Hey, don't be an asshole. Of course, I love her. I'm in this for the long haul. I don't want to get married."

"Ever?"

"Maybe. I don't know. I have more pressing things to think about, like having a kid," I tell him. Remi frowns at me. "It's like asking you when you and Nell are going to have kids?"

"They are a way off yet," he tells me.

"See, I'm the exact way about marriage," I explain to him.

"You will not break Portia's heart?" he questions me.

"Why would you think that?" I ask.

"Um, because of your reputation. I can't imagine you've gone from this playboy doctor to family man so quickly. You better not be cheating on her?" Remi points his finger at me.

"Look, finding out you accidentally knocked up your parents' best friend's youngest daughter shakes that ego up good. Seeing those first images of your child, I can't describe the feeling, but it changed me. I knew the way I was living my life, the relationships I was having are not what I want to show my little man. I was a dick. Even after getting involved with Tracey; the cluster fuck that turned into couldn't even stop me from hooking up with other staff members. I nearly lost my career and I've fucked my career at my current hospital with my antics and yet I still didn't stop. Like, what the hell? This baby made me reassess my life. It told me I needed to do better, and I have been," I explain to Remi.

"But what about Portia?" he asks.

"I wasn't expecting to fall for her. She's gorgeous. I'm not blind. I wanted us to have a healthy relationship, at least be friends. I've seen too many doctors at work go through horrible custody battles with their exes. Knock 'em down, drag them out into fights and I never wanted that for my baby. I attempted to hang out and get to know Portia, other than what I remembered from her growing up. We started spending time together and the more time I spent with her, the more I realized how incredible she was. I never let myself think of a future with a woman before. Why would I, when I was on to the next? But with Portia I had to because of the baby. When we were looking for homes to bring up our little man in that's when I saw what I wanted. I wanted a future where I had someone to come home to and a little person wrapping their pudgy little arms around me thinking I was the best thing in the world. I didn't realize how hot it was having a partner to come home to. To share your day with, especially when it's been a hard one. I found myself excited to come home to Portia and share my day with her. And for her to do the same. I loved the fact that Mom and Dad love her too. Let's be serious. They've liked no one we've brought home," I say, looking over at my brother, who cracks a smile. "I worry Portia is young. If I push her for more of a commitment than we already have I'm robbing her of, I don't know, life."

"So, you want her to go out partying and sleeping with a heap of college guys?" Remi asks.

"Fuck no," I say, which makes my brother laugh. "I guess I feel bad for ruining her college experience. She should be out at the frat house, instead, she's at home curled up on the sofa because she's exhausted from the baby. I remember how awesome college was. It feels like it's what you do in life, like a passageway from being a kid to an adult. I've robbed her of it," I try to explain to my brother.

"If it is what Portia wanted, then you two would not be having this baby," Remi tells me. Maybe he's right. I guess if this isn't what Portia wanted, she would have chosen differently. I don't know. "As long as you don't fuck over my soon to be sister-in-law than we are all good." Remi grins, slapping me on the back.

"I'm supposed to be giving you life advice, not the other way around."

"It's not my fault I have my shit together." Remi grins.

We sit down to a gorgeous spread of seafood and some traditional Thanksgiving food. It's a little hot for the full-on roast turkey, but there are cold cuts of turkey anyway. Everyone is in a cheerful mood, chatting away. The moms are already onto their second bottle of champagne and their cheeks are rosy. I can see as the dinner progresses, the sweat drips down Remi's face, he is freaking out.

"Miles, your turn. What are you thankful for?" Mom asks me. It's a tradition in our home to go around the table and ask everyone what they are thankful for.

"I am thankful for Portia and our little man. And I can't wait because this time next year we will have an extra seat at the table," I say, holding my glass up in the air as I look over at Portia, who gives me a warm smile.

"I can't wait either," Mom says, clapping her hands loudly together. Which has Allison joining in. They go off on a baby tangent for a little while before coming back to the table. "Remi, sweetheart, your turn. What are you thankful for?" Mom throws the question over to my brother, and that is his cue. I wait on the edge of my seat for his moment. Remi pushes his chair out and stands up. He turns and looks down at Nell.

"I am so thankful I have you in my life. After everything we have been through all these years you still love me. I will never take your love for granted ever again, Nell," Remi says seriously, looking down at Nell. The entire table is quiet, staring at Remi. Then Remi falls to his knee and a soft gasp float over the table as realization of what is happening kicks in. "There is no one else in this world I want to walk this road called life together with. I have loved you since the moment I saw you and I will love you till the moment I take my last breath. Will you marry me, Nell?"

All the women at the table are crying at Remi's beautiful words. Not going to lie, I got choked up a little too. He opens the red leather box and produces a massive diamond ring. Nell's eyes widen as she takes in the ring.

"Yes. Yes!" she screams as Remi slips the ring on her finger before she jumps into his arms, nearly toppling him over. The Thanksgiving table erupts in squeals of delight at the engagement.

39

PORTIA

I can't believe it's already a New Year. Falling asleep before midnight was not the normal way I would ring in the New Year. I would still be out till who knows what time in the morning. I would be party hopping like Cora and Hannah did last night. I don't blame them; they came over to see me for a bit before going out to celebrate. Then Remi and Nell also popped by. Miles's friends came over too. Most ended up staying over after they partied a little too hard. Honestly, looking at the snow outside, I don't know how I used to party in it. All I can think now is how cold it is and having to deal with all those crowds and I'm glad I have an excuse to crash on the sofa stuffing my face with chocolate.

Stirling and Audrey are in Turks and Caicos. Rhys, his best friend, had organized a holiday for his girlfriend and all her friends. Thank goodness he and Audrey sorted out their shit and are now happily together. She has turned the grumpiest Hartford brother into a low-grade grump because she's nothing but pure sunshine.

"Babe. Oh my god. Babe." Miles comes rushing in to where I'm lying on the sofa watching the repeat of the fireworks from last night. "Stirling called me freaking out. Audrey is pregnant. They found out last night when Audrey fainted."

"Is she okay?" I ask him.

"Yeah, she's all good. He called to double check with me as he was ready to rush off the island at sunup. Can you believe it?" he asks with the biggest smile on his face. "They weren't trying. It's come as a surprise, so he's a little freaked. Also, Rhys popped the question to Ariana last night too."

"Look at you with all the gossip," I say, smiling up at him.

"I'm going to be a dad and an uncle all in the same year. Our kids are going to grow up together. It's exciting." He grins. He's right. Audrey is a good couple of months behind me then, and our babies are going to be cousins.

"Guessing the beach house you bought us for Christmas is going to come in handy for family holidays." I smile. It was the biggest surprise I got for Christmas; keys to the beach house we both fell in love with months ago. To say I was beyond excited was an understatement. We took the family that afternoon to see the house. My parents are very excited it's close to them, but it's far enough for us they won't be in our pocket. "I'm so happy for them. They must be freaked out though. I bet Rhys didn't take the news well?"

"Shit no, apparently he and my brother fought," Miles states.

Oh, no, that would have been horrible for Audrey, an unexpected pregnancy and your brother and partner fighting, not good.

"Guess your parents are going to be ecstatic having another little bundle on the way."

"We need Remi and Nell to have a baby this year and the trifecta is complete." Miles chuckles.

"Yeah, don't hold your breath on that." I laugh.

"Aw, look at the two of you. I'm so happy for you both for finally getting it together." Jenny, our OBGYN, grins at Miles and me. Jenny walks us through the scan, checking every inch of our little man until Miles gets paged via the hospital directly into our room.

"Sorry, babe, I have to go. I'll see you when I get home. I won't be long, okay," he says, kissing my forehead before rushing out the door. I let out a sigh. I'm becoming used to the calls at all hours of the night.

"The joys of being with an ER doctor. Never know when an emergency strikes." Jenny chuckles. "It will get worse in his new job. That hospital is one of the busiest in the country," Jenny tells me as she continues moving the ultrasound wand across my stomach. *New job?* What is she talking about? "You must be so proud of Miles to be offered the position. It's his dream job," Jenny continues, oblivious to the turmoil I'm currently sitting in.

What new job is she talking about? Why has he told her and not me? I thought we were a partnership or was he never going to tell me and be like, oh yeah, got a job across the country and I'm taking it, let's go. As if I would follow him.

"Where is it again? I've totally forgotten. Pregnancy brain," I ask her.

"Oh, it's in Orlando," Jenny tells me excitedly. "It's one of the busiest teaching hospitals. Such a great opportunity for him, especially at his young age. Ever since Tracey, they have over-looked him for every promotion. Even when he's the most quali-fied. His indiscretion will forever haunt him there. It's not fair, Miles is a brilliant doctor," she says sadly, shaking her head. "I'm glad he has you Portia. He's changed so much for the better. You made him shed his ego and become the man I knew he could be."

"Thanks," I say, controlling my emotions, which is hard when they are dialed up to one hundred percent. I don't know how I feel about everything she's said.

By the time I get home to the townhouse, I'm fuming. My head is about to explode. I stomp into the townhouse, slamming doors. I rush up to my room and search through Miles's things but find nothing. This is something so important in his life he's told other people, but not me. The one he's supposed to love. The one carrying his baby. Not that there is anything wrong with Florida, but it is not where I want to live. My life is here in New York. This may be a great opportunity for him, but what about me? I've given up everything to have this baby and I would never change it for the world, but I want to have a career too. I want to join Carrie and design wealthy people's homes. I've been busting my ass off during these holidays to get ahead in my degree so I can finish it earlier. Now he's going to take all that away from me. Also, our families aren't in Florida, they are all here. I don't know what I'm doing. I can't do this on my own. If what Jenny says is true and it's a busy hospital, then will I ever see him? Will he work longer hours? I thought he wanted to spend time with our baby.

I need time to think. So I pack a bag of clothes. I need to go home and have some space between us because the anger I'm feeling in this moment I'm likely to say something I will regret and once it's out you can't put it back into the box.

This time I leave a note for him where he can see it.

Miles,

Congrats!

I heard about your job offer in Orlando.

I'm so angry with you for not telling me about it. I thought we were a team. I need some space because I'm likely to throw something at you if I see you. I've gone to my parents' place for a couple of days.

Portia

As soon as I get out of the city, I call my sister.

"Hey, how did the checkup go?" Nell asks, answering the phone.

"Okay." I sniffle.

"Portia, what's the matter? Are you okay?" she asks. I can hear the concern in her voice.

"He lied to me," I tell her as I burst into tears. I quickly swipe them away as they blur my vision.

"Who lied to you? Is it Miles? What happened? Where are you? I'm on my way," she tells me.

"I'm on my way home." I sniffle.

"Portia, you shouldn't be driving in this state. Pull over and tell me where you are," Nell yells at me.

"I thought we were building a future together, Nell. I fell in love with him," I say to her.

"I know, sweetie. Please, you've got me worried. Where are you? I'll come and get you. Remi can bring your car home. I want you safe at home with us so we can sort out what's going on," Nell says calmly, trying not to spook me.

"I'm fine, Nell. I'll be there soon," I tell her.

"Please, Portia," my sister pleads with me.

"Fine, let me find somewhere I can pull over and I'll call you back, okay," I tell her before hanging up on her. I have a look around, but when I turn a certain way, an almighty pain in my stomach hits me and I panic and try to keep the car on the road. My heart is racing a million miles a minute and I feel like I'm going to have a heart attack. Something funny is going on with the baby. Oh, no. Please don't tell me I'm going into labor, not now, it's too early. I can't. Panic is coursing through my veins. I need to find a hospital. I ask Siri where the closest hospital is, and I head toward it.

40

MILES

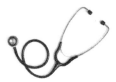

"Excuse me, Dr. Hartford, I have an urgent message for you," Lisa, the nurse, says, interrupting my lesson. I excuse myself from my students, who are doing rounds with me to follow Lisa. "We have a message from the emergency department at Southampton Hospital. They have admitted your partner, Portia." Every ounce of blood drains from my body. No. I left her hours ago with Jenny getting a checkup. Why is she on the way to The Hamptons? "They said she has high blood pressure and may have had an episode in the car. She drove herself to the emergency department and gave them your name upon check in to contact you. I've already organized the schedule and got you tomorrow off as well."

"Lisa, you are an angel, thank you," I tell her as my mind races at what Portia must think and feel at the moment. Why does she have high blood pressure? I've made sure her stress levels have been kept at a minimum. Did something happen at the appointment with Jenny? I rush out of the emergency department and down the halls toward my locker to grab my things. I left my phone in my locker today as I was called at the last minute to help with an emergency, and then I got roped in helping the interns. I should have been with her. If I hadn't had put work before Portia's well-being, this wouldn't have happened. Fuck. I grab my things from my locker and rush down toward the basement parking garage. I search through my missed calls. There's a message from Remi; I hit play.

"What the fuck did you do?" he screams down the phone line. "Portia called Nell in tears, saying you lied to her. Did you fucking cheat on her? I told you if you ever did something like that to her, I would fucking kill you. She's in hospital now because of you, you selfish dick. If she loses this baby, no one will ever forgive you." And with that warning, he hangs up on me.

What the hell is he talking about? What does Portia think is going on? I have done nothing. I haven't lied to her. I'm not cheating on her. Who the hell told her I was? Did some vengeful ex try to put crazy ideas in Portia's head? I call my brother as soon as I have reception and he picks up.

"What the fuck do you want?" he answers angrily.

"What the hell is going on? I ask him.

"You fucking tell me?" he curses.

"I'm not cheating on Portia. I haven't looked at another woman since her. I love her. Now tell me what the hell is going on!" I scream at my brother.

"Then why the hell does Portia think you lied to her?" he questions me.

"I have no fucking idea. They called me away from our checkup for an emergency at work and next thing I know I'm being given a message from the nurses Portia is in hospital. Is she okay? What's going on?" I ask him.

There's silence for a couple of beats, and it's driving me crazy.

"Portia is fine. She has high blood pressure from stress of whatever the fuck you did. The doctor is monitoring her. They said she is going to have to be on bed rest for the next week and if there is no improvement than she is going to have to be on bed rest until the end of her pregnancy," he tells me. Shit.

"I'm going to be there as soon as I can. I've organized to take a helicopter, so I'll be there within the hour," I tell him before hanging up.

Next phone call is to Jenny to find out what happened at the appointment.

"Hey, you, how's it going?" Jenny answers happily.

"Not good. Portia is in the hospital up in Southampton with high blood pressure. Did something happen at the appointment? I don't know what happened. She seemed fine before I left."

"No. I don't think so, we were chatting about you and your job." Jenny falls silent on the other end of the phone. "Shit," she curses.

"What the hell did you say, Jenny?" I say, raising my voice at her.

"I might have put my foot in it by accident. I assumed Portia knew. I wouldn't have said anything otherwise. I was talking about the job offer to Orlando and how proud I was you got it," she explains. Shit. Shit. Shit. No wonder she freaked out. "I had no idea you hadn't spoken to Portia yet."

"I hadn't told her because I declined the offer when I arrived back at the hospital today. Because I was actually offered a position at, ironically enough, the Southampton Hospital," I tell her. "I was going to talk to Portia about it tonight."

"Fuck, Miles, I'm so sorry. Shit. Me and my big mouth have fucked everything up. Is she okay? Please tell me she's okay?" Jenny asks.

"From what I know, yes. I'll keep you in the loop." And with that, I hang up. This has turned into a complete and utter cluster fuck for no reason.

After the longest helicopter ride in history, I am finally arriving at the hospital. Remi is there, out the front, meeting me. He's on bodyguard duty.

"I have to let you in as you're the baby's father, but if you upset Portia at any point, I'm going to take you out back and punch the living daylights out of you. Do you hear me?" Remi warns me as he grips my shirt.

"For fuck's sake, Remi. She thinks I took a job in Florida and didn't tell her about it. That's what has her upset; not her thinking I've been unfaithful!" I scream at my brother as I shove him off me.

"But I thought?" he asks, confused.

"You didn't get the entire story and jumped to conclusions about me. Fuck you," I spit, storming into the hospital. No one is going to get between Portia and me. "What room is she in?" I turn to Remi, who is hot on my heels.

"Room 1254," he tells me.

I stride off down the corridors, searching for the room. The door is closed when I get there.

"Fair warning, bro, no one is happy with you," Remi tells me.

"I don't fucking care. All I care about is Portia and my baby," I tell him as I open the door to Portia's room. Her parents and sister turn to see who is entering the room and when they see it's me, their faces turn to hate.

"Get the hell out of here!" Nacho screams at me as he strides toward me ready to punch me out.

"Lay one hand on me, Nacho, and I will make one phone call and have you and your family banned from this hospital. Do you hear me?" I tell him, standing my ground.

"You fucking little shit. How dare you?" Nacho curses at me.

"Dad!" Portia screams from her bed. She looks so pale and gaunt. "Please, don't," she tells him.

"Nacho, don't," Remi adds, standing behind me in solidarity. My brother's mentor's eyes widen at my brother's stance. "I think the best thing we can do is leave these two to it," he says to the room. Nell glares at Remi as if he's lost his mind.

"I think that might be best," Allison states, ushering her husband out of the room. Remi holds out his hand for Nell. She hesitates for a moment, but Portia gives her a reassuring nod.

Once the door is closed, I rush toward her and take a seat beside her, pulling her hand in mine, which she snatches straight back from me. She's upset, I get it, but does she not realize how freaked out I was getting a call from emergency that my partner is in hospital.

"First, let me say I was never moving to Orlando," I tell her. This gets her attention as she turns and looks at me fully. "Jenny was out of line saying what she did today. Yes, she knew about the job offer as we have mutual friends that work in the hospital who spilled the beans. What she didn't know when she opened her mouth to you today was I had turned the job down."

"You did?"

"Of course. Why would I want to move you so close to giving birth and away from your family?" I explain to her.

"You don't want to go to Orlando?" she asks.

"The hospital is fantastic, but it doesn't fit in with my life. My life is here with you, wherever it is," I tell her. Tears fall down her cheeks.

"Sweetheart, no. Please don't cry," I tell her, jumping up and wiping her tears away.

"I thought you were leaving me, Miles." She breaks down, sobbing. I crawl up into the bed and pull her against me, trying to calm her down as I don't want her blood pressure to spike.

"Never, you're stuck with me. I'm not going anywhere," I tell her, dragging my fingers through her hair.

"I love you, Miles," she says, burying her face in my chest.

"I know you do, sweetheart. I love you too. But please, next time you think I've done something, can you come to me first?" I tell her.

"I'm sorry. I've messed everything up. I was devastated when Jenny told me about your job and then my mind went into overdrive and all I wanted to do was leave." She sobs into my chest.

"I'm sorry too. I should have spoken to you about the offer earlier. I knew I would not take it so thought nothing of it," I explain to her.

"Guess we need to work on our communication, then." Portia sighs.

Yeah, we probably do. I need no more threats to my life from my brother or her family again. Speaking of communication, I should probably tell her about my other job offer. "Well, in the name of communication, I received another job offer yesterday, and I had been waiting for that one as I think it might be the better option for us. But I can still say no, whatever is best for our family is what I'll do," I explain to her.

"Where is it?" she asks quietly. Her body stiffens, waiting for the fallout.

"Funny enough, right here, in this hospital," I tell her.

"Here as in Southampton?"

"Yep. I was coming home tonight to talk to you about it. But then things got a little lost in translation," I say as I run my hand down her face. "I have a couple of days to give them my answer and I don't have to take it if you want to stay in the city."

"Is this a good hospital?" she asks.

"Yeah, it is. Not as busy as the city, but I think I'd be happier with a slower pace. Means more time at home with you and little dude. Plus, we already have the house up here. Your family isn't far. Mine will come up and visit most weekends. But I know how much you love the townhouse and all the effort you have put into it," I explain to her.

"Would you be happy up here, away from your friends?" she asks.

"Would you?" I question her back.

"Honestly, I don't know," she tells me.

"Then that's okay, babe. We don't have to go anywhere," I

tell her as I place kisses on her temple. "All that matters is we keep your blood pressure down. You had me so worried."

"When's the deadline to tell them?" she asks.

"Next week." She nods.

"Can we talk about this tomorrow? Today has sucked and I don't know if I'm in the right headspace to make life-changing decisions," she grumbles, curling up into my side.

"There's no rush," I tell her.

"Good, you guys have sorted out your drama. So, you are moving then?" Nell says, stepping into the room. I'm still lying in the hospital bed with Portia curled up against me. I feel her chuckle against my chest.

"Guess it's tomorrow then."

"We have made no decisions yet," I tell Nell.

"What's there to decide. We are all here. You will have a ton of babysitters. We can teach little one to ride horses. He might be a brilliant polo player like his uncle and grandpa," she says excitedly.

"Or he might be a doctor and follow in his daddy's footsteps," I add, not too keen on this polo stuff.

"Nah, you're outnumbered by the horsey side, Miles." Nell chuckles.

My phone rings in my pocket and I look down and see it's Mom. "Babe, it's Mom. She's probably heard you're in the hospital. I'm going to take it." I press a kiss to her forehead and walk out of the room to take Mom's call. After reassuring her Portia and the baby are okay, I hang up and head back to Portia's room. But Nacho stops me from entering.

"I owe you an apology, Miles," Nacho says grumpily, which I think is his normal disposition.

"It's okay. You didn't know the real reason. So, I understand how you all jumped to those kinds of conclusions," I tell him.

"I love my daughter. And you will soon realize when your son is born you will do everything in your power to protect your children. But I also know you. I was there when you were born, right beside your father. He was so proud of you. You're a good boy, Miles, and I know I haven't been one hundred percent on board with you and Portia. But I see how much you love my daughter and that's all a father could ever want."

Is Nacho giving me his seal of approval?

"Remi explained you were offered a job up here. If you take it, you would make my wife very happy, which would improve my life," he says with a grin.

"Ultimately, it's up to your daughter. Whatever makes her happy I'm down with," I tell him.

"Happy wife, happy life. You're catching on real quick," he says, slapping me on the back and bursting out laughing.

41

MILES

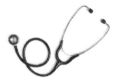

"Babe, my waters just broke!" Portia screams from the bathroom. I jump up, ready for action.

"It's go-time!" I call out to her, trying to orientate myself in the darkness.

"Yes, babe, it's go-time." She laughs from the bathroom.

I mentally run through my checklist. As a doctor you would think I would be better under pressure than I am at what the hell time is it, turning I press my phone and the time 2:28 a.m. flashes on the screen. Oh, come on, little man, couldn't you come at a more civilized time after I've had my coffee?

Regarding my job at Southampton, literally a day before I was going to accept it, someone contacted me regarding an offer here in the city at another hospital. As soon as I told Portia she was *"take this one"*. We both knew we wanted to stay in the city. I didn't want to stay at the hospital I was working in. We both agreed maybe in a couple more years' time we might see if Southampton has any openings again, but for the moment, we are happy being where we need to be.

"Ooohh!" Portia screams from the bathroom with a contraction. Get it together boy your woman is about to give birth and if you don't hurry, you will deliver it in your bathroom, and she will not be happy ruining her new tiles.

"Where's the grandbaby?" Allison calls out, rushing in with my mom hot on her heels. We have kept them at bay for long enough. They are dying to see our little dude.

"Let me introduce you all to little Hunter Garcia Hartford," I tell the room as I pick up my little boy from the crib and hand him off to the grandmas to swoon over.

"Congratulations, man," Remi says, slapping me on the back. "You did good." I can feel my heart swelling with pride. When I saw that little red face for the first time, I was gone for. Couldn't believe he was finally here. When the nurse placed him on an exhausted Portia, and he suckled straight away, I didn't think I could be any more in love with her than I was in that moment. She's stuck with me forever.

It's our first holiday as a family and we've headed to the south of France to watch Uncle Remi play polo and defend his number one world title. We've hired a chateau large enough to house all of us now there are two grandbabies here. Stirling and Audrey had a little boy called Archie shortly after us and the two of them are already the best of friends. Stirling proposed to Audrey in the hospital not long after she gave birth. As he was so overwhelmed with love, he couldn't wait any longer. I get it. I wanted to do the same thing, but I knew Portia would kill me. She was not ready for marriage then, but I'm about to surprise her this trip. How could I come to France and not propose to her? Seems criminal. She won't be expecting it and I hope she says yes, otherwise this is going to be awkward.

I've left Hunter with Mom and told Portia I organized a child-free picnic for the two of us and honestly, we need it.

"Be good for Grandma, okay?" Portia tells Hunter, giving him a kiss on his forehead as he bounces happily in Grandma's arms. He waves his pudgy little hands at us and we high tail it before he realizes it means we are not coming back. "This is exactly what I needed." Portia sighs as she takes my hand, and we wander the lavender-filled gardens. "This place is gorgeous. I've always wanted to live in France. The architecture, the romance, the cheese," she says with a giggle.

"Luckily I packed a lot of cheese for you then," I say, giving her a wink.

The chateau has organized a gorgeous picnic set up in a small glasshouse hidden away in the rose gardens.

"Oh, my, this is gorgeous." Portia squeals seeing the setup. They have laid out a linen tablecloth across the wooden table. There are crystal glasses and a chilled bottle of champagne in a bucket of ice. A vase of pink roses and peonies in the center and a charcuterie board set to the side with meats, cheeses, olives, and fruits. "This is perfect, thank you," Portia exclaims, pulling me into a heated kiss. I wanted her to sit down and eat first, but of course Portia doesn't play to my rules.

"I love you so much, Portia," I say, cupping her face.

"I love you too." She smiles up at me.

"I never knew I could be as happy as I am when I am with you and Hunter," I tell her. Those chocolate eyes glisten with emotion. "We didn't have the most conventional start to our relationship, but I don't think I would do a single thing differently because I don't know if the outcome would be where we are today, and I would never want my life to be any other way."

"Stop it, you're making me cry," she says playfully slapping my chest.

"I'm going to make you cry some more," I tell her as I drop to one knee and pull out the ring box I've carried halfway across the world. Portia gasps and her hands cover her mouth in surprise. "I know you and I have said we don't need a piece of paper to tell us we are a family, but I wouldn't mind you wearing my ring letting the world know you're mine," I tell her, opening the ring box and showing her the three-carat emerald cut black diamond with a band of sparkling white diamonds around it. As soon as I saw it, I knew it was her.

"Will you, Portia Garcia, be my partner in love and life forever?" I ask her.

"Yes. Yes. Yes!" she screams, wrapping her arms around me and kissing me. "I'm all yours," she tells me as I slip the ring on her finger.

"I love you, Portia."

"I love you too," she says, laughing as I swing her around.

"Now is it cheese time?"

EPILOGUE

PORTIA

W here are we all now?

Well, things have certainly changed. Miles and I moved from the city to The Hamptons and took over running Carrie and Leon's Hamptons office. Miles moved from working in the ER to opening his own practice and becoming a GP with better hours, and more time with the family.

Speaking of the family, we have had three more kids after Hunter. I know, sucker for punishment, or I have a handsy husband who can't keep his penis to himself, and I wind up pregnant. We had River, Tennessee, and our little girl Alexis.

Did Miles and I get married? Yes. In Vegas on a no kids weekend ten years later. We were very drunk and thought it was a great idea at the time. When we came home and told everyone, our moms had a fit and made us have another ceremony at our home in The Hamptons with the kids as our witnesses.

Stirling and Audrey moved to Greenwich to be closer to her brother and friends. They have a beach house near us and spend a lot of the summer there. Stirling and Audrey had their little one, Archie, and a couple of years later, they had a little girl called Bonnie.

They got married in a glamorous wedding at the Waldorf Astoria. Audrey made all the fashion magazines with her dress, and all the social pages lived on every aspect of her day for an entire year.

The same happened with my sister too. Nell's wedding was an equally extravagant affair. It was held at my parents' home instead. My mother went crazy organizing the event. Carrie, Leon, and I were roped into designing the new buildings on the property. We worked with Rhys's wife's company as she's an architect. She also designed their dream home, which is situated at the far end of the property, and I got to decorate it.

They waited a little longer to have kids until Remi slowed down as they didn't want to drag kids around to all the competitions. They eventually had two kids, McKenna and Madeline.

Nell took over Mom's label and turned it into an equestrian lifestyle brand. She has fashion, homewares, saddlery, shoes; you name it. Nell made it onto the Forbes list of 30 under 30 the first year she took over from Mom. And her career has skyrocketed ever since.

And we all lived happily ever after!

THE END

ACKNOWLEDGMENTS

Thanks for finishing this book.
Really hope you enjoyed it.
Why not check out my other books.
Have a fantastic day !

Don't forget to leave a review.
xoxo

ABOUT THE AUTHOR

JA Low lives in the Australian Outback. When she's not writing steamy scenes and admiring hot cowboy's, she's tending to her husband and two sons, and dreaming up the next epic romance.

Come follow her

Facebook: www.facebook.com/jalowbooks
TikTok: www.tiktok.com/@jalowbooks
Instagram: www.instagram.com/jalowbooks
Pinterest: www.pinterest.com/jalowbooks
Website: www.jalowbooks.com
Goodreads: https://www.goodreads.com/author/show/14918059.J_A_Low
BookBub: https://www.bookbub.com/authors/ja-low

ABOUT THE AUTHOR

Come join JA Low's Block
www.facebook.com/groups/1682783088643205/

www.jalowbooks.com
jalowbooks@gmail.com

INTERCONNECTING SERIES

Reading order for interconnected characters.

Dirty Texas Series

Suddenly Dirty

Suddenly Together

Suddenly Bound

Suddenly Trouble

Suddenly Broken

Paradise Club Series

Paradise

Playboys of New York

Off Limits

Strictly Forbidden

The Merger

Without Warning

The Hartford Brother's Series

Tempting the Billionaire

ALSO BY JA LOW

ALSO BY JA LOW

The Dirty Texas Box Set

Five full length novels and Five Novellas included in the set.

One band. Five dirty talking rock stars and the women that bring them to their knees.

Suddenly Dirty

A workplace romance with your celebrity hall pass.

Suddenly Together

A best friend to lover's romance with the one man who's off limits.

Suddenly Bound

An opposites attract romance with family loyalty tested to its limits.

Suddenly Trouble

A brother's best friend romance with a twist.

Suddenly Broken

A friend's with benefits romance that takes a wild ride.

One little taste can't hurt; can it?

If you like your rock stars dirty talking, alpha's with hearts of gold this series is for you.

ALSO BY JA LOW

The Paradise Club Series

Book 1 - Paradise

Spin off from the Dirty Texas Series

My name's Nate Lewis, owner of The Paradise Club.

I can bring every little dirty fantasy you have ever dreamed of to reality.

My business is your pleasure. I'm good at it.

So good it's made me a wealthy and powerful man.

I have one rule—never mix business and pleasure, and I've lived by it from day one.

Until her.

** WARNING: If you do not like your books with a lot of heat then do not read this book. **

ALSO BY JA LOW

International Bad Boys Set

Standalone Books

Book 1 - The Sexy Stranger (Italian)

Book 2 - The Arrogant Artist (French)

Book 3 - The Hotshot Chef (Spanish)

INTERCONNECTING SERIES

Reading order for Interconnecting Series

Bratva Jewels Series

The Sexy Stranger

ALSO BY JA LOW

Bratva Jewels Duet Box Set

SAPPHIRE - BOOK 1

An unconventional love is tested to its limits.

Mateo is used to being in the spotlight, he craves it in everything he does . . . except when it comes to his love life - that is firmly in the closet.

Tomas shuns the spotlight, the one he was born into, he wants nothing to do with it or his high-flying family who now reject him for his choices in love.

But Tomas' and Mateo's carefully constructed lives are turned inside out when they discover a beautiful, battered woman on their doorstep. The woman with the sapphire eyes has no memory of who she is or how she got there. She doesn't know about the Bratva Jewels - the Russian mafia's most desired escorts - or how her story intersects with theirs. Can Tomas and Mateo help her remember before the men who are after her find her first?

DIAMOND - BOOK 2

Round 2 with the Devil begins.

Grace thought she had left the nightmare of the Bratva Jewels behind her. Her days spent as one of the Russian Mafia's most desired escorts were some of the darkest of her life, but she was safe now. Or so she thought.

When Russian mobster Dmitri seeks revenge, he gets it, and Grace knows she must call on every ounce of inner strength she has to withstand what he has in store for her. What she didn't expect was to meet someone like Maxim . . .

Maxim is one of the Bratva's most skilled, and most feared, assassins. But his relationship to the Bratva is a complicated one. And when he meets Grace, suddenly everything becomes clear.

Printed in Great Britain
by Amazon